Mary Higgins Clark has written twenty bestselling novels and three short story collections since 1975. She has served as president of the Mystery Writers of America and lives in Saddle River, New Jersey.

On the Street Where You Live

MARY HIGGINS CLARK

POCKET
BOOKS

LONDON · SYDNEY · NEW YORK · TOKYO · SINGAPORE · TORONTO

First published in Great Britain by Simon & Schuster UK Ltd, 2001
This edition first published by Pocket Books, 2002
An Imprint of Simon & Schuster UK Ltd
A Viacom company

Copyright © Mary Higgins Clark, 2000

This book is copyright under the Berne Convention.
No reproduction without permission.
® and © 1997 Simon & Schuster Inc. All rights reserved.
Pocket Books & Design is a registered trademark of Simon & Schuster Inc

The right of Mary Higgins Clark to be identified as author of this work has
been asserted in accordance with sections 77 and 78 of the Copyright,
Designs and Patents Act, 1988.

1 3 5 7 9 10 8 6 4 2

Simon & Schuster UK Ltd
Africa House
64-78 Kingsway
London WC2B 6AH

www.simonsays.co.uk

Simon & Schuster Australia
Sydney

A CIP catalogue record for this book is available from the British Library

This book is a work of fiction. Names, characters, places and incidents are
either a product of the author's imagination or are used fictitiously. Any
resemblance to actual people living or dead, events or locales is entirely
coincidental.

Typeset in Sabon & Galliard
Printed and bound in Great Britain by
Bookmarque Ltd, Croydon, Surrey

Acknowledgments _____

Once again it is time to say a thousand thanks to everyone who has been so much a part of the journey of this book.

My gratitude is endless to my long time editor, Michael Korda. It is hard to believe that twenty-six years have passed since we first started putting our heads together with *Where Are the Children?* It is a joy to work with him and for the last ten years his associate, senior editor, Chuck Adams. They are marvelous friends and advisors along the way.

Lisl Cade, my publicist, is truly my right hand—encouraging, perceptive, helpful in ways too numerous to mention. Love you, Lisl.

My gratitude continues to my agents Eugene Winick and Sam Pinkus. Truly friends for all seasons.

Associate Director of Copyediting Gypsy da Silva and I have once again shared an exciting journey. Many, many thanks Gypsy.

Thank you also to copyeditor Carol Catt, scanner Michael Mitchell, and proofreader Steve Friedeman for your careful work.

John Kaye, Prosecutor of Monmouth County, has been kind enough to answer this writer's questions about the role of the prosecutor's office as this book was being written.

I am most grateful, and if any way I have misinterpreted, I plead guilty.

Sgt. Steven Marron and Detective Richard Murphy, Ret., NYPD, New York County District Attorney's Office, have continued to advise me on how the real world investigators respond to the situations depicted within these pages. I am so grateful for all the help.

Again and always thanks and blessings to my assistants and friends Agnes Newton and Nadine Petry and reader-in-progress, my sister-in-law, Irene Clark.

Judith Kelman, author and friend, has always responded instantly when I needed a difficult question answered. She is a master at research and a master at friendship. Bless you, Judith.

My daughter, fellow author Carol Higgins Clark, has been in the throes of writing her book as I write mine. This time our paths are parallel but separate but not our ability to communicate the highs and lows of creativity.

I have studied the writings of specialists in the fields of reincarnation and regression and with gratitude acknowledge the contributions I have gleaned from their writing. They are: Robert G. Jarmon, M.D., Ian Stevenson and Karlis Osis.

For Fr. Stephen Fichter, many thanks for a last minute biblical confirmation.

I close with my thanks to my husband, John, and our wonderful combined families, children and grandchildren, who are named in the dedication.

And now my readers, past, present, and future, thank you for selecting this book. I truly hope you enjoy.

For my nearest and dearest—
John Conheeney—Spouse Extraordinaire

The Clark offspring—
Marilyn, Warren and Sharon, David, Carol and *Pat*

The Clark grandchildren—
Liz, Andrew, Courtney, David, Justin and *Jerry*

The Conheeney children—
*John and Debby, Barbara and Glenn, Trish, Nancy
& David*

The Conheeney grandchildren—
*Robert, Ashley, Lauren, Megan, David, Kelly,
Courtney, Johnny* and *Thomas*

You're a grand bunch and I love you all.

Tuesday, March 20

one _____

HE TURNED ONTO THE BOARDWALK and felt the full impact of
the stinging blast from the ocean. Observing the shifting
clouds, he decided it wouldn't be surprising if they had a snow
flurry later on, even though tomorrow was the first day of
spring. It had been a long winter, and everyone said how
much they were looking forward to the warm weather ahead.
He wasn't.

He enjoyed Spring Lake best once late autumn set in.
By then the summer people had closed their houses, not ap-
pearing even for weekends.

He was chagrined, though, that with each passing year
more and more people were selling their winter homes and
settling here permanently. They had decided it was worth the
seventy-mile commute into New York so that they could
begin and end the day in this quietly beautiful New Jersey seaside community.

Spring Lake, with its Victorian houses that appeared
unchanged from the way they had been in the 1890s, was
worth the inconvenience of the trip, they explained.

Spring Lake, with the fresh, bracing scent of the ocean
always present, revived the soul, they agreed.

Spring Lake, with its two-mile boardwalk, where one

could revel in the silvery magnificence of the Atlantic, was a treasure, they pointed out.

All of these people shared so much—the summer visitors, the permanent dwellers—but none of them shared *his* secrets. He could stroll down Hayes Avenue and visualize Madeline Shapley as she had been in late afternoon on September 7, 1891, seated on the wicker sofa on the wraparound porch of her home, her wide-brimmed bonnet beside her. She had been nineteen years old then, brown-eyed, with dark brown hair, sedately beautiful in her starched white linen dress.

Only he knew why she had had to die an hour later.

St. Hilda Avenue, shaded with heavy oaks that had been mere saplings on August 5, 1893, when eighteen-year-old Letitia Gregg had failed to return home, brought other visions. She had been so frightened. Unlike Madeline, who had fought for her life, Letitia had begged for mercy.

The last one of the trio had been Ellen Swain, small and quiet, but far too inquisitive, far too anxious to document the last hours of Letitia's life.

And because of her curiosity, on March 31, 1896, she had followed her friend to the grave.

He knew every detail, every nuance of what had happened to her and to the others.

He had found the diary during one of those cold, rainy spells that sometimes occur in summer. Bored, he'd wandered into the old carriage house, which served as a garage.

He climbed the rickety steps to the stuffy, dusty loft, and for lack of something better to do, began rummaging through the boxes he found there.

The first one was filled with utterly useless odds and ends: rusty old lamps; faded, outdated clothing; pots and pans and a scrub board; chipped vanity sets, the glass on the mirrors cracked or blurred. They all were the sorts of items one shoves out of sight with the intention of fixing or giving away, and then forgets altogether.

Another box held thick albums, the pages crumbling,

filled with pictures of stiffly posed, stern-faced people refusing to share their emotions with the camera.

A third contained books, dusty, swollen from humidity, the type faded. He'd always been a reader, but even though only fourteen at the time, he could glance through these titles and dismiss them. No hidden masterpieces in the lot.

A dozen more boxes proved to be filled with equally worthless junk.

In the process of throwing everything back into the boxes, he came across a rotted leather binder that had been hidden in what looked like another photo album. He opened it and found it stuffed with pages, every one of them covered with writing.

The first entry was dated, September 7, 1891. It began with the words "Madeline is dead by my hand."

He had taken the diary and told no one about it. Over the years, he'd read from it almost daily, until it became an integral part of his own memory. Along the way, he realized he had become one with the author, sharing his sense of supremacy over his victims, chuckling at his playacting as he grieved with the grieving.

What began as a fascination gradually grew to an absolute obsession, a need to relive the diary writer's journey of death on his own. Vicarious sharing was no longer enough.

Four and a half years ago he had taken the first life.

It was twenty-one-year-old Martha's fate that she had been present at the annual end-of-summer party her grandparents gave. The Lawrences were a prominent, long-established Spring Lake family. He was at the festive gathering and met her there. The next day, September 7th, she left for an early morning jog on the boardwalk. She never returned home.

Now, over four years later, the investigation into her disappearance was still ongoing. At a recent gathering, the prosecutor of Monmouth County had vowed there would be no diminution in the effort to learn the truth about what had happened to Martha Lawrence. Listening to the empty vows, he chuckled at the thought.

How he enjoyed participating in the somber discussions about Martha that came up from time to time over the dinner table.

I could tell you all about it, every detail, he said to himself, and I could tell you about Carla Harper too. Two years ago he had been strolling past the Warren Hotel and noticed her coming down the steps. Like Madeline, as described in the diary, she had been wearing a white dress, although hers was barely a slip, sleeveless, clinging, revealing every inch of her slender young body. He began following her.

When she disappeared three days later, everyone believed Carla had been accosted on the trip home to Philadelphia. Not even the prosecutor, so determined to solve the mystery of Martha's disappearance, suspected that Carla had never left Spring Lake.

Relishing the thought of his omniscience, he had lightheartedly joined the late afternoon strollers on the boardwalk and exchanged pleasantries with several good friends he met along the way, agreeing that winter was insisting on giving them one more blast on its way out.

But even as he bantered with them, he could feel the need stirring within him, the need to complete his trio of present-day victims. The final anniversary was coming up, and he had yet to choose her.

The word in town was that Emily Graham, the purchaser of the Shapley house, as it was still known, was a descendant of the original owners.

He had looked her up on the Internet. Thirty-two years old, divorced, a criminal defense attorney. She had come into money after she was given stock by the grateful owner of a fledgling wireless company whom she'd successfully defended pro bono. When the stock went public and she was able to sell it, she made a fortune.

He learned that Graham had been stalked by the son of a murder victim after she won an acquittal for the accused killer. The son, protesting his innocence, was now in a psychiatric facility. Interesting.

More interesting still, Emily bore a striking resemblance to the picture he'd seen of her great-great-grandaunt, Madeline Shapley. She had the same wide brown eyes and long, full eyelashes. The same midnight-brown hair with hints of auburn. The same lovely mouth. The same tall, slender body.

There were differences, of course. Madeline had been innocent, trusting, unworldly, a romantic. Emily Graham was obviously a sophisticated and smart woman. She would be more of a challenge than the others, but then again, that made her so much more interesting. Maybe *she* was the one destined to complete his special trio?

There was an orderliness, a rightness to the prospect that sent a shiver of pleasure through him.

two

EMILY GAVE A SIGH OF RELIEF as she passed the sign indicating she was now in Spring Lake. *"Made it!"* she said aloud. "Hallelujah."

The drive from Albany had taken nearly eight hours. She had left in what was supposed to have been "periods of light to moderate snow," but which had turned into a near blizzard that only tapered off as she exited Rockland County. Along the way the number of fender benders on the New York State Thruway reminded her of the bumper cars she had loved as a child.

In a fairly clear stretch, she had picked up speed, but then witnessed a terrifying spinout. For a horrible moment it had seemed as though two vehicles were headed for a head-on collision. It was avoided only because the driver of one car had somehow managed to regain control and turn right with less than a nanosecond to spare.

Kind of reminds me of my life the last couple of years, she had thought as she slowed down—constantly in the fast lane, and sometimes almost getting clobbered. I needed a change of direction and a change of pace.

As her grandmother had put it, "Emily, you take that job in New York. I'll feel a lot more secure about you when you're living a couple of hundred miles away. A nasty ex-husband and a stalker at one time are a little too much on your plate for my taste."

And then, being Gran, she continued, "On the bright side, you never should have married Gary White. The fact that three years after you're divorced he'd have the gall to try to sue you because you have money now only proves what I always thought about him."

Remembering her grandmother's words, Emily smiled involuntarily as she drove slowly through the darkened streets. She glanced at the gauge on the dashboard. The outside temperature was a chilly thirty-eight degrees. The streets were wet—here the storm had produced only rain—and the windshield was becoming misted. The movement of the tree branches indicated sharp gusts of wind coming in from the ocean.

But the houses, the majority of them restored Victorians, looked secure and serene. As of tomorrow I'll officially own a home here, Emily mused. March 21st. The equinox. Light and night equally divided. The world in balance.

It was a comforting thought. She had experienced enough turbulence of late to both want and need a period of complete and total peace. She'd had stunning good luck, but also frightening problems that had crashed like meteors into each other. But as the old saying went, everything that rises must converge, and God only knows she was living proof of that.

She considered, then rejected, the impulse to drive by the house. There was still something unreal about the knowledge that in only a matter of hours, it would be hers. Even before she saw the house for the first time three months ago, it had been a vivid presence in her childhood imaginings—half real, half blended with fairy tales. Then, when she stepped into it that first time, she had known immediately that for her the place held a feeling of coming home. The real estate agent had mentioned that it was still called the Shapley house.

Enough driving for now, she decided. It's been a long, long day. Concord Reliable Movers in Albany were supposed to have arrived at eight. Most of the furniture she wanted to keep was already in her new Manhattan apartment, but when her grandmother downsized she had given her some fine antique pieces, so there was still a lot to move.

"First pickup, guaranteed," the Concord scheduler had vehemently promised. "Count on me."

The van had not made its appearance until noon. As a result she got a much later start than she'd expected, and it was now almost ten-thirty.

Check into the inn, she decided. A hot shower, she thought longingly. Watch the eleven o'clock news. Then, as Samuel Pepys wrote, "And so to bed."

When she'd first come to Spring Lake, and impulsively put a deposit down on the house, she had stayed at the Candlelight Inn for a few days, to be absolutely sure she'd made the right decision. She and the inn's owner, Carrie Roberts, a septuagenarian, had immediately hit it off. On the drive down today, she'd phoned to say she'd be late, but Carrie had assured her that was no problem.

Turn right on Ocean Avenue, then four more blocks. A few moments later, with a grateful sigh, Emily turned off the ignition and reached in the backseat for the one suitcase she'd need overnight.

Carrie's greeting was warm and brief. "You look exhausted, Emily. The bed's turned down. You said you'd stopped for dinner, so there's a thermos of hot cocoa with a couple of biscuits on the night table. I'll see you in the morning."

The hot shower. A nightshirt and her favorite old bathrobe. Sipping the cocoa, Emily watched the news and felt the stiffness in her muscles from the long drive begin to fade.

As she snapped off the television, her cell phone rang. Guessing who it was, she picked it up.

"Hi, Emily."

She smiled as she heard the worried-sounding voice of Eric Bailey, the shy genius who was the reason she was in Spring Lake now.

As she reassured him that she'd had a safe, relatively easy trip, she thought of the day she first met him, when he moved into the closet-sized office next to hers. The same age, their birthdays only a week apart, they'd become friendly, and she recognized that underneath his meek, little-boy-lost exterior, Eric had been gifted with massive intelligence.

One day, when she realized how depressed he seemed, she'd made him tell her the reason. It turned out that his fledgling dot-com company was being sued by a major software provider who knew he could not afford an expensive lawsuit.

She took the case without asking for a fee, expecting it to be a pro bono situation, and joked to herself that she would be papering the walls with the stock certificates Eric promised her.

But she won the case for him. He made a public offering of the stock, which immediately rose in value. When her shares were worth ten million dollars, she sold them.

Now Eric's name was on a handsome new office building. He loved the races and bought a lovely old home in Saratoga from which he commuted to Albany. Their friendship had continued, and he'd been a rock during the time she was being stalked. He even had a high-tech camera installed at her townhouse. The camera had caught the stalker on tape.

"Just wanted to see that you made it okay. Hope I didn't wake you up?"

They chatted for a few minutes and promised to talk again soon. When she put the cell phone down, Emily went to the window and opened it slightly. A rush of cold, salty air made her gasp, but then she deliberately inhaled slowly. It's crazy, she thought, but at this moment it seems to me that all my life I've been missing the smell of the ocean.

She turned and walked to the door to be absolutely sure it was double locked. Stop *doing* that, she snapped at herself. You already checked before you showered.

But in the year before the stalker was caught, despite her efforts to convince herself that if the stalker wanted to hurt her he could have done so on many occasions, she had begun to feel fearful and apprehensive.

Carrie had told her that she was the only guest at the inn. "I'm booked full over the weekend," she'd said. "All six bedrooms. There's a wedding reception at the country club on Saturday. And after Memorial Day, forget it. I don't have a closet available."

The minute I heard that only the two of us were here, I started wondering if all the outside doors were locked and if the alarm was on, Emily thought, once again angry that she could not control her anxiety.

She slipped out of her bathrobe. Don't think about it now, she warned herself.

But her hands were suddenly clammy as she remembered the first time she had come home and realized he'd been there. She had found a picture of herself propped up against the lamp on her bedside table, a photograph showing her standing in the kitchen in her nightgown, a cup of coffee in her hand. She had never seen the picture before. That day she'd had the locks of the townhouse changed and a blind put on the window over the sink.

After that there'd been a number of other incidents involving photographs, pictures taken of her at home, on the street, in the office. Sometimes a silky-voiced predator would call to comment on what she was wearing. "You looked cute jogging this morning, Emily . . ." "With that dark hair, I didn't think I'd like you in black. But I do. . . ." "I love those red shorts. Your legs are really good . . ."

And then a picture would turn up of her wearing the described outfit. It would be in her mailbox at home, or stuck on the windshield of her car, or folded inside the morning newspaper that had been delivered to her doorstep.

The police had traced the telephone calls, but all had been made from different pay phones. Attempts to lift fingerprints from the items that she had received had been unsuccessful.

For over a year the police had been unable to apprehend the stalker. "You've gotten some people acquitted who were accused of vicious crimes, Miss Graham," Marty Browski, the senior detective, told her. "It could be someone in a victim's family. It could be someone who saw you in a restaurant and followed you home. It could be someone who knows you came into a lot of money and got fixated on you."

And then they'd found Ned Koehler, the son of a woman whose accused killer she had successfully defended, lurking outside her townhouse. He's off the streets now, Emily reassured herself. There's no need to worry about him anymore. He'll get the care he needs.

He was in a secure psychiatric facility in upstate New York, and this was Spring Lake, not Albany. Out of sight, out of mind, Emily thought, prayerfully. She got into bed, pulled up the covers, and reached for the light switch.

Across Ocean Avenue, standing on the beach in the shadows of the deserted boardwalk, the wind from the ocean whipping his hair, a man watched as the room became dark.

"Sleep well, Emily," he whispered, his voice gentle.

Wednesday, March 21 —————

three _____

HIS BRIEFCASE UNDER HIS ARM, Will Stafford walked with long, brisk strides from the side door of his home to the converted carriage house that, like most of those still existing in Spring Lake, now served as a garage. The rain had stopped sometime during the night and the wind diminished. Even so, the first day of spring had a sharp bite, and Will had the fleeting thought that maybe he should have grabbed a topcoat on the way out.

Shows what happens when the last birthday in your thirties is looming, he told himself ruefully. Keep it up and you'll be looking for your earmuffs in July.

A real estate attorney, he was meeting Emily Graham for breakfast at Who's on Third?, the whimsical Spring Lake corner café. From there they would go for a final walk-through of the house she was buying, then to his office for the closing.

As Will backed his aging Jeep down the driveway, he reflected that it had been a day not unlike this in late December when Emily Graham had walked into his office on Third Avenue. "I just put down a deposit on a house," she'd told him. "I asked the broker to recommend a real estate lawyer. She named three, but I'm a pretty good judge of witness testimony. You're the one she favored. Here's the binder."

She was so fired up about the house that she didn't even introduce herself, Will remembered with a smile. He got her name from her signature on the binder—"Emily S. Graham."

There weren't too many attractive young women who could pay two million dollars cash for a house. But when he'd suggested that she might want to consider taking a mortgage for at least half the amount, Emily had explained that she just couldn't imagine owing a million dollars to a bank.

He was ten minutes early, but she was already in the café, sipping coffee. One-upmanship, Will wondered, or is she compulsively early?

Then he wondered if she could read his mind.

"I'm not usually the one holding down the fort," she explained, "but I'm so darn excited about closing on the house that I'm running ahead of the clock."

At that first meeting in December, when he had learned that she'd only seen one house, he said, "I don't like to talk myself out of a job, but Ms. Graham, you're telling me that you just saw the house for the first time? You didn't look at any others? This is your first time in Spring Lake? You didn't make a counteroffer but paid full price? I suggest you think this over carefully. By law you have three days to withdraw your offer."

That was when she'd told him that the house had been in her family, that the middle initial in her name was for Shapley.

Emily gave her order to the waitress. Grapefruit juice, a single scrambled egg, toast.

As Will Stafford studied the menu, she studied him, approving of what she saw. He was certainly an attractive man, a lean six-footer with broad shoulders and sandy hair. Dark blue eyes and a square jawline dominated his even-featured face.

At their first meeting she had liked his combination of easygoing warmth and cautious concern. Not every lawyer would practically try to talk himself out of a job, she thought. He really was worried that I was being too impulsive.

Except for that one day in January when she had flown

down in the morning and back to Albany in the afternoon, their communication had been either by phone or mail. Still, every contact with him confirmed that Stafford was indeed a meticulous attorney.

The Kiernans, who were selling the house, had owned it only three years and spent that entire time faithfully restoring it. They were in the final stage of the interior decoration when Wayne Kiernan was offered a prestigious and lucrative position which required permanent residence in London. It had been obvious to Emily that giving up the house had been a wrenching decision for them.

On that hurried visit in January, Emily went through every room with the Kiernans and bought the Victorian-era furniture, carpets, and artifacts they had lovingly purchased and were now willing to sell. The property was spacious, and a contractor had just completed a cabana and had just started excavating for a pool.

"The only thing I regret is the pool," she told Stafford as the waitress refilled their cups. "Any swimming I do will be in the ocean. But as long as the cabana is already in place, it seems a little silly not to go ahead with the pool as well. Anyhow, my brothers' kids will love it when they visit."

Will Stafford had handled all the paperwork covering the various agreements. He was a good listener, she decided, as over breakfast she heard herself telling him about having grown up in Chicago. "My brothers call me 'the afterthought,' " she said, smiling. "They're ten and twelve years older than I am. My maternal grandmother lives in Albany. I went to Skidmore College in Saratoga Springs, which is a stone's throw away, and spent a lot of my free time with her. *Her* grandmother was the younger sister of Madeline, the nineteen-year-old who disappeared in 1891."

Will Stafford noticed the shadow that came over Emily's face, but then she sighed and continued, "Well, that was a long time ago, wasn't it?"

"A *very* long time," he agreed. "I don't think you've told me how much time you expect to spend down here. Are you planning to move in immediately, or use the house week-ends, or what?"

Emily smiled. "I plan to move in as soon as we pass title this morning. All the basic stuff that I need is there, in-cluding pots and pans and linens. The moving van from Albany is scheduled to arrive tomorrow with the relatively few things I'm bringing here."

"Do you still have a home in Albany?"

"Yesterday was my last day there. I'm still settling my apartment in Manhattan, so I'll be back and forth between the apartment and this house until May 1st. That's when I start my new job. After that I'll be a weekend and vacation kind of resident."

"You realize that there's a great deal of curiosity in town about you," Will cautioned. "I just want you to know that I'm not the one who leaked that you're a descendant of the Shapley family."

The waitress was putting their plates on the table. Emily did not wait for her to leave before she said, "Will, I'm not trying to keep that a secret. I mentioned it to the Kiernans, and to Joan Scotti, the real estate agent. She told me that there are families whose ancestors were here at the time that my great-great-grandaunt disappeared. I'd be interested to know what if anything any of them have heard about her—other, of course, than the fact that she seemingly vanished from the face of the earth.

"They also know I'm divorced and that I'll be working in New York, so I have no guilty secrets."

He looked amused. "Somehow I don't visualize you as harboring guilty secrets."

Emily hoped her smile did not look forced. I *do* intend to keep to myself the fact that I've spent a fair amount of time in court this past year that had nothing to do with practic-ing law, she thought. She had been a defendant in her ex-husband's suit, claiming he was entitled to half the money she had made on the stock, and also had been on the witness stand testifying against the stalker.

"As for myself," Stafford continued, "you haven't asked, but I'm going to tell you anyway. "I was born and raised about an hour from here, in Princeton. My father was CEO and chairman of the board of Lionel Pharmaceuticals in Manhattan. He and my mother split when I was sixteen, and since my father traveled so much, I moved with my mother to Denver and finished high school and then college there."

He ate the last of his sausage. "Every morning I tell myself I'll have fruit and oatmeal, but about three mornings a week I succumb to the cholesterol urge. You obviously have more character than I do."

"Not necessarily. I've already decided that the next time I come here for breakfast it will be to have exactly what you just finished."

"I'd have given you a bite. My mother taught me to share." He glanced at his watch and signaled for the check. "I don't want to hurry you, Emily, but it's nine-thirty. The Kiernans are the most reluctant sellers I've ever bumped into. Let's not keep them waiting and give them a chance to change their minds about the house."

While they waited for the check, he said, "To finish the not very thrilling story of my life, I married right after law school. Within the year we both knew it was a mistake."

"You're lucky," Emily commented. "My life would have been a lot easier if I had been that smart."

"I moved back East and signed on with the legal department of Canon and Rhodes, which you may know is a high-powered Manhattan real estate firm. It was a darn good job, but pretty demanding. I wanted a place for weekends and came looking down here, than bought an old house that needed a lot of work. I love to work with my hands."

"Why Spring Lake?"

We used to stay at the Essex and Sussex Hotel for a couple of weeks every summer when I was a kid. It was a happy time." He shrugged.

The waitress put the check on the table. Will glanced at it and got out his wallet. "Then twelve years ago I realized

I liked living here and didn't like working in New York, so I opened this office. A lot of real estate work, both residential and commercial.

"And speaking of that, let's get going to the Kiernans." They got up together.

BUT THE KIERNANS had already left Spring Lake. Their lawyer explained he had power of attorney to execute the closing. Emily walked with him through every room, taking fresh delight in architectural details she had not fully appreciated before.

"Yes, I'm absolutely satisfied that everything I bought is here and the house is in perfect condition," she told him. She tried to push back her increasing impatience to get the deed transferred, to be in the house alone, to wander through the rooms, to rearrange the living room furniture so that the couches faced each other at right angles to the fireplace.

She needed to put her own stamp on the house, to make it *hers*. She'd always thought of the townhouse in Albany as a stopgap place, although she had been in it three years—ever since she'd returned from a visit to her parents in Chicago a day early and found her husband in an intimate embrace with her closest friend, Barbara Lyons. She picked up her suitcases, got back in the car, and checked into a hotel. A week later she rented the townhouse.

The house she had lived in with Gary was owned by his wealthy family. It had never felt like hers. But walking through this house seemed to evoke sensory memory. "I almost feel as though it's welcoming me," she told Will Stafford.

"I think it might be. You should see the expression on your face. Ready to go to my office and sign the papers?"

THREE HOURS LATER Emily returned to the house and once more pulled into the driveway. "Home sweet home," she said joyously as she got out of the car and opened the trunk to collect the groceries she'd purchased after the closing.

An area near the new cabana was being excavated for the pool. Three men were working on the site. After the walk-through she'd been introduced to Manny Dexter, the foreman. Now he caught her eye and waved.

The rumble of the backhoe drowned out her footsteps as she hurried along the blue flagstone walk to the back door. This I could do without, she thought, then reminded herself again that the pool would be nice to have when her brothers and their families came to visit.

She was wearing one of her favorite outfits, a dark green winter-weight pantsuit and white turtleneck sweater. Warm as they were, Emily shivered as she shifted the grocery bag from one arm to the other and put the key in the door. A gust of wind blew her hair in her face, and as she shook it away, she jostled the bag and a box of cereal dropped onto the flooring of the porch.

The extra moment it took to pick up the box meant that Emily was still outside when Manny Dexter shouted frantically to the operator of the backhoe. "Turn that thing off! Stop digging! *There's a skeleton down there!*"

four _____

DETECTIVE TOMMY DUGGAN did not always agree with his boss, Elliot Osborne, the Monmouth County prosecutor. Tommy knew Osborne considered his unceasing investigation into the disappearance of Martha Lawrence an obsession that might only succeed in keeping her killer in a state of high alert.

"That is unless the killer is a drive-through nut who grabbed her and dumped her body hundreds of miles from here," Osborne would point out.

Tommy Duggan had been a detective for the last fif-teen of his forty-two years. In that time he'd married, fathered two sons, and watched his hairline go south while his waistline traveled east and west. With his round, good-humored face and ready smile, he gave the impression of being an easygoing fellow who had never encountered a problem more serious than a flat tire.

In fact, he was a crackerjack investigator. In the department, he was admired and envied for his ability to pick up a seemingly useless piece of information and follow it until it proved to be the break in his case. Over the years, Tommy had turned down several generous offers to join private security firms. He loved the job.

All his life he had lived in Avon by the Sea, an oceanside town a few miles from Spring Lake. As a college student he had been a busboy and then a waiter at the Warren Hotel in Spring Lake. That was how he had come to know Martha Lawrence's grandparents, who regularly dined there.

Again today, as he sat in his private cubbyhole, he spent the short lunch break he allotted himself glancing once more through the Lawrence file. He knew that Elliot Osborne wanted to nail Martha Lawrence's killer as much as he did. The only thing that differed was their ideas of how to go about solving the crime.

Tommy stared at a picture of Martha that had been taken on the boardwalk in Spring Lake. She'd been wearing a tee shirt and shorts. Her long blond hair caressed her shoulders, her smile was sunny and confident. She had been a beautiful twenty-one-year-old who, when that picture was taken, should have had another fifty or sixty years of life. Instead she had had less than forty-eight hours.

Tommy shook his head and closed the file. He was convinced that by continuing to make the rounds of people in Spring Lake he eventually would stumble upon some crucial fact, some bit of information previously overlooked, that would lead him to the truth. As a result he was a familiar figure to the neighbors of the Lawrences and to all the people who had been in contact with Martha in those last hours of her life.

The staff of the caterer who had serviced the party at the Lawrence home the night before Martha disappeared were longtime employees. He had talked repeatedly to them, so far without garnering any helpful information.

Most of the guests who had attended the party were locals, or summer residents who kept their homes open year-round and would come down regularly for weekends. Tommy always kept a copy of the guest list folded in his wallet. It wasn't a big effort for him to drive to Spring Lake and look up a couple of them just to chat.

Martha had disappeared while jogging. A few of the regular early morning joggers reported they had seen her near the North Pavilion. Each of them had been checked out thoroughly and cleared.

Tommy Duggan sighed as he closed the file and put it back in his top drawer. He didn't believe that some drive-by had randomly stopped in Spring Lake and waylaid Martha. He was sure that whoever had abducted her was someone she trusted.

And I'm working on my own time, he thought sourly as he observed the contents of the lunch bag his wife had packed for him.

The doctor had told him to take off twenty pounds. As he unwrapped a tuna on whole wheat, he decided that Suzie was hell-bent on making the weight loss happen by starving him to death.

Then he smiled reluctantly and admitted that it was this lousy diet that was getting to him. What he really needed was a nice thick ham and cheese on rye, with potato salad on the side. And a pickle, he added.

As he bit into the tuna sandwich, he reminded himself that even if Osborne *had* just made another remark about him overdoing his efforts on the Lawrence case, Martha's family didn't see it that way.

In fact Martha's grandmother, a handsome and naturally elegant eighty-year-old, had looked happier than he'd have thought possible when he stopped in on her last week. Then she told him the good news: Martha's sister, Christine, just had a baby.

"George and Amanda are so thrilled," she told him. "It's the first time I've seen either one of them really smile in the last four and a half years. I know that having a grandchild will help them get over losing Martha."

George and Amanda were Martha's parents.

Then Mrs. Lawrence had added, "Tommy, on one level we all accept that Martha is gone. She never would have voluntarily disappeared. What haunts us is the terrible possibility that some psychotic person kidnapped her and is keeping her prisoner. It would be easier if we only knew for certain that she's gone."

"Gone," meaning dead, of course.

She had been seen last on the boardwalk at 6:30 A.M. on September 7, four-and-a-half years ago.

As Tommy unenthusiastically finished his sandwich, he made a decision. As of 6:00 A.M. tomorrow, he was going to become one of the joggers on the Spring Lake boardwalk.

It would help him to shed the twenty pounds, but there was something else. Like an itch he couldn't scratch, he was getting a feeling that sometimes came when he was working intensely on a homicide, and try as he might to escape it, it wouldn't go away.

He was closing in on the killer.

His phone rang. He picked it up as he bit into the apple that was supposed to pass for dessert. It was Osborne's secretary. "Tommy, meet the boss down at his car right away."

Elliot Osborne was just getting in the backseat when Tommy, puffing slightly, arrived at the reserved parking section. Osborne did not speak until the car pulled out and the driver turned on the siren.

"A skeleton has just been uncovered on Hayes Avenue in Spring Lake. Owner was excavating for a pool."

Before Osborne could continue, the phone in the squad car rang. The driver answered and handed it back to the prosecutor. "It's Newton, sir."

Osborne held up the phone so that Tommy could hear what the forensics chief was saying. "You've got yourself a hell of a case, Elliot. There are remains of two people buried here, and from the look of it, one has been in the ground a lot longer than the other."

five

AFTER MAKING THE 911 CALL, Emily ran outside and stood at the edge of the gaping hole and looked down at what appeared to be a human skeleton.

As a criminal defense attorney she had seen dozens of graphic pictures of bodies. The expressions on the faces of many of them had been frozen in fear. In others she'd been sure she could detect lingering traces of pleading in their staring eyes. But nothing had ever affected her the way the sight of this victim did now.

The body had been bound in heavy, clear plastic. The plastic was shredding but, although the flesh had crumbled, it had done a good job of keeping the bones intact. For a moment it crossed her mind that the remains of her great-great-grandaunt had been accidentally discovered.

Then she rejected that possibility. In 1891, when Madeline Shapely disappeared, plastic had not yet been invented, so this could not be her.

When the first police car raced up the driveway, its siren screeching, Emily returned to the house. She knew it was inevitable that the police would want to speak to her, and she felt the need to collect her wits.

"Collect her wits"—her grandmother's expression.

The bags of food were on the kitchen counter where she had dropped them in her rush to phone. With robotlike precision she filled the kettle, placed it on the stove, turned on the flame, then sorted through the bags and put the perishables in the refrigerator. She hesitated for a moment, then began opening and closing cabinets.

"I don't remember where the groceries belong," she

said aloud, fretfully, then recognized that the stab of childish irritation was the result of shock.

The kettle began whistling. A cup of tea, she thought. That will clear my head.

A large window in the kitchen overlooked the grounds behind the house. Teacup in hand, Emily stood at it, observing the quiet efficiency with which the area around the excavation was being cordoned off.

Police photographers arrived and began snapping picture after picture of the site. She knew it had to be a forensic expert who scrambled into the excavation, near the place where the skeleton was lying.

She knew that the remains would be taken to the morgue and examined. And then a physical description would be issued, giving the sex of the victim, along with the approximate size and weight and age. Dental records and DNA would help to match the description with that of a missing person. And for some unfortunate family the agony of uncertainty would be ended, along with the forlorn hope that maybe the loved one would return.

The bell rang.

A GRIM-FACED TOMMY DUGGAN stood next to Elliot Osborne on the porch and waited for the door to be opened. From their whispered consultation with the forensics chief, both men were sure that the search for Martha Lawrence was over. Newton had told them that the condition of the skeletal frame wrapped in plastic indicated it was that of a young adult who, as far as he could tell, had perfect teeth. He refused to speculate on the loose human bones that he had found near the skeleton until the medical examiner could examine them in the morgue.

Tommy glanced over his shoulder. "There are people starting to gather out there. The Lawrences are sure to hear about this."

"Dr. O'Brien is going to rush the autopsy," Osborne

said crisply. "He understands that everyone in Spring Lake is going to jump to the conclusion that it's Martha Lawrence."

When the door opened, both men had their identification badges in hand. "I'm Emily Graham. Please come in," she said.

She had expected the visit to be little more than a formality. "I understand that you only closed on the house this morning, Ms. Graham," Osborne began.

She was familiar with government officials like Elliot Osborne. Impeccably dressed, courteous, smart, they were also good public relations people who left the nitty-gritty to their underlings. She knew that he and Detective Duggan would be comparing notes and impressions later on.

She also knew that behind his appropriately serious demeanor, Detective Duggan was studying her with appraising eyes.

They were standing in the foyer, where the only piece of furniture was a quaint Victorian loveseat. When she had seen the house that first day and said she wanted to buy it, adding that she would be interested in purchasing some of the furnishings as well, Theresa Kiernan, the former owner, had pointed to the love seat with a faint smile. "I love this piece, but trust me, it's purely for atmosphere. It's so low that it defies the force of gravity to get up from it."

Emily invited Osborne and Detective Duggan into the living room. I was planning to move the couches this afternoon, she thought as they followed her through the archway. I wanted to have them face each other at the fireplace. She tried to fight back a growing sense of unreality.

Duggan had quietly taken out a notebook.

"We'd just like to ask you a few simple questions, Ms. Graham," Osborne said sympathetically. "How long have you been coming to Spring Lake?"

To her own ears, her story of driving down for the first time three months ago and immediately buying the house sounded almost ludicrous.

"You'd never been here before and bought a house like

this on impulse?" There was a distinct tone of incredulity in Osborne's voice.

Emily could see that the expression in Duggan's eyes was speculative. She chose her words carefully. "I came to Spring Lake on an impulse because all my life I've been curious about it. My family built this house in 1875. They owned it until 1892, selling it after the older daughter, Madeline, disappeared in 1891. In looking up the town records to see where the house was, I found it was for sale. I saw it, loved it, and bought it. More than that I can't tell you."

She did not understand the startled expression on both their faces. "I didn't even realize this was the Shapley house," Osborne said. "We're expecting that the remains will be those of a young woman who disappeared over four years ago while visiting her grandparents in Spring Lake." With a brief shake of his hand, he signaled to Duggan that now was not the right time to mention the second set of remains.

Emily felt the color drain from her face. "A young woman disappeared over four years ago and is buried here?" she whispered. "Dear God, how can that be?"

"It's a very sad day for this community." Osborne got up. "I'm afraid we'll have to keep the scene under protection until they have finished processing it. As soon as it is, you'll be able to have your contractor resume digging for your pool."

There isn't going to be a pool, Emily thought.

"There's bound to be a lot of media people around. We'll keep them from bothering you as best we can," Osborne said. "We may want to talk to you further."

As they walked to the door, the bell pealed insistently.

The moving van from Albany had arrived.

six _____

FOR THE RESIDENTS of Spring Lake, the day had begun in its usual, orderly fashion. Most of the commuters had gathered at the train station for the hour-and-a-half ride to their jobs in New York City. Others had parked their cars in neighboring Atlantic Highlands and caught the jet water launch which whisked them to a pier at the foot of the World Financial Center.

There, under the watchful gaze of the Statue of Liberty, they had hurried to their various offices. Many of them worked in the financial community as traders on the stock exchange or executives in brokerage houses. Others were lawyers and bankers.

In Spring Lake the morning passed in reassuring regularity. Children filled the classes at the public school and St. Catherine's. The tasteful shops on quaint Third Avenue opened for business. At noon a favorite spot for lunch was the Sisters Café. Realtors brought prospective buyers to see available properties and explained that, even with the escalating prices, a home here was an excellent investment.

The disappearance of Martha Lawrence four and a half years earlier had hung like a pall over the consciousness of the residents, but other than that terrible event, serious crime was virtually nonexistent in this town.

Now, on this wind-driven first day of spring, that local sense of security was shaken to the core.

Word of the police activity on Hayes Avenue spread through the town. Rumors of the discovery of human remains followed quickly. The operator of the backhoe quietly used his cell phone to call his wife.

"I heard the forensics chief say that from the condition of the bones he thinks it's a young adult," he whispered.

"There's something else down there too, but they're not letting on what it is."

His wife rushed to call her friends. One of them, a stringer for the CBS network, phoned in the tip. A helicopter was dispatched to cover the story.

Everyone knew that the victim was going to be Martha Lawrence. Old friends gathered one by one in the Lawrence home. One of them took it upon herself to dial Martha's parents in Philadelphia.

Even before the official word came, George and Amanda Lawrence canceled their planned visit to the home of their older daughter in Bernardsville, New Jersey, to see their new granddaughter. With a sense of heartsick inevitability, they set out for Spring Lake instead.

By six o'clock, as dark settled over the East Coast, the pastor of St. Catherine's accompanied the prosecutor to the Lawrence home. Martha's dental records, accurate in their description of the teeth that had given Martha her brilliant smile, matched exactly the impression Dr. O'Brien had made during the autopsy.

A few strands of what had been long blond hair still clung to the back of the skull. They matched the strands the police had taken from Martha's pillow and hairbrush after her disappearance.

A sense of collective mourning settled over the town.

The police had decided to withhold, for the present, information about the second skeletal remains. They were also those of a young woman, and the forensics chief estimated that they had been in the ground for over one hundred years.

In addition, it would not be revealed that the instrument of Martha's death had been a silk scarf with metallic beading, knotted tightly around her throat.

However, the most chilling fact that the police were not ready to share was the revelation that, within her plastic shroud, Martha Lawrence had been buried with the finger bone of the century-old victim, and that a sapphire ring still dangled from that bone.

seven

NEITHER THE STATE-OF-THE-ART security system nor the presence of a policeman in the cabana to guard the crime scene could reassure Emily the first night in her new home. The bustle of the moving men, followed by the need to unpack and restore the house to orderliness, had distracted her for the afternoon. As far as was humanly possible, she tried to take her mind off the activity in the backyard, the presence of the quiet and orderly spectators gathered in the street, and the penetrating noise of the helicopter hovering overhead.

At seven o'clock she made a salad, baked a potato, and broiled the baby lamb chops that had been part of her celebratory food shopping after she took title to the house.

But even though she drew all the blinds and turned the fire in the kitchen hearth to the highest setting, she still felt completely vulnerable.

To distract herself, she brought the book she'd been looking forward to reading to the table, but, despite her efforts, nothing relieved her anxiety. Several glasses of Chianti neither warmed nor relaxed her. She loved to cook, and friends had always commented that she could make even a simple meal seem special. Tonight she could barely taste what she was eating. She reread the first chapter of the book twice, but the words seemed meaningless, without coherence.

Nothing could overcome the haunting knowledge that a young woman's body had been found on this property. She told herself that it had to be an ironic coincidence that her great-great-grandaunt had disappeared from these grounds and that today another young woman who had disappeared in Spring Lake had been found here.

But as she tidied the kitchen, turned off the fire, checked all the doors, set the alarm to go off at any attempt to open the doors or a window, Emily was unable to either ignore or escape the growing certainty that the death of her ancestor and the death of that young girl four and a half years ago were inexorably linked.

The book under her arm, she climbed the stairs to the second floor. It was only nine o'clock, but all she wanted to do was to shower, change into warm pj's and go to bed, where she would read or watch television or both.

Like last night, she thought.

The Kiernans had suggested she would be pleased with their twice-a-week housekeeper, Doreen Sullivan. At the closing their lawyer had said that as a welcoming present they had engaged Doreen to go through the house and put fresh linens on the beds and fresh towels in the bathrooms.

The house was on the corner, one street from the ocean. There were ocean views from the south and east sides of the master bedroom. Twenty minutes after she reached the second floor, Emily was showered and changed, and now somewhat relaxed, pulled the coverlet back from the matching headboard.

Then she hesitated. Had she bolted the front door?

Even with the security system on, she had to be sure.

Annoyed at herself, she hurried out of the bedroom and down the hall. At the head of the stairs, she flipped the switch that lit the foyer chandelier, then hurried down the stairs.

Before she reached the front door she saw the envelope that had been slipped under it. Please, God, not again, she thought as she bent down to pick it up. *Don't* let that business begin again!

She ripped open the envelope. As she had feared, it contained a snapshot, the silhouette of a woman at a window, the light behind her. For a moment she had to focus on it to realize she was the woman in the picture.

And then she knew.

Last night. At the Candlelight Inn. When she'd opened the window she had stood there looking out before she lowered the shade.

Someone had been standing on the boardwalk. No,

that wasn't possible, she thought. She had looked at the boardwalk and it was deserted.

Someone standing on the *beach* had snapped her picture and had it developed, then slipped it under the door within the last hour. It hadn't been there when she went upstairs.

It was as though the person who had stalked her in Albany had followed her to Spring Lake! But that was impossible. Ned Koehler was in Gray Manor, a secure psychiatric facility in Albany.

The house phone had not yet been connected. Her cell phone was in the bedroom. Holding the picture, she ran to pick it up. Her fingers trembling, she dialed information.

"Welcome to local and national information . . ."

"Albany, New York. Gray Manor Hospital." To her dismay she could barely speak above a whisper.

A few moments later she was talking to the evening supervisor of the unit where Ned Koehler was confined.

She identified herself.

"I know your name," the supervisor said. "You're the one he was stalking."

"Is he out on a pass?"

"Koehler? Absolutely not, Ms. Graham."

"Is there a chance he managed to get out on his own?"

"I saw him at bed check less than an hour ago."

A vivid image of Ned Koehler flashed through Emily's mind: a slight man in his early forties, balding, hesitant in speech and manner. In court he had wept silently throughout the trial. She had defended Joel Lake, who had been accused of murdering Ned's mother during a bungled robbery.

When the jury acquitted Lake, Ned Koehler had gone berserk and had lunged across the room at her. He was screaming obscenities, Emily remembered. He was telling me I'd gotten a killer off. It had taken two sheriff's deputies to restrain him.

"How is he doing?" she asked.

"Singing the same old song—that he's innocent." The

supervisor's voice was reassuring. "Ms. Graham, it's not uncommon for stalking victims to feel apprehensive even after the stalker is under lock and key. Ned isn't going anywhere."

When she replaced the receiver, Emily made herself study the picture. In it she was framed in the center of the window, an easy target for someone with a gun instead of a camera, it occurred to her.

She had to call the police. What about the policeman in the back, in the cabana. I don't want to open the door. Suppose he isn't there. Suppose someone else is there.

911—

No, the number of the police station was on the calendar in the kitchen. She didn't want the police to arrive with screaming sirens. The alarm system was on. No one could get in.

The officer who took the call sent a car immediately. The lights were flashing, but the driver did not turn on the siren.

The cop was young, probably not more than twenty-two. She showed him the picture, told him about the stalker in Albany.

"You're sure he hasn't been released, Ms. Graham?"

"I just called there."

"My guess is that a smart-alec kid who knows you had this problem is playing a practical joke," he said soothingly. "Have you got a couple of plastic bags you could give me?"

He held the snapshot and then the envelope at the corner as he dropped them into the bags. "These will be checked for fingerprints," he explained. "I'll be on my way now." She walked with him to the door.

"Tonight we'll be keeping a close watch on the front of the house and we'll alert the officer in the back to keep his eyes open," he told her. "You'll be fine."

Maybe, Emily thought as she bolted the door behind him.

Getting into bed, she pulled up the covers and forced

herself to turn off the light. There was plenty of publicity when Ned Koehler was caught and then put away, she thought. Maybe this person is a copycat.

But *why?* And what other explanation could there be? Ned Koehler was guilty. Of course he was. The supervisor's voice: "singing the same old song"—that he was innocent.

Was he? If so, was the real stalker still free and ready to renew his unwelcome attentions?

It was nearly dawn when, with the reassurance of the early morning light, Emily finally fell asleep. She was woken at nine by the barking of the dogs the police had brought to assist them in their search for other possible victims buried on her property.

eight

CLAYTON AND RACHEL WILCOX had been guests at the Lawrence home the night before Martha Lawrence disappeared. Since then, like all the other guests, they had been visited regularly by Detective Tom Duggan.

They had heard the shocking news that Martha's body had been discovered, but unlike many of the other guests at that final festive gathering, they had not gone immediately to the Lawrence home. Rachel had pointed out to her husband that only the very closest friends would be welcome at such a time of grief. The finality in her voice left no room for discussion.

Sixty-four-years old, Rachel was handsome, with shoulder-length iron-gray hair that she looped neatly around her head. Tall and with impeccable carriage, she exuded authority. Her skin, devoid of even a touch of makeup, was clear and firm. Her eyes, a grayish blue, had a perpetually stern expression.

Thirty years ago, when, as a shy, nearly forty-year-old assistant dean, Clayton had been courting her, he had lovingly compared Rachel to a Viking. "I can imagine you at the helm of a ship, armed for battle, with the wind blowing through your hair," he had whispered.

He now mentally referred to Rachel as "The Viking." The name, however, was no longer an endearment. Clayton lived in a constant state of high alert, ever anxious to avoid his wife's blistering wrath. When he nonetheless somehow provoked it, her caustic tongue lashed him mercilessly. Early in their marriage he had learned that she neither forgave nor forgot.

Having been a guest at the Lawrence home hours before Martha disappeared seemed to him to be sufficient reason to pay a brief condolence call, but Clayton wisely did not make that suggestion. Instead, as they watched the eleven o'clock news broadcast, he listened in suffering silence to Rachel's caustic comments.

"It's very sad, of course, but at least this should put an end to that detective coming around here and annoying us," she said.

If anything, this will bring Duggan around *more* often, Clayton thought. A large man, with a leonine head of shaggy gray hair and knowing eyes, he looked the academic he had been.

When, twelve years ago, at age fifty-five, he retired from the presidency of Enoch College, a small but prestigious institution in Ohio, he and Rachel had moved permanently to Spring Lake. He had first come to the town as a young boy, visiting an uncle who had moved there, and over the years he had come back for occasional visits. As a hobby, he had delved with enthusiasm into the history of the town and was now known as the unofficial local historian.

Rachel had become a volunteer at several local charities, where she was admired for her organizational abilities and energies, although no one particularly liked her. She had also made sure that everyone knew that her husband was a former college president, and that she herself was a graduate of Smith. "All the women in our family, starting with my grandmother, have been graduates of Smith," she would explain. She had never forgiven Clayton for an indiscretion with a fellow professor three years after their marriage. Later, the mistake that had caused him to retire abruptly from Enoch College, a place where she had enjoyed the lifestyle, had permanently embittered her.

As a picture of Martha Lawrence filled the television screen, Clayton Wilcox felt his hands go moist with fear. There had been someone else with long blond hair and an exquisite body. Now that Martha's remains had been found, how intensely would the police probe into the backgrounds of the people who had been at the party that night? He swallowed over the dryness in his mouth and throat.

"Martha Lawrence had been visiting her grandparents before returning to college," the CBS anchorwoman, Dana Tyler, was saying.

"I gave you my scarf to hold at the party," Rachel complained for the millionth time. "And naturally, you managed to lose it."

nine

TODD, SCANLON, KLEIN AND TODD, a nationally known criminal defense law firm located on Park Avenue South in Manhattan, had been founded by Walter Todd. As he put it, "Forty-five years ago I hung out a shingle in a storefront near the courthouse. Nobody came. I started making friends with the bail bondsmen. They took a liking to me and began telling their clients that I was a good lawyer. And, even better than that, I was cheap."

The other Todd in the partnership was Walter's son, Nicholas. "Looks like me, sounds like me, and before he's finished, he'll be as good a lawyer as I am," Walter Todd would brag. "I swear Nick could get Satan off the hook."

He always ignored Nick's protest. "I would hardly consider that a compliment, Dad."

On March 21st, Nick Todd and his father worked late on an impending trial, then Nick joined his parents for dinner in their spacious U.N. Plaza apartment.

At ten minutes of eleven he started to leave, but then decided to wait and watch the CBS eleven o'clock news with them. "There may be something about the trial," he said. "There's a rumor floating that we're working on a plea bargain."

The Martha Lawrence story was the breaking headline. "That poor family," his mother said, sighing. "I guess it's better for them to know, but to lose a child . . ." Anne Todd's voice trailed off. When Nick was two, she had given birth to a baby girl whom they named Amelia. She had lived only a day.

She would have been thirty-six next week, Anne thought. Even as a newborn she looked like me. In her mind she could see Amelia alive, a young woman with dark hair and blue-green eyes. I know she would have loved music as much as I do. We'd have gone to concerts together . . .

She blinked back the tears that always welled in her eyes when she thought of her lost daughter.

Nick realized what had been pricking at his subconscious. "Isn't Spring Lake the place where Emily Graham bought a house?" he asked.

Walter Todd nodded. "I still wonder why I let her get away with waiting until May to come into the office," he said, gruffly. "We could use her now."

"Maybe because, after seeing her in Albany, you thought she had something worth waiting for," Nick suggested amiably.

An image of Emily Graham floated through his mind. Before they offered her the job, he and his father had gone up to Albany to observe her in court. She had been brilliant, getting an acquittal for a client who had been charged with criminally negligent homicide.

She had gone out to lunch with them. Nick remembered the eloquent praise his usually taciturn father had heaped on her.

They're as alike as two peas in a pod, he thought now. Once they take on a case they'd just about kill for the client.

Since she'd taken the New York apartment, Emily had been in to see them several times, settling her office and getting to know the staff. Nick realized that he was looking forward very much to having her there every day.

His lanky six-foot-two frame unfolded as he stood up. "I'm on my way. I want to hit the gym early tomorrow, and it's been a long day."

His mother accompanied him to the door. "I wish you'd wear a hat," she fretted. "It's terribly cold out."

He bent down and kissed her cheek. "You forgot to tell me not to forget to wear a scarf."

Anne hesitated, then glanced into the living room where her husband was still intent on hearing the news. Dropping her voice, she begged, "Nick, please tell me what's wrong, because, don't deny it, there is something wrong. Are you sick and not letting me know?"

"Trust me. I'm in perfect health," he reassured her. "It's just that the Hunter trial is worrying me."

"*Dad* isn't worried about it," Anne protested. "He said he's sure the worst possible scenario is a hung jury. But you're like me. You always were a worrier."

"We're even. You're worried about me and I'm worried about the trial."

They smiled together. Nick is like me inside, Anne thought, but in looks he's all Walter, even to wrinkling his forehead when he's concentrating.

"Don't frown," she told him as he opened the door.

"I know. It makes wrinkles."

"And don't worry about the trial. You know you'll win in court."

On the way down in the elevator from the 36th floor, Nick thought, That's just it, Mom. We will win, on a technicality, and that scum will get off scot-free. Their client was a sleazy lawyer who had invaded the trust accounts of estate heirs, many of them people who desperately needed their inheritance.

He decided to walk downtown and then take a subway to his co-op in SoHo. But even the crisp night air did not relieve the depression that was increasingly becoming part of his psyche. He passed through Times Square barely aware of its glittering marquees.

You don't have to be Lady Macbeth and kill someone to feel as if you have blood on your hands, he thought grimly.

Thursday, March 22 ═══════════

ten _____

EVER SINCE THEY BEGAN digging for the pool, he had known they might come across Martha's remains. He could only hope that the finger bone was still intact within the plastic shroud. But even if it wasn't, they were bound to find the ring. All the reports said that every inch of the excavation area was being sifted by hand.

Of course it was too much to expect the medical examiner to realize that Martha and Madeline had died exactly the same way. Martha with the scarf tightened around her neck, Madeline with the starched white linen sash torn from around her waist as she tried to flee.

He could recite *that* passage from the diary from memory.

It is curious to realize that without a single gesture on my part, Madeline knew she had made a mistake in coming into the house. There was a nervous plucking at her skirt with those long, slender fingers, even though her facial expression did not change.

She watched as I locked the door.

"Why are you doing that?" she asked.

She must have seen something in my eyes, because her

hand flew to her mouth. I watched the muscles in her neck move as she vainly tried to scream. She was too frightened to do anything but whisper, "Please."

She tried to run past me to the window, but I grabbed her sash and pulled it from her, then grasped it in two hands and wrapped it around her neck. At that, with remarkable strength, she tried to punch and kick me. No longer a trembling lamb, she became a tigress fighting for her life.

Later, I bathed and changed and called on her parents, who by then were deeply concerned as to her whereabouts.

Ashes to ashes. Dust to dust.

There was a front page picture of Martha in all the papers, even the *Times*. Why not? It was newsworthy when the body of a beautiful young woman was found, especially when she was from a privileged family in an upscale and picturesque community. How much more newsworthy it would be if they announced they had found a finger bone with a ring inside the plastic. If they had found it, he hoped they would realize that he had closed Martha's hand over it.

Her hand had been still warm and pliable.

Sisters in death, one hundred and ten years apart.

It had been announced that the prosecutor was holding a news conference at eleven. It was five of eleven now.

He reached over and turned on the television set, then leaned back and chuckled in anticipation.

eleven _____

FIFTEEN MINUTES before his scheduled news conference, Elliot Osborne briefed his top aides on what he would and would not tell the press.

He would report the findings of the autopsy, and that

the cause of death was strangulation. He would not, repeat *not*, tell them a scarf had been the murder weapon or about the metallic beading that had edged it. He would say that the victim's body had been wrapped in thick layers of plastic that, though separating and crumbling, had kept the skeletal remains intact.

"Are you going to talk about the finger bone, sir? That's gonna really stir up a hornet's nest."

Pete Walsh had just been promoted to the rank of detective. He was smart and he was young. He also couldn't wait to get his two cents in, Tommy Duggan thought sourly. It gave him a small measure of satisfaction to hear the boss tell Walsh to let him finish, although he felt like a louse as Walsh's face turned beet red.

He and Osborne had been back here at dawn. They had gone over every detail of O'Brien's completed autopsy report and rehashed every detail of the case.

They didn't need Pete Walsh to tell them the media would have a field day with this one.

Osborne continued: "In my statement I will say that we never expected to find Martha Lawrence alive; that it is not unusual for the remains of a victim to be found buried near the place where death had occurred."

He cleared his throat. "I will have to reveal that, for some bizarre and twisted reason, Martha Lawrence was buried in contact with other human remains, and those remains are over a century old.

"As you know, four and a half years ago, when Martha disappeared, *The Asbury Park Press* dug up the old story about the disappearance of nineteen-year-old Madeline Shapley in 1891. It is very likely that the media will jump to the conclusion that the finger bone found with Martha belonged to Madeline Shapley, particularly since the remains are on the Shapley property."

"Is it true that the new owner of that property is a descendant of the Shapleys?"

"That is true, yes."

"Then can't you check her DNA against the finger bone?"

"If Ms. Graham is willing, we can certainly do that. However, last night I ordered that all available records of Madeline Shapley's disappearance be examined and a search be made for any other cases of missing women in Spring Lake around that time."

It was just a blind stab, Duggan thought, but we hit the jackpot.

"Our researchers found that two other young women had been listed as missing at around that same time" Osborne continued. "Madeline Shapley had last been seen on the porch of the family home on Hayes Avenue when she disappeared on September 7, 1891.

"Letitia Gregg of Tuttle Avenue disappeared on August 5, 1893. According to the police file, her parents feared that she might have gone swimming alone, which was why that case was never classified as suspicious.

"Three years later, on March 31, 1896, Letita's devoted friend Ellen Swain disappeared. She had been observed leaving a friend's home as dusk was settling in."

And that's when the media starts screaming about a turn-of-the-century serial killer in Spring Lake, Tommy thought. Just what we need.

Osborne glanced at his watch. "It's one minute of eleven. Let's go."

The briefing room was packed. The questions thrown at Osborne were rapid and hard-hitting. There was no way he could argue with the *New York Post* reporter who said that the finding of the two skeletal remains on the same site could not be a bizarre coincidence.

"I agree," Osborne said. "The finger bone with the ring was deliberately placed inside the plastic with Martha's body."

"*Where* inside the plastic?" the ABC crime reporter asked.

"Within Martha's hand."

"Do you think it was a coincidence that the killer

found the other remains when he dug Martha's grave, or could he possibly have chosen that spot because he knew it had been used as a burial ground?" Ralph Penza, a senior reporter from NBC, asked quietly.

"It would be ridiculous if I were to suggest that someone anxious to bury his victim and avoid possible detection would happen upon the bones of another victim and make the snap decision to place a finger bone within the shroud he was creating."

Osborne held up a photograph. "This is an enlarged aerial shot of the crime site." He pointed to the excavation pit in the backyard. "Martha's killer dug a relatively shallow grave, but it might never have been found except for the pool excavation. Until a year ago a very large holly tree totally blocked that section of the backyard from the view of anyone in the house or on the street."

In response to another question, he verified that Emily Graham, the new owner of the property, was a descendant of the original owners, and that, yes, if she were willing, DNA testing would establish whether or not the remains found with Martha's were those of Ms. Graham's great-great-grandaunt.

The question that Tommy Duggan knew was inevitable came: "Are you suggesting that this perhaps was a serial killing, tied into a murder in Spring Lake one hundred and ten years ago?"

"I'm suggesting nothing."

"But both Martha Lawrence and Madeline Shapley disappeared on September 7th. How do you explain that?"

"I don't."

"Do you think Martha's killer is a reincarnation?" Reba Ashby from *The National Daily* asked eagerly.

The prosecutor frowned. "Absolutely *not!* No more questions."

Osborne caught Tommy's eye as he exited the room. Tommy knew they were sharing the same thought. Martha Lawrence's death had just become a juicy headline story, and the only way to stop it was to find the killer.

The remnants of a scarf with metallic edging was the only clue they had with which to begin the search.

That, and the fact that whoever the killer was, he—and for now they were assuming it was a "he"—knew about a grave that had been dug on the Shapley property secretly over one hundred years ago.

twelve

AT NINE O'CLOCK Emily awoke from the uneasy sleep she'd fallen into after she closed the windows and blocked out the sounds from the backyard.

A long shower helped to diffuse the sense of heaviness that was gripping her.

The body of the missing girl in the backyard . . .

The snapshot slipped under the door . . .

Will Stafford had cautioned her that she was being too impulsive in buying this house. But I *wanted* it, she thought, as she tightened the belt of her terry-cloth robe around her waist. I *still* want it.

She stuffed her feet into slippers and went downstairs to make coffee. Ever since her college days it had been her routine to shower, make coffee, then dress, with a cup of coffee nearby. She had always sworn she could feel lights go on in different sections of her brain as she sipped.

Even without looking outside she could see that it was going to be a beautiful day. Rays of sunshine were streaming through the stained-glass window at the landing of the staircase. When she passed the living room, she paused to admire the decorative fireplace screen and andirons she'd put in place yesterday. "I'm almost positive they were bought for the Spring Lake house when it was built in 1875," her grandmother had told her.

They looked as if they belonged there. And I *feel* as if I belong here, Emily thought.

In the dining room she saw the oak sideboard with boxwood panels, another piece that the movers had brought down from Albany. That sideboard had definitely been purchased for this house. Years ago her grandmother had found the receipt for it.

While she waited for the coffee to brew, Emily stood at the window and watched the police squad carefully sifting the dirt at the excavation site. What kind of evidence would they find four and a half years after Martha's death? she wondered.

And why the dogs this morning? Did they seriously believe that someone else was buried here?

When the coffee was ready she poured a cup and took it upstairs, then turned on the radio as she dressed. The lead story was the discovery of Martha Lawrence's body, of course. Emily winced as she heard her own name on the news, and that "The new owner of the property where Martha Lawrence's remains were found is the great-great-grandniece of another young woman who mysteriously disappeared over one hundred years ago."

She snapped off the radio as her cell phone rang. It's going to be Mom, she thought. Hugh and Beth Graham, her father and mother, both pediatricians, had been at a medical seminar in California. She knew they had been due back in Chicago the night before.

Her mother had not been comfortable with the idea of her buying the house in Spring Lake. She's not going to like what I have to tell her, Emily thought. But there's no way I can avoid it.

Dr. Beth Graham was clearly distressed at what had occurred. "Good God, Em, I remember as a child hearing the story of Madeline and how her mother had lived her whole life still hoping that one day Madeline would walk through the door. You mean to say that another young girl in Spring Lake was missing and her remains were found on the property?"

She did not give Emily a chance to answer before continuing. "I'm so sorry for her family, but for the love of heaven the one thing I hoped was that you'd at least be safe there. After that stalker was arrested, I breathed easy for the first time in a year."

Emily could picture her mother in her office, standing small but ramrod straight at her desk, her pretty face creased with worry. She shouldn't be worrying about me, she thought. I'm sure right now the waiting room is filled with babies.

Her parents shared a medical practice. Though in their early sixties, neither one of them even considered retirement. Growing up, her mother had often told her and her brothers, "If you want to be happy for a year, win the lottery. If you want to be happy for life, love what you do."

Her mother and father loved every one of their little patients.

"Mom, look at it this way. At least the Lawrence family will have closure, and there's no reason to worry about me."

"I suppose not," her mother admitted reluctantly. "There's no chance they'd let that stalker out, is there?"

"Not a chance," Emily said heartily. "Now go take care of your babies. Give my love to Dad."

When she pushed the OFF button of the cell phone it was with the quiet resolve that there was no way her parents were going to hear about the copycat stalker. She also was glad she had made the decision to report the snapshot pushed under the door to the Spring Lake police, just in case her parents ever *did* get to hear of it.

She had dressed in jeans and a sweater. As much as possible, she wanted this day to go ahead as she had planned. The Kiernans had taken the furniture from the small bedroom next to the master suite, and that space would make a perfect office. Her desk and files and bookcases were in it now. She needed to set up her computer and fax and unpack the books. The phone company was coming this morning to install new telephone lines, one of which would be computer dedicated.

She wanted to place family pictures throughout the

house. As she twisted her hair into a knot and caught it up with a comb, Emily thought of the pictures she had weeded out before the move to the Manhattan apartment.

All the pictures with Gary were gone.

Also all the college pictures with Barb in them. Her best friend. Her best buddy. Emily and Barbara. Where you find one, you find the other.

Uh-huh, Emily thought as the familiar stab of pure pain shot through her. Meet my ex-husband. Meet my used-to-be best friend.

I wonder if they're still seeing each other? I always knew Barb had a yen for Gary, but I never dreamed it was reciprocated.

After three years there was no question. The residual pain was caused by the enormity of the betrayal, although on the personal level, both of them had lost their ability to cause her sorrow.

She made the bed, pulling the sheets tight, tucking them in. The cream-colored coverlet complemented the sparkling green-and-rose print of the bed skirt and the window treatments. She would eventually trade the chaise lounge for a pair of comfortable chairs at the bay window. But for now, it matched the decor and would do.

The firm ring of the doorbell meant one of two things, either the telephone service was there or the media. She glanced out the window and was relieved to see the panel truck with the familiar Verizon logo on it.

By five of eleven the technicians from the phone company were gone. She went into the study and turned on the television to catch the news.

". . . century-old finger bone with a ring . . ."

When the program ended, Emily turned off the TV and sat quietly. As the screen went black she continued to stare at it, her mind a kaleidoscope of childhood memories.

Gran telling the stories about Madeline over and over again. I always wanted to hear about her, Emily thought. Even when I was little I found her fascinating.

Gran's eyes would get a faraway look as she talked about her. "Madeline was my grandmother's older sister. . . . My grandmother always looked so sad when she talked about her. Madeline was her big sister, and she worshiped her. She would tell me how beautiful she was. Half the young men in Spring Lake were in love with her.

"They all made it their business to walk past the house, hoping to see her sitting on the porch. That last day she was so excited. Her beau, Douglas Carter, had spoken to her father and received permission to propose to her. She expected him to bring her an engagement ring. It was late afternoon. She was wearing a white linen dress. Madeline showed my grandmother how she had changed her sixteenth birthday ring from her left to her right hand so that she wouldn't have to take it off when Douglas came . . ."

Two years after Madeline disappeared, Douglas Carter had killed himself, Emily remembered.

She got up. How much more could her grandmother recall of the events she had been told about as a child?

Her eyesight was failing, but she was still in remarkably good health. And, like many very elderly people, her long-term memory had strengthened with age.

She and a couple of her old friends had moved at the same time to an assisted-living facility in Albany. Emily dialed the number and heard the phone picked up on the first ring.

"Tell me about the house," her grandmother ordered after a quick greeting.

There was no easy way to tell her what had happened. "A young woman who disappeared has been found there? Oh, Emily, how could that happen?"

"I don't know, but I want to find out. Gran, remember you told me that Madeline had had a ring on the day she disappeared?"

"She was expecting that Douglas Carter would bring her an engagement ring."

"Didn't you say something about her wearing a ring that had been her sixteenth-birthday present?"

"Let me see. Oh, yes, I did, Em. It was a sapphire ring

set with tiny diamonds. From the description of it, I had one like it made for your mother when she was sixteen. Didn't she give it to you?"

Of *course,* Emily thought. Someone swiped it at a youth hostel that summer I went hiking in Europe with Barbara.

"Gran, by any chance do you still have that recorder I gave you?"

"Yes, I do."

The several summers she had been in Europe during her college days they had made tapes and sent them to each other.

"I want you to do something. Start talking into it. Tell me everything that you can remember having heard about Madeline. Try to remember names of people she may have known. I want to know anything that comes back to you about her or her friends. Would you do that?"

"I can try. I just wish I had those old letters and albums that got burned in the garage fire years ago. But I'll see what I can dredge up."

"Love you, Gran."

"You're not trying to figure out what happened to Madeline after all these years?"

"You never know."

Emily's next call was to the prosecutor's office. When she gave her name she was put through immediately to Elliot Osborne.

"I watched the news," she said. "By any chance was the ring you found a sapphire surrounded by small diamonds?"

"It was."

"Was it on the ring finger of the right hand?"

There was a pause. "How do you know that, Ms. Graham?" Osborne asked.

After she had hung up, Emily walked across the room, opened the door, and stepped out onto the porch. She walked around the side of the house to the back, where the investigative unit was still sifting through the dirt.

They had found Madeline's ring and finger bone in

with Martha Lawrence. The rest of Madeline's remains were found just inches below the plastic shroud. In her mind's eye, Emily could vividly see her great-great-grandaunt as she must have been on that sunny afternoon. Sitting on the porch, in a white linen dress, dark brown hair cascading around her shoulders, nineteen years old, and in love. Awaiting her fiancé, who was bringing an engagement ring to her.

Was it possible after one hundred and ten years to learn what had happened to her? *Someone* found out where she was buried, Emily thought, and chose to bury Martha Lawrence with her.

Deep in thought, her hands in the pockets of her jeans, she went back inside.

thirteen _____

WILL STAFFORD HAD a 9:00 A.M. closing on a commercial office building in Sea Girt, the next town from Spring Lake. As soon as he returned to his office, he tried to call Emily, but her phone had not yet been connected, and he didn't have the number of her cell phone.

It was nearly noon when he reached her. "I went to New York right after your closing yesterday," he explained, "and didn't know what was going on until I heard it on the news late last night. I'm so sorry for the Lawrences, and I'm sorry for you."

It was gratifying to hear the concern in his voice. "By any chance did you see the interview with the prosecutor?" she asked.

"Yes, I did. Pat, my receptionist, came in to tell me it was on. Do you think that by any chance . . . ?"

She knew the question he was going to ask. "Do I think that the ring they found in Martha Lawrence's hand belonged to Madeline Shapley? I know it did. I spoke to my grandmother, and she was able to describe the ring from what she'd heard about it."

"Then all these years your great-great-grandaunt has been buried on the property."

"It would seem so," Emily said.

"Someone knew that, and put Martha's body with hers. But how would anyone have known where Madeline Shapley was buried?" Will Stafford sounded as puzzled as Emily felt.

"If there is an answer to that, I intend to try to find it," she told him. "Will, I'd like to meet the Lawrences. Do you know them?"

"Yes, I do. They used to entertain pretty frequently before Martha disappeared. I was often at their house, and, of course, I see them around town."

"Would you call and ask if they would allow you to bring me over for a short visit whenever they're up to it?"

He did not question her reason for asking. "I'll get back to you," he promised.

Twenty minutes later the voice of the receptionist, Pat Glynn, came over the intercom. "Mr. Stafford, Natalie Frieze is here. She wants to see you for a few minutes."

Just what I need, Will thought. Natalie was the second wife of Bob Frieze, a longtime Spring Lake resident. Nearly five years ago, Bob had retired from his brokerage firm and fulfilled a lifelong dream by opening a decidedly upscale restaurant in Rumson, a town twenty minutes away. He'd called it The Seasoner.

Natalie was thirty-four. Bob was sixty-one, but clearly each had gotten what was wanted from the marriage. Bob had a trophy wife, and Natalie a luxurious lifestyle.

She also had a roving eye that sometimes settled on Will.

But today, when she came in, Natalie was not her normal flirtatious self. She skipped her usual effusive greeting to him, which always included a warm kiss, and flopped into a chair. "Will, it's so terribly sad about Martha Lawrence," she said, "but is this going to stir up a hornet's nest? I'm worried *sick.*"

"With all due respect, Natalie, you don't look worried sick. In fact, you look as though you just came back from a shoot for *Vogue.*"

She was wearing a three-quarter-length chocolate-brown leather coat with a sable collar and cuffs, and matching leather slacks. Her long blond hair hung straight past her shoulders. The even tan, which Will knew had been recently acquired in Palm Beach, accentuated her turquoise-blue eyes. She slouched back in the chair as though too burdened to sit up straight and crossed one long leg over the other, revealing a slender, high-arched foot in an open-backed sandal.

She ignored the compliment. "Will, I came straight over to talk to you after I saw that news conference. What do you think about that finger bone in Martha's hand. Isn't that a little *weird?*"

"It's certainly very strange."

"Bob almost had a heart attack. He stayed to watch the prosecutor finish his statement before he left for the restaurant. He was so upset I didn't even want him to drive the car."

"What would make him so upset?"

"Well, *you* know how that Detective Duggan keeps coming around to talk to all of us who were at that damn party at the Lawrence house the night before Martha disappeared."

"What are you getting at, Natalie?"

"What I'm getting at is that if we thought we saw a lot of Duggan before, it won't begin to compare with how much we'll see of him now that the investigation has heated up. It's obvious that Martha was murdered, and if people around here get the idea that one of us was responsible for her death it's going to be pretty damn bad publicity."

"*Publicity!* For godssake, Natalie, who's worried about publicity?"

"I'll tell you who's worried about it. My *husband* is. Every nickel Bob owns is sunk into his fancy restaurant. Why he thought that he could make a success of one without knowing about the restaurant business is a question only a shrink could answer. Now his guts are all tied up in a knot because he has the idea that if there's a lot of attention aimed our way because we were at the party, it might hurt his business. Such as it is, I might add—he's gone through three chefs so far."

Will had gone to the restaurant a few times. The decor was heavy-handed and luxurious, jacket and tie were required in the evening, which didn't sit well with people on vacation. I suggested he drop the requirement for a tie, Will thought. The food had been only average, and the prices much too steep.

"Natalie," he said, "I understand that Bob is under a lot of stress, but the idea that all of us being at the Lawrence party would keep anyone away from his restaurant is really reaching."

And if it fails with a pile of money lost in it, your pre-nup won't be worth much, he thought.

Natalie sighed and untangled herself from the chair. "I hope you're right, Will. Bob is one big quivering sea of nervous tension. Barks at me if I make even the smallest suggestion."

"What *kind* of suggestion?" I can only imagine what kind, Will thought.

"That maybe before he fires another chef he'd better take a cooking class so he can step in and take over the kitchen himself." Natalie shrugged and grinned. "I feel better talking to you. You can't have had lunch yet. Let's go get something to eat."

"I was going to send out for a sandwich."

"No you're not. We're going to eat at The Old Mill. Come on. I need company."

When they went out to the street, she tucked her hand under his arm.

"People may talk," he suggested, smiling.

"Oh, so what? They all resent me anyhow. I told Bob we should have moved. This town is too small for me and his first wife."

As he held the car door open for Natalie and she ducked her head to get in, sunbeams made her long blond hair glisten and sparkle.

For a reason unknown to him the prosecutor's statement raced through Will's mind. "Strands of long blond hair were found on the remains."

Bob Frieze, like his trophy wife, was known to have a roving eye.

Especially for beautiful women with long blond hair.

fourteen _____

DR. LILLIAN MADDEN, a prominent psychologist who used hypnosis regularly in her practice, firmly believed in reincarnation and would regress appropriate patients to previous lifetimes. She believed that emotional trauma suffered in other lives might be the source of emotional pain in present-day experience.

Very much in demand on the speakers' circuit, she expounded a favorite premise, that the people we know in this life were most likely people we knew in other lives. "I do not mean that your husband was your husband three hundred years ago," she would tell her enthralled listeners, "but I do believe he may have been your best friend. In the same way, a person with whom you have had a problem may also have been an adversary in another life."

A childless widow with her home and office in Belmar, a town bordering Spring Lake, she had heard about the discovery of Martha Lawrence's body the night before and experienced the communal sorrow that afflicted the residents of all the nearby towns.

The idea that a grandchild was not safe while jogging on a summer morning seemed incomprehensible to all of them. To find that the slain body of Martha Lawrence had been buried so near her grandparents' home convinced everyone that someone who had seemed trustworthy must be guilty of the crime. Someone who conceivably would be welcome in any one of their homes.

After she heard the report, Lillian Madden, a lifelong insomniac, had spent sleepless hours meditating on the finality of the tragic discovery. She knew that Martha's family had undoubtedly still been hoping against hope that one day, miraculously, she would return unharmed.

Instead they now lived with the cruel knowledge that any number of times they had passed by the property where her body was buried.

Four and a half years had passed. Had Martha returned in a new incarnation? Did the baby just born to Martha's older sister house the soul that had at one time dwelt in Martha's body?

Lillian Madden believed it was possible. Her prayer for the Lawrence family was that they might sense that in welcoming and loving the baby they might also be welcoming Martha home.

Her morning schedule of patients began at 8:00 A.M., an hour before her secretary, Joan Hodges, came in. It was noon before Dr. Madden talked to Joan at her desk in the reception room.

Joan, dressed in a tailored black pantsuit that showed off her recently achieved size 12, did not hear her come in. She was pushing back a strand of frosted blond hair from her forehead with one hand and scribbling a message with the other.

"Anything important?" Dr. Madden asked.

Startled, Joan looked up. "Oh, good morning, Doctor. I don't know how important they are, but you're not going to like these messages," she said bluntly. A forty-four-year-old grandmother, Joan was, in Lillian Madden's opinion, the perfect person to work in a psychologist's office. Breezy, matter-of-fact, unflappable, and naturally sympathetic, she had the gift of putting people at ease.

"What about them am I not going to like?" Lillian Madden asked mildly as she reached for the notes on Joan's somewhat cluttered desk.

"The prosecutor held a news conference, and in this past hour you've gotten calls about it from three of the most sensational tabloids in the country. Let me tell you why."

Lillian listened in startled silence as her secretary described the discovery of the ringed finger of another woman in Martha Lawrence's skeletal hand, and the fact that Madeline Shapley, like Martha, had disappeared on September 7th.

"Surely they don't think that Martha was Madeline reincarnated and destined for the same terrible death?" Lillian demanded. "That would be absurd."

"They didn't ask that," Joan Hodges said grimly. "They want to know if you think Madeline's killer is the one who's been reincarnated." She looked up at Madden. "Come to think of it, Doctor, you can't blame them for wondering that, can you?"

fifteen _____

AT TWO O' CLOCK, Tommy Duggan got back to his office, trailed by Pete Walsh. After the press conference ended, a team from the prosecutor's office had begun poring over the Martha Lawrence file. Every detail, from the first phone call four and a half years ago reporting Martha missing, to the finding of her body, was being scrutinized and analyzed to see if anything had been overlooked.

Osborne had put Tommy in charge of the investigation

and made Pete Walsh his assistant. Walsh had been a police officer in Spring Lake for eight years before joining the prosecutor's office two months ago.

He also had been a member of the research team that had spent the night at the Hall of Records in the courthouse going through the dusty bins, searching for material relating to the disappearance of Madeline Shapley in 1891.

It was Walsh who had suggested looking to see if there were any other reports of women missing around that time, and he had come up with the names of Letitia Gregg and Ellen Swain.

Now Tom Duggan looked at Walsh with sympathy. "If I haven't mentioned it before, you look like a chimney sweep," he told him.

Despite his efforts to clean up, dust and grime from the nightlong search were ground into Pete's skin and clothes. His eyes were bloodshot and though he had the build of a linebacker, his shoulders were drooping with fatigue. At thirty, even with a hairline that was already receding, he looked to Tom like a tired kid.

"Why don't you just go home, Pete?" he asked. "You're asleep on your feet."

"I'm fine. You talked about phone calls you wanted to make. I'll split them with you."

Tom shrugged. "Have it your way. The morgue will release Martha's remains to the family later today. They've arranged for a funeral director to pick them up and take them to the crematorium. The immediate family will be there and will escort the urn with her ashes to the family mausoleum in St. Catherine's cemetery. Just so you know, that information is not to be leaked to the public. The family wants it to be absolutely private."

Pete nodded.

"By now a spokesman for the family will have announced to the press that a memorial Mass will be held for Martha on Saturday at St. Catherine's."

Tommy was sure that most if not all of the people who

had been at the party the night before Martha vanished would be in attendance at the Mass. He had already told Pete that he wanted to get them under the same roof somewhere and then question them individually. Inconsistencies in their recollections could be straightened out much faster if they were together—or perhaps *not* straightened out, he thought grimly.

There had been twenty-four guests and five catering staff in the Lawrence home the night before Martha vanished.

"Pete, after we assemble them, we'll do the usual. Have a little talk with them, one by one, and try to find out if any of them lost anything at the party. Our top priority is to learn if anyone had been wearing or carrying a gray silk scarf with metallic beading."

Tommy pulled out the list of the guests who had been at the party and laid it on the desk. "I'm going to call Will Stafford and ask if I can have everyone meet at his house after the memorial Mass," he said. "If I clear that with him, we'll start making phone calls."

He reached for the phone.

Stafford had just returned from lunch. "Sure you can meet at my house," he agreed, "but you'd better schedule it a little later. There's a message on my desk that says the Lawrences are inviting some close friends back to the house for a buffet luncheon after the Mass. I'm sure most of the people who were at the party will be included in that."

"Then I'll ask them to be at your place at three o'clock. Thanks, Mr. Stafford."

I'd give a lot to be at that luncheon, Tommy thought. He nodded at Pete. "Now that we have the place and the time, let's start making these calls. We're supposed to be at Emily Graham's house in an hour. We're going to try to sweet-talk her into letting that backhoe dig up the rest of her yard."

They began making the phone calls and reached everyone except Bob Frieze. "He'll call you back presently," an employee at the restaurant promised.

"Tell him to call me back fast," Tommy ordered. "I have to leave here *soon*, not presently."

"Better than I expected," he told Pete as they compared the results of the other calls. With the exception of two elderly couples who could not possibly have been involved in Martha's death, all the other people who had been at the party were planning to attend the Mass on Saturday.

He dialed The Seasoner restaurant again, and this time Bob Frieze accepted the call. The request to meet at Stafford's house brought a vigorous protest.

"Saturday afternoon and evening are very busy in my restaurant," he snapped. "We've spoken any number of times, Detective Duggan. I can assure you I have nothing further to add to what I've already told you."

"I don't think you'd want it leaked to the press that you're resisting cooperating with the police," Tommy retorted.

When he hung up with Frieze, he smiled in satisfaction. "I like leaning on that guy," he told Walsh. "It feels good."

"It felt good listening to you lean on him. When I was on the force in Spring Lake everyone had that guy's number. The first Mrs. Frieze is a lovely woman who got dumped after giving him three nice kids and putting up with his little escapades for over thirty years. We all knew that Bob Frieze was a womanizer. And he's got a lousy disposition. When I was a rookie eight years ago, I ticketed him for speeding, and trust me, he did everything he could to get me fired."

"What I'm beginning to wonder is whether or not his second marriage has cured him of womanizing," Tommy said thoughtfully. "He's suddenly getting mighty defensive."

He got up. "Come on. We have just enough time to grab some lunch before we meet Graham."

Tommy suddenly realized that he hadn't had a bite of food since someone had brought in coffee and bagels hours earlier. For a moment he wrestled with his own demons, then settled on the order he would place at McDonald's. A Super Mac, complete with a double order of french fries. And a large Coke.

sixteen _____

AT TWO FORTY-FIVE, Emily parked in front of the home of Clayton and Rachel Wilcox, on Ludlam Avenue. Half an hour earlier, she had called Will Stafford and asked him to suggest where she should begin her research into the disappearance of Madeline Shapley.

A hint of apology in her voice, she said, "Will, I know you thought you'd be finished with me after we closed on the house yesterday, and you should have been. I feel as if I'm in danger of becoming a pest to you, but I *do* want to get some background on Spring Lake at the time my family lived here. I intend to ask about obtaining police reports of Madeline's case, if they still exist, and there may be newspaper stories somewhere as well. I just don't know where to start."

"Our own library on Third Avenue has excellent reference material," he told her, "but the Monmouth County Historical Society in Freehold is undoubtedly the primary resource."

She thanked him and was about to hang up when he said, "Wait a minute, Emily. A good shortcut might be to talk to Dr. Clayton Wilcox. He's a retired college president, and has become the town's unofficial historian. Something else may interest you about him: he and his wife, Rachel, were guests at the Lawrence home the night before Martha Lawrence disappeared. Let me give him a ring."

He called her back fifteen minutes later. "Clayton would enjoy meeting you. Go right over. I told him what you wanted, and he's already putting together some material for you. Here's the address."

And here I am, Emily thought as she got out of the car. The morning had been bright and relatively warm, but the fading mid-afternoon sunshine and the light wind had combined to create a chilled and somber atmosphere.

She quickly walked up the steps to the porch and rang the bell. A moment later the door opened.

Even if no one had told her, she would have guessed instinctively that Dr. Clayton Wilcox was an academic. The full head of shaggy hair, the glasses perched on the end of his nose, the heavy-lidded eyes, the bulky sweater over a shirt and tie. The only thing that's missing is a pipe, she thought.

His voice was deep and the tone pleasant when he greeted her. "Miss Graham, please come in. I wish I could say, 'Welcome to Spring Lake,' and leave it at that, but under the tragic circumstances of the discovery of the Lawrence girl's body on your property, that doesn't seem appropriate, does it?" He stood aside, and as she passed him, Emily was surprised to realize that he was almost six feet tall. He had a way of slouching forward that at first impression had minimized his height.

He took her coat, then led her down the hall, past the living room. "When we decided to move to Spring Lake twelve years ago, my wife did the house hunting," he explained, as he waved her into a room where, except for the window, all four walls were lined floor to ceiling with bookshelves. "My one criterion was that I have a true Victorian and that one room would provide ample space for my books, my desk, my couch, and my chair."

"That's quite an order." Emily smiled as she glanced around. "But you got what you asked for."

It was the kind of room she liked. The wine-colored leather couch was deep and comfortable. She would have liked to have the opportunity to peruse the bookshelves. Most of the books appeared to be old, and she guessed that the ones in a glass-enclosed section were probably rare.

A stack of books and papers was piled haphazardly on the left-hand corner of the massive desk. At least a dozen notebooks were crisscrossed around an open laptop computer. Emily could see that the screen was lit.

"I've interrupted you," she said. "I'm terribly sorry."

"Not at all. My writing wasn't going well, and I looked forward to meeting you."

He settled in the club chair. "Will Stafford tells me that you are interested in learning about the history of Spring Lake. I've been listening to the news reports, so I know that your ancestor's remains were found along with those of poor Martha Lawrence."

Emily nodded. "Martha's murderer obviously knew that Madeline Shapley had been buried there, but the question is how *could* he know?"

"*He?* You're assuming the present day killer is a man?" Wilcox raised an eyebrow.

"I think it's more than likely," Emily said. "But can I be sure? Of course not. Nor do I have any certainty about the killer over one hundred years ago. Madeline Shapley was my great-great-grandaunt. If she'd lived to be eighty, she would have died a couple of generations ago and been forgotten by now, as we all will be in time. Instead, she was murdered when she was only nineteen years old. In a peculiar way, to our family she's not dead. She's unfinished business."

Emily leaned forward and clasped her hands together. "Dr. Wilcox, I'm a criminal defense attorney and a pretty good one. I have a lot of experience collecting evidence. There's a *connection* between the deaths of Martha Lawrence and Madeline Shapley, and when one of those murders is solved, it may be that the other one will be solved too. It may sound ridiculous, but I believe that whoever learned that Madeline Shapley was buried on the grounds of her family home also learned how and why she died."

He nodded. "You may be right. It's possible there's a record somewhere. A written confession perhaps. Or a letter. But then you're suggesting that whoever found such a document not only concealed it but used the grave-site information in it when he committed his own crime."

"I guess that *is* what I'm suggesting, yes. And something else. I believe neither Madeline in 1891, nor Martha four and a half years ago, was the kind of young woman who would have gone off with a stranger. More likely both of them let themselves get trapped by someone they trusted."

"I think that's a big leap, Miss Graham."

"Not necessarily, Doctor Wilcox. I know Madeline's mother and sister were in the house when she vanished. It was a warm September day. The windows were open. They would have heard her if she had screamed.

"Martha Lawrence was jogging. It was early, but she surely wasn't the only jogger. There are houses overlooking the boardwalk. It would have been pretty daring, and pretty tough, to somehow overcome her and drag her into a car or van without being observed."

"You've done a good deal of thinking about this, haven't you Miss Graham?"

"Please call me Emily. Yes, I guess I *have* done a good deal of thinking about it. It isn't hard to focus on the subject when a forensic team is sifting through my backyard for bones of murder victims. Fortunately, I don't start my new job in Manhattan until May 1st. I can do a lot of crash research till then."

She stood up. "I've taken enough of your time, Doctor Wilcox, and I must get back to meet with a detective from the prosecutor's office."

Wilcox hoisted himself to his feet. "When Will Stafford phoned, I pulled out some books and articles about Spring Lake that might be helpful to you," he told her. "There are also some copies of newspaper clippings from the 1890s. These are only the tip of the iceberg, but they'll keep you busy for a while."

The pile of books and papers she'd noticed on the desk was what he had put together for her. "Wait a minute. You can't possibly carry them like this," he said, more to himself than to her. He opened the bottom drawer of the desk and pulled out a folded cloth bag with the words "Enoch College Book Store" printed across it.

"If you always keep my books in this, they won't get separated," he suggested. He gestured to the desk. "I'm writing a historical novel set in Spring Lake in 1876, the year the Monmouth Hotel was opened. It's my first attempt at fiction, and I find it quite a challenge." He smiled. "I've done a fair amount of academic writing, of course, but I'm learning that it's much easier to write about factual subjects than to write fictional ones."

He walked with her to the door. "I'll put together more material for you, but let's talk after you've had a chance to go through all these references. You may have some questions."

"You've been very kind," she said as she shook his hand at the door. Emily did not know why she had a sudden feeling of discomfort, even claustrophobia. It's that house, she thought as she went down the steps and got into the car. Except for his office, it's utterly cheerless.

She had glanced into the living room as she passed it. The dark upholstery and heavy draperies were the worst of the Victorian-era decor, she decided, everything heavy, dark, formal. I wonder what *Mrs*. Wilcox is like?

FROM THE WINDOW, Clayton Wilcox watched Emily drive away. A most attractive young woman, he decided, as he reluctantly turned and went back to his study. He sat at the desk and pushed the ENTER key on the computer.

The screen saver disappeared, and the page he had been working on came into view. It concerned the frantic search for a young woman who had come to Spring Lake with her parents to attend the gala opening of the Monmouth Hotel in 1876.

From his top drawer, Clayton Wilcox took out the copy he had made from microfilm of a front-page story in the *Seaside Gazette* of September 12, 1891.

It began: "Foul play is suspected in the mysterious disappearance five days ago of Miss Madeline Shapley of Spring Lake . . ."

seventeen _____

"I CAN'T DO IT ANYMORE," Nick said aloud. He was standing at the window of his corner office in the law firm of Todd, Scanlon, Klein and Todd, looking down at the street thirty floors below. He watched as cars disappeared into the tunnel that ran from Fortieth to Thirty-third Street under Park Avenue South.

The only difference between the cars and me is that I'm stuck in the tunnel, he thought. *They* come out the other side.

The morning had been spent in the conference room working on the Hunter case. Hunter's going to go scot-free, and I'll have helped to make that possible. The absolute certainty made Nick feel physically sick.

I don't want to hurt Dad, but I can't do it anymore, he acknowledged to himself.

He thought about the old words of wisdom: "This above all: To thine own self be true and it must follow as the day the night thou canst not then be false to any man."

I can't be false to myself any longer. I don't *belong* here. I don't want to be here. I want to prosecute these creeps, not defend them.

He heard the door of his office open. Only one person would do that without knocking. He turned around slowly. As he expected, his father was framed in the doorway.

"Nick, we've got to do something about Emily Graham. I must have been out of my mind when I told her she could wait until May 1st to start work. A case just came in that's tailor-made for her. I want you to go down to Spring Lake and tell her that we need her to be in here within the week."

Emily Graham. The thought that had struck Nick when he saw her in action in court ran through his mind.

Emily and his father were like two peas in a pod. They were born to be criminal defense attorneys.

He'd been within inches of telling his father that he had to resign from the firm.

I can wait a little longer, he decided. But once Emily Graham's on board, I'm out of here.

eighteen _____

THE QUESTION to the prosecutor from the shrill reporter during the televised new conference delighted him: *Do you think Martha's killer is a reincarnation?*

But then the prosecutor's brusque dismissal of the possibility affronted him.

I *am* reincarnated, he thought. We have become one.

I can prove it

I shall prove it.

By late afternoon he had decided the way in which he would reveal the truth about himself to the skeptic.

A simple ordinary postcard would be sufficient, he thought. A crude drawing, no better than what a child might send.

He would mail it on Saturday.

On his way to church.

nineteen _____

TOMMY DUGGAN and Pete Walsh were on the porch waiting for Emily when she arrived home.

Tommy brushed aside her apology for keeping them waiting. "We're a little early, Ms. Graham." He introduced Pete, who promptly reached down and picked up the bag of books Clayton Wilcox had given Emily.

"You must be planning to do a lot of reading, Ms. Graham," he commented as she unlocked the door.

"I guess I am."

They followed her into the foyer. "Let's talk in the kitchen," she suggested. "I'd love a cup of tea, and maybe I can persuade you to join me."

Pete Walsh accepted. Tommy Duggan passed on the tea, but could not resist helping himself to a couple of the chocolate-chip cookies she put out on a plate.

They sat at the kitchen table. The big window afforded a stark view of the excavation site and the piles of dirt around it. The words CRIME SCENE, NO TRESPASSING, were printed on the tapes that cordoned off the area. They could see the policeman guarding the site looking out the window of the cabana.

"I see that the forensic team is gone," Emily said. "I hope that means you're through with the investigation here? I want the contractor to get that pit filled in. I've decided I'm not going ahead with a pool."

"That's just what we want to discuss, Ms. Graham," Tommy said. "While the backhoe is here, we'd like to have the rest of your yard dug up."

Emily stared at him. "What purpose would that serve?"

"A very important one. You should have the reassurance of knowing that you will never face another shock like the one you experienced yesterday."

"Surely you don't believe there are *other* bodies buried out there?" The shock in her voice was unmistakable.

"Ms. Graham, I know you watched the prosecutor on TV, because you phoned in about the ring that was found."

"Yes."

"Then you heard him say that after your—What is

it, great-great-grandaunt?—disappeared in 1891, two other young women vanished from Spring Lake."

"Dear God, do you think they may be buried out there?" Emily gestured toward the backyard.

"We'd like to find out. We'd also like to get a blood sample from you so that we can verify through DNA that it really is Madeline Shapley's finger bone."

Tom Duggan realized that he was suddenly feeling the absolute exhaustion that sets in when you've barely slept in a day and a half. He felt dull and heavy eyed. He felt sorry for Emily Graham. She looked shocked and distressed.

They had run a check on her yesterday—top criminal defense attorney going to one of those fancy law firms in Manhattan. Divorced from a jerk who tried to horn in on her when she came into money. Victim of a stalker who was now in a psychiatric facility. But someone had taken her picture the night she arrived in Spring Lake and slipped it under the door.

Anyone could have looked her up on the Internet and found out about the stalker. There'd been a lot of publicity when they finally caught him. Some stupid kid from around here might have thought it funny to try to scare her. The Spring Lake cops were good. They'd keep their eyes out for anyone hanging around here. Maybe they'd be able to lift fingerprints off the snapshot or the envelope.

And now she's sitting in this beautiful house, with the backyard looking like a bomb site because the remains of two murder victims, one of them her own relative, were buried here. It was sad.

Tommy knew his wife Suzie would want to know about Emily Graham. What she looked like. What she was wearing. Suzie had found his description of his meeting with Emily Graham yesterday totally inadequate. Tommy tried to sum up the impressions he would pass on to her when he went home this evening.

Emily Graham was wearing blue jeans, a red sweater with a big collar, and ankle boots. Her clothes sure didn't come from a discount house. Plain gold earrings. No rings.

Dark brown hair, soft, shoulder length. Big brown eyes that were now worried and apprehensive. Really pretty, maybe even beautiful.

My God, I'm falling asleep talking to her, he thought.

"Ms. Graham, this summer I don't want you to be sitting outside with your friends and wondering if more human bones may suddenly work their way to the surface."

"But isn't it a fact that if two other young women vanished in the 1890s, and their bodies *are* found here, it will prove that there *was* a serial killer in this town one hundred and ten years ago?"

"Yes, it would," Duggan said. "However, my concern is to get my hands on the guy who killed Martha Lawrence. I've always believed it was somebody from around here. A lot of people have roots in this town going back three and four generations. Others spent summers here or worked in the hotels when they were college kids."

"Tom and I worked at the Warren," Walsh observed. "Ten years apart, of course."

Duggan shot a look at him. It as much as said, "Don't interrupt."

"The bones we found here underneath Martha's skeleton were in a relatively shallow grave," he continued. "They'd have been found long ago if that tree hadn't been there. A few might have surfaced over the years. I think what happened is that somebody came across them at some point, maybe even found the finger bone with the ring, kept it, and when he killed Martha decided to bury her there with it."

He looked at her. "You're shaking your head," he said. "You don't agree."

"I'm letting my guard down," Emily said. "A good defense attorney keeps a poker face. No, Mr. Duggan, I can't agree. It's too much for me to believe that someone found the bone, never told anyone about it, murdered that poor Lawrence girl, then decided to bury her here. I don't buy that."

"How would you explain it?"

"I think whoever murdered Martha Lawrence knew *exactly* what happened in 1891, and has committed a copycat murder."

"You're not into that reincarnation theory, I hope?"

"No, I'm not, but I do believe that Martha's killer knows a whole lot about Madeline Shapley's death."

Tom stood up. "Ms. Graham, this house has turned over ownership quite a few times during all those years. We're going to look up the records, find out who those owners were, and see if any of them are still around here. Will you allow us to dig up your yard?"

"Yes, I will." Her voice was resigned.

"And now I'm going to ask *you* something. Let me see the records you found about Madeline Shapley's disappearance and the disappearance of those other two young women in the 1890s."

They looked at each other. "I'd have to check with the boss, but I don't see a problem there," Duggan told her.

She walked to the front door with them.

"The contractor told me he can start again first thing in the morning," she told them. "I had hoped he'd be here filling in the hole, but if the whole yard has to be dug up, so be it."

"We'll have the forensic unit here sifting. They shouldn't take more than a day, or at the most two, then you can put all this behind you," Duggan promised.

Back in the car, they drove in silence for five minutes. Then Duggan said, "Are you thinking the same thing I am, Pete?"

"Maybe."

"That girl, Carla Harper, from Philadelphia?"

"Right."

"She disappeared two years ago, in August."

"Right. An eyewitness swears she saw her talking to a guy at a rest stop just outside Philadelphia. Claims they were driving separate cars, but when they left he followed her. Eyewitness swears he had Pennsylvania plates. Then a couple of days later Harper's purse with apparently nothing missing was found in a wooded area not far from that rest stop. The case has been handled by the Philadelphia prosecutor."

Tommy picked up the phone and called the office and asked to be put through to Len Green, one of the other detectives working closely on the case.

"Len, when did the second woman disappear in the 1890s?"

"Give me a minute?" There was a pause. "Here it is, August 5, 1893."

"When was Carla Harper reported missing?"

"Be right back to you."

Tommy held the phone until he heard the words he'd been expecting to hear. "August 5th."

"We're on the way. See you in twenty minutes. Thanks, Len."

Tommy Duggan was no longer sleepy. They had to talk to the Philadelphia detective who had handled the case of Carla Harper immediately. The fact that both Madeline Shapley and Martha Lawrence had disappeared on September 7th, even though separated by one hundred and ten years, might have been coincidental; the fact that then two young women had disappeared on August 5th in the same time frame could not be coincidental.

They *did* have a copycat killer on their hands in Spring Lake. "You know what this means, Pete?" he asked.

Pete Walsh did not answer. He knew Tommy Duggan was thinking aloud.

"It means that if this guy is following a pattern, he's going to target one more young woman, on March 31st."

"*This* March 31st?"

"I don't know yet. In the 1890s the three women vanished several years apart." He got back on the phone. "Len, now check this out," he began.

When he had the information he wanted, he said. "There was a difference of twenty-three months between the disappearances of the first two women in the 1890s. There was exactly that same number of months between the disappearance of Martha Lawrence and Carla Harper."

They were pulling into the parking lot at the prosecutor's office. "If some woman vanishes in Spring Lake next week on March 31st, the cycle will be complete. And to add to the fun, we may have a copycat stalker of Emily Graham on our hands too."

As Pete Walsh got out of the car, he wisely did not tell Tommy Duggan that his mother-in-law believed in reincarnation and that he too was beginning to think there might be something to it.

twenty

WHEN SHE HAD DONE the food shopping after the closing on the house, Emily had purchased a package of chicken parts with the idea of making a pot of soup. After the detectives left, she decided to prepare it now and have it for dinner tonight.

The open pit in the backyard and the possibility that other bodies were buried there made her feel as if the scent of death were permeating the very air around her. Besides, she thought, I always do my best thinking when my hands are chopping vegetables or kneading dough.

Chicken soup does do something for the psyche, and right now, Emily admitted to herself, mine needs some help.

She went into the kitchen and drew the blinds, grateful to block out the dismal scene in the yard. Her hands worked independently, scraping carrots, cutting up celery and onions, reaching for seasonings. By the time she had turned on the flame under the pot, she had made a decision.

It had been foolish not to call the Albany police immediately and report what had happened last night. They should be aware of it.

Why didn't I call them?

She answered her own question. Because I don't want

to believe that it's going to begin again. I've been burying my head in the sand since I saw that photograph slipped under the door last night.

She knew what she had to do. Detective Walsh had carried the bag of books into the kitchen. She picked it up, went into the study, and laid it by the ottoman in front of the deep armchair. She went over to the desk, got the portable phone, and perched on the ottoman.

Her first call was to Detective Marty Browski in Albany. He had been the one who collared Ned Koehler lurking outside her townhouse. Browski's response to what she told him was both astonishment and concern. "My guess is that you've got a copycat, either that or one of Koehler's friends is picking up where he left off. We'll look into it. Emily, I'm glad you called the local police. Tell you what. I'll give them a call down there and alert them to the seriousness of the problem. I can fill them in on the background."

Her next call was to Eric Bailey. It was after five, but he was still in the office and delighted to hear from her. "Albany's not the same without you," he said.

She smiled at the familiar worried tone. Even with millions of dollars, Eric would never change, she thought. Shy, little-boy-lost, but a genius. "I miss you too," she assured him. "And I've got a favor to ask."

"Good. Whatever you want, you've got it."

"Eric, the security camera you put in the townhouse was the reason the cops got Ned Koehler. You offered me one for Spring Lake. I want to take you up on that offer. Can you send someone down to put it in?"

"I can send myself down. I want to see you anyhow. The next few days are really busy. Is Monday okay?"

She could visualize him, his forehead creased, his fingers restlessly toying with some gadget on his desk. When he became successful he traded his blue jeans and tee shirts and parkas for an expensive wardrobe. She hated the sly jokes people told about him, that he still looked the same: woebegone. The poor soul.

"Monday is fine," she said.

"How's everything going with your house?"

"Interesting. I'll fill you in on Monday." And that's about as much as I can do, Emily thought as she replaced the receiver. Now to get into these books.

She spent the next three hours curled up in the big chair, absorbed in the books Wilcox had lent her. He had chosen well, she decided. She found herself pulled into an era of horse-drawn carriages, oil lamps, and stately summer "cottages."

With the awareness of the price she had just paid for her house still fresh in her mind, the ordinance that the minimum amount a property owner could spend building a new home was three thousand dollars made her smile.

The report from the president of the Board of Health in 1893 over the need to stop the dumping of garbage in the ocean "to keep our beach free from offensive matter washed thereupon day to day" was a wry reminder that some things never change.

A book with many photographs included one of a Sunday school picnic in 1890. The list of the children in attendance included the name of Catherine Shapley.

Madeline's sister. My great-great grandmother, Emily thought. I wish I could pick her out. In the sea of faces it was impossible to match one of them with the few family photos that had survived the storeroom fire.

At eight o'clock she went back into the kitchen and completed preparing dinner. Once again she propped a book up on the table. This one she had deliberately saved because it looked the most interesting. *Reflections of a Girlhood* was the title. It had been published in 1938. The author, Phyllis Gates, had summered in Spring Lake in the late 1880s and early 1890s.

The book was well written and gave a vivid picture of the social life of those days. Picnics and cotillions, splendid events at the Monmouth Hotel, bathing in the ocean, horseback riding and bicycling were described. What intrigued Emily most were the copious excerpts from a diary Phyllis Gates had kept during those years.

Emily had finished dinner. Her eyes were burning with

fatigue, and she was about to close the book for the night when she turned the page and saw Madeline Shapley's name in a diary excerpt.

June 18, 1891. This afternoon we attended a festive luncheon at the Shapley home. It was to celebrate Madeline's nineteenth birthday. Twelve tables beautifully decorated with flowers from the garden had been placed on the porch. I sat at Madeline's table as did Douglas Carter, who is so very much in love with her. We tease her about him.

In an 1891 excerpt, the author wrote:

We had just closed our cottage and returned to Philadelphia when we learned of Madeline's disappearance. It was a great grief to all of us. Mother hurried back to Spring Lake to express her condolences and found the family to be in a state of profound grief. Madeline's father confided that for the sake of his wife's health he will remove the family from the area.

About to close the book, Emily skimmed through the pages. An October 1893 entry caught her eye.

Douglas Carter committed suicide. He had missed the early train from New York on that tragic day and was forced to wait for a later one. He became obsessed with the idea that had he been there earlier he might have saved her.

My mother felt that it had been a grave mistake for Douglas's parents not to move from their home, directly across the street from the Shapleys. She felt that the melancholy that overcame Douglas might have been avoided, had he not sat hour after hour staring at the porch of the Shapley home.

Emily set down the book. I knew Douglas Carter had committed suicide, she thought. I *didn't* know he lived directly across the street.

I'd like to find out a lot more about him, she thought. I wonder how sure they were that he did in fact miss the train?

Friday, March 23 ═══════════

twenty-one _____

THE RUMOR HAD BEGUN with the question of *The National Daily* reporter to the prosecutor: "Do you think Martha's killer is a reincarnation?"

Dr. Lillian Madden's phone started to ring without stopping on Thursday afternoon. On Friday morning Joan Hodges, her secretary, had a stock answer, which she delivered crisply over and over again: "Dr. Madden has deemed it inappropriate to discuss the subject of reincarnation in regard to the Spring Lake murder case."

At lunchtime on Friday, Joan Hodges had no problem discussing the matter with her boss. "Dr. Madden, look at what the newspapers are saying, and they're right. It was no coincidence that Martha Lawrence and Madeline Shapley both disappeared on September 7th. And you want to know the latest?"

Pause now for dramatic effect, Lillian Madden thought wryly.

"On August 5, 1893, Letitia Gregg—listen to me, Doctor—'failed to return *home*.'" Joan's eyes widened. "Doctor, there was a girl, Carla Harper, who spent the weekend at the Warren Hotel two years ago, then just vanished into thin air. I remember reading about it. She checked out of the Warren and got in her car. Some woman swears she saw her near Philadelphia. That's where she was going. She lived in Rosemont, on the Main Line. But now according to the *New York Post,* that eyewitness starts to sound like looney-tunes."

Then Joan's eyes, wide open and demanding, bored into Dr. Lillian Madden's face. "Doctor, I don't think Carla Harper ever left Spring Lake. I think—and apparently lots of people think—that there was a serial killer in Spring Lake in the 1890s and that he's been reincarnated."

"That's utter nonsense," Lillian Madden said brusquely. "Reincarnation is a form of spiritual growth. A serial murderer from the 1890s would be paying for his transgressions now, not *repeating* them."

With decisive steps, her entire posture telegraphing her disapproval of the tone of the conversation, Lillian Madden went into her private office and closed the door. There, she sank into her desk chair and put her elbows on the desk. Her eyes closed, she massaged her temples with her index fingers.

Before too much longer, human beings will be cloned, she thought. All of us in the medical field understand that. Those of us who believe in reincarnation believe that pain we endured in other lifetimes may affect us in our present existence. But *evil?* Could someone knowingly or unknowingly repeat *exactly* the same kind of evil deeds he committed over a century ago?

What was bothering her? What memory was trying to force itself into her conscious mind?

Lillian wondered if she could skip her lecture tonight. No, that wouldn't be fair to the students, she decided. In ten years she hadn't missed one session of the course in Regression she gave every spring at Monmouth Community College.

There were thirty students enrolled in the course. The college was allowed to sell ten more single-session tickets for each lecture. Would some of those reporters who had been phoning find out about those tickets and be there tonight?

In the second half of the session it was her practice to ask for volunteers to be hypnotized and regressed. That sometimes resulted in vivid and detailed recollections of other incarnations. She made the decision to eliminate the hypnosis section tonight. During the last ten minutes she always took questions from the students and visitors. If reporters were there, she would have to respond to them. There was no way around that.

She always prepared her lectures well in advance. Each one was carefully integrated with both its predecessor and successor. Tonight's lecture was based on the observations of Ian Stevenson, a professor of psychology at the University of Virginia. He had tested the hypothesis that in order to identify two different life histories as belonging to the same person, there would have to be continuity of memories and/or personality traits.

It was not exactly the lecture she would have chosen to give tonight. As she went over her notes shortly before she left home, Lillian became painfully aware that Stevenson's findings could be interpreted as bolstering the theory about a reincarnated serial killer.

Lillian was so deep in thought that she was startled by Joan's brisk knock on the door. It opened and Joan was in the room before she could be invited to enter.

"Mrs. Pell is here, Doctor, but she's early, so take your time. Look what she brought to show you."

Joan was holding a copy of *The National Daily*. SPECIAL EDITION was enblazoned across the logo. The headline read SERIAL KILLER RETURNS FROM THE GRAVE.

The story continued onto the second and third pages. Pictures of Martha Lawrence and Carla Harper, side by side, were captioned, "Sisters in Death?"

The story began, "Red-faced police are admitting that the eyewitness who claimed to have seen twenty-year-old Carla Harper at a rest stop not far from her home in Rosemont, Pennsylvania, may have been mistaken. They now admit it is entirely possible that Harper's purse was planted near that rest stop by her killer after the eyewitness account was widely published. The focus of the investigation is now centered in Spring Lake, New Jersey."

"It's just what I told you, Doctor. The last time that girl was seen was in Spring Lake. And she disappeared on August 5th, the same day as Letitia Gregg—isn't that a great name?—did in 1893!"

The newspaper also had sketches of three young women in the high-necked, long-sleeved, ankle-length garb of the late nineteenth century. The caption read, "The 19th Century Victims."

A photograph of a tree-lined street of Victorian homes of that time was placed side by side with the picture of a remarkably similiar present-day street. The caption was, "Then and Now."

The report that followed had the byline and picture of a columnist, Reba Ashby. It began: "A visitor to the lovely seaside town of Spring Lake has the sense of stepping back into a more peaceful and tranquil era. But in that time, as in the present, the peace was broken by a sinister and evil presence . . ."

Lillian folded the paper and handed it back to Joan. "I've seen enough of it."

"Don't you think you should cancel your class tonight, Doctor?"

"No, I don't, Joan. Will you ask Mrs. Pell to come in, please?"

THAT EVENING, as Lillian Madden had expected, all the available guest passes for her lecture had been sold. She sensed that several people who had arrived early enough to get front-row seats might be from the media. They were carrying notebooks and recorders.

"My regular students understand that no recorders are permitted in this class," she said looking pointedly at one thirtyish woman who seemed vaguely familiar.

Of course! She was Reba Ashby from *The National Daily,* the one who'd penned the "Then and Now" story.

Lillian took a moment to adjust her glasses. She did

not want to appear nervous or ill at ease in front of Ms. Ashby.

"In the Middle East, Asia, and other locations," she began, "there are thousands of cases where children under the age of eight will talk about a previous identity. They will recall in vivid detail the life they previously lived, including the names of members of their former families.

"Dr. Stevenson's monumental empirical research explores the possibility that images in a person's mind and physical modifications in that person's body may manifest themselves as characteristics in a newborn."

Images in a person's mind, Lillian thought. I'm feeding Ashby her next column. She went on.

"Some people can choose their future parents, and rebirth tends to happen in a geographical area quite close to where the earlier incarnation led his life."

The questioning, when it began, was heated. Ms. Ashby led off: "Dr. Madden," she said, "everything I heard you say tonight seems to me to validate the idea that a serial killer who lived in the 1890s has been reincarnated. Do you think that the present-day killer has images of what happened to the three women in the 1890s?"

Lillian Madden paused before answering. "Our research shows that memories of past lives cease to exist at about age eight. That is not to say that we may not experience a sense of familiarity with a person we have just met or a place we have visited for the first time. But that is not the same as vivid, recent images."

There were other questions, and then Ashby cut in again. "Doctor, don't you usually include hypnotizing a few volunteers as part of your lecture?"

"That is correct. I have chosen not to do so tonight."

"Will you explain how you go about regressing someone?"

"Certainly. Three or four people usually volunteer for the experiment, but some of them may not cooperate with the hypnosis. I speak, one at a time, with those who are clearly in a hypnotic state. I invite them to travel back in time through a warm tunnel. I tell them it will be a pleasant journey. Then I pick dates at random and ask if a picture forms in their mind. Often the answer is no, and I keep going backward, until they have reached a previous incarnation."

"Dr. Madden, did you ever have anyone specifically ask to be regressed to the late 1800s?"

Lillian Madden stared at the questioner, a heavyset man with brooding eyes. Probably another reporter, she thought, but that wasn't the point. He had brought to the surface the memory that had been eluding her all day. It must have been four, maybe five, years ago that someone *had* in fact asked her that very question. He had been in her office, with an appointment, and told her that he was sure he had lived in Spring Lake at the end of the nineteenth century.

But then he resisted hypnosis, indeed, he almost seemed frightened of it, and left before the hour was up. She could see him clearly in her mind. But what was his name? What was it?

It will still be in my appointment book, she thought. I'll recognize it when I see it.

She could hardly wait to get home.

twenty-two

IN ALBANY, Marty Browski walked up the path to Gray Manor, the psychiatric hospital where Ned Koehler, the man who had been convicted of stalking Emily Graham, was being treated.

A short, trim, fifty-year-old with a stern face and deepset eyes, Marty had made the trip across town from the precinct because he had to satisfy himself that Koehler was still where he belonged.

While there was no question that the man was potentially dangerous, there had always been something about the case that bothered Marty. No question Ned Koehler had taken that final step stalkers often take: he had cut the telephone wires to shut down the alarm system in Graham's apartment and tried to enter it.

Fortunately the security camera her friend Eric Bailey—the dot-com big-bucks guy—had installed not only went on high-tech backup, automatically, but summoned the police and also took a picture of Koehler, knife in hand, jimmying the lock on the bedroom window!

Koehler was screwy, no question of *that*. Probably always had been on the edge, then the mother's death pushed him all the way over. He was right. Joel Lake, the bum whom Graham got acquitted, was the mother's killer.

But Graham was a damn good defense lawyer, Browski told himself, and our side just didn't prove our case.

And now Graham was the victim of another stalking episode, this one in Spring Lake. I've always wondered about Graham's ex-husband, Browski thought, as he opened the main door of the hospital and went into the reception room.

There were a couple of people at the desk, waiting to be escorted into the locked-up areas. He dropped himself into a chair and looked around.

The walls were painted a soft yellow and had some fairly decent prints tastefully arranged on them. Imitation leather chairs in small conversational groupings looked comfortable enough. Several side tables were covered with magazines that appeared to be of recent vintage.

Still, no matter how hard you try to brighten them up, these places are grim, Browski thought. *Any* place that you can't leave of your own free will is grim.

While he waited, he found himself weighing the possibility that Gary Harding White might have been—and might still *be*—the stalker. The White family had been prominent in Albany for generations, but Gary Harding White wasn't cut from the same cloth as the rest of the clan, all of them high achievers. Despite the privileged background, good looks, and a good education, Gary failed at everything and was getting a reputation as something of a con man. A womanizer too.

After Harvard Business School, White settled down in Albany and joined the family business. He hadn't lasted.

Then his father dropped a bundle staking him to his own company, but that went bust. Now he was into something else, and that too was limping along financially. The word around town was that his father was sick of bankrolling him.

It had obviously driven Gary White up the wall that his ex-wife had a financial windfall. The way he'd sued for half of it appalled everyone, and in the process he'd lied like a rug in court and looked like a fool.

Had he been bitter enough to try to destroy Emily Graham's peace of mind by stalking her? Browski wondered. Was he still doing it?

But, Koehler was potentially dangerous. After all, he'd tried to attack Emily Graham in the courtroom, and he had tried to break into her house. *But was* he *the stalker?*

Seeing that the receptionist had taken care of the people waiting around her desk, he approached and pulled out his wallet. Holding up his ID, he said, "Marty Browski. I'm expected. Will you let Dr. Sherman know I'm here to question Ned Koehler. Is his lawyer here yet?"

"Mr. Davis went upstairs a short time ago," she told him.

A few minutes later, Marty was sitting at a table opposite Koehler and Hal Davis, his lawyer. The door was closed, but a guard was watching through the window.

Ned's the kind of guy you want to feel sorry for but can't, Browski thought. A singularly unattractive man, Koehler was in his early forties. He was rawboned with narrow eyes and a sharp chin. On someone else, his head of thinning salt-and-pepper hair might have been faintly attractive, but somehow it only contributed to his overall disheveled appearance.

"How's it been going, Ned?" Browski asked in a friendly voice.

Tears welled in Koehler's eyes. "I miss my mother."

It was the reaction Browski expected. "I know you do."

"It was that woman lawyer's fault. *She* got him off. He should be in prison."

"Ned, Joel Lake was in your building that night. He admitted he burglarized your apartment. But your mother was in the bathroom. He could hear the water running in the tub. She never saw him. He never saw her. Your mother was on the phone talking to her sister after Joel was seen leaving the building."

"My aunt has no sense of time."

"The jury thought she did."

"That Graham woman twisted the jury around her little finger."

Maybe she didn't twist the jury, Browski thought, but she *did* make them believe Joel's version. Not too many lawyers could get a suspect acquitted of a homicide when the guy admitted he was in the victim's apartment and burglarized it around the time of the murder.

"I hate Emily Graham, but I didn't follow her around or take pictures of her."

"You were trying to break into her home that night. You were carrying a knife."

"I wanted to scare her. I wanted her to see how scared my mother must have been when she saw that intruder pick up that knife."

"You were just planning to scare her?"

"You don't have to answer that, Ned," Hal Davis warned.

Koehler ignored him and looked at Browski with unblinking eyes. "I was just going to scare her. I just wanted to make her understand what my mother felt when she looked up and . . ."

He started to cry again. "I miss my mother," he repeated.

Davis patted his client on the shoulder and stood up. "Satisfied, Marty?" he asked Browski as he nodded to the guard to take Koehler back to his unit.

twenty-three _____

NICK TODD had picked up the phone to call Emily Graham a half dozen times and each time had replaced the receiver. *When I ask her to come into the office sooner than agreed, I'll be stressing the volume of work and the fact that we need her,* he thought. *Then, as soon as she's in place—I'm on my way out.*

But no, he decided, it wasn't fair to do it that way, and it certainly wasn't fair to disclose his plans to her until he had talked to his father.

On Friday morning, Walter Todd called his son on the intercom. "Have you spoken to Emily Graham?"

"Not yet."

"I thought we decided you'd go down and see her in the next day or two."

"I intend to do that." Nick hesitated. "I'd like to buy you lunch."

There was a similiar hesitation at the other end of the phone. "It seems to me that we have an office account at a number of restaurants."

"We have one at The Four Seasons. But this one is on me, Dad."

THEY WALKED UP Park Avenue together to Fifty-second Street. They agreed that the hint of mildness in the air after the cold, wet snap felt good. Spring was around the corner, they decided.

They discussed the stock market. No one could be sure if the dot-coms would recover.

They discussed the headlines about the Spring Lake case. "I'd like to throttle the people who turn a young woman's tragic death into a lurid, weirdo, media event," Walter Todd said.

As usual The Four Seasons was filled with recognizable faces. A former president was in the Grill Room in deep discussion with a prominent publisher. A former mayor was at his usual table. Nick recognized heads of studios and networks, well-known authors and business tycoons—the typical luncheon mixture of the well-known and well-heeled.

They stopped at several tables to greet friends. Nick winced hearing his father's proud introduction of him to a retired judge, "My son and partner . . ."

But when they were seated in the Pool Room and had ordered Perrier, he got right to the point. "All right, Nick, what's up?"

It was misery for Nick to see the tightening of muscles in his father's throat, the flash of anger in his eyes, the bleak pain that settled over his face, as he heard his son's plans.

Finally Walter Todd swallowed and said, "So that's it. A pretty big decision, Nick. Even if you get a job in the U.S. Attorney's office, it isn't going to pay you the kind of salary you make now, you know."

"I know, and don't think I'm so altruistic that I won't miss the big bucks." He broke off a piece of roll and crumbled it in his fingers.

"You do realize that being the arm of the law isn't all putting the bad guys away? You have to prosecute a lot of people you might wish you were defending."

"That's something I'll have to face."

Walter Todd shrugged. "Obviously I have to accept your decision. Am I happy about it? No. Am I disappointed? Yes. How soon does this Don Quixote scenario begin?"

You're also sore as hell about it, Nick thought, but that's to be expected.

The captain came by with menus and recited the specials of the day. A longtime fixture at the Four Seasons, he smiled benignly at them. "Always a pleasure to see the two Mr. Todds lunching together."

They ordered, and when the waiter was out of earshot, Walter Todd smiled grimly. "The cafeteria in the courthouse isn't listed in Zagat's, Nick."

It was a relief to see his father recover his cutting edge. "Well, maybe you'll invite me up here for a good meal every so often, Dad."

"I'll take it under consideration. Have you discussed this with your mother yet?"

"No, I haven't."

"She's been fretting that something is bothering you a great deal. She'll be relieved it isn't some mysterious illness. I confess I'm relieved too."

The two men looked across the table at each other, mirror images distinguished only by thirty years of the inevitable toll of the aging process. Rangy shoulders; lean, disciplined bodies; sandy hair that was now totally gray in the older man. Crease marks on Nick's forehead, deep furrows on his father's. Firm jaws and hazel eyes. Walter Todd's eyes framed with rimless glasses, Nick's eyes more vivid in color, the expression quizzical rather than stern.

"You're a damn good trial lawyer, Nick, the best. After me, of course. When you pull out, it will leave a mighty big hole in the firm. Good lawyers are a dime a dozen. Good, make that *very, very* good trial lawyers, aren't easy to come by."

"I know it, but Emily Graham is going to fill the bill for you. My heart's just not in it. I'd have started to slip. I can feel it. She has your passion for the job, but when I go down to see her, I've got to tell her that the workload is going to be heavier than she expected, at least for a while."

"How soon do you want to leave?"

"As soon as Emily Graham can take over my office. I'll move my stuff to one of the smaller ones in the transition phase."

Walter Todd nodded. "If she balks about coming in before May lst?"

"Then, of course, I'll wait it out."

She's not going to balk about coming in earlier, Nick thought.

No matter what it takes, I'll make sure of that.

twenty-four

THE WHINE AND CLATTER of the backhoe began promptly at 8:00 A.M. on Friday morning. When she looked out the kitchen window as she made coffee, Emily winced at the destruction of flower beds and decorative shrubs and lawn. The sprinkler system is being ripped up too, she thought, with a sigh.

It was clear that an expensive relandscaping project would have to be scheduled.

So be it, she thought, as she went back upstairs to shower and dress, carrying the coffee. Forty minutes later she was settled in the study, a second coffee in her hand, her notebook on the ottoman.

The book *Reflections of a Girlhood* remained a treasure trove of background and information. The author, Phyllis Gates, continued to visit Spring Lake for three more summers after Madeline disappeared. In a diary excerpt in 1893, she referred to the fear that Letitia Gregg might have drowned:

Letitia loved to swim and was very daring. August 5th was a warm and sultry day. The beach was crowded with visitors, and the surf dreadfully rough. In the midafternoon, Letitia was alone in the house. Her mother was out visiting, and the maid was enjoying her weekly afternoon off. Letitia's bathing costume was missing, which is the reason behind the belief that she went by herself to cool off with a dip in the ocean.

Following the disappearance of Madeline Shapley two

years ago, the sadness throughout the community is palpable, and a sense of fear is apparent. Since Letitia's body has not washed up, there is always the possibility that she met with foul play on her way to, or returning from, the beach.

Mother has become a fierce guardian, unwilling to have me even stroll down the street unless I am accompanied. I shall be quite glad to return to Philadelphia at the end of the season.

The author continued:

I remember how we young people would gather on each other's porches, endlessly discussing what might have happened to Madeline and Letitia. The young men included Douglas Carter's cousin, Alan Carter, and Edgar Newman. I always sensed a bond of unspoken sorrow between these two young men, because Edgar had been very sweet on Letitia, and we all knew Alan had been smitten with Madeline, even though she was about to be engaged to Douglas when she disappeared. Another member of our group who is very low in spirits is Ellen Swain. She was Letitia's bosom friend and misses her dreadfully.

At that time, Henry Gates, a junior at Yale, was beginning to stop by more and more frequently. I had already set my heart on marrying him, but of course in those days a young lady was very proper and most circumspect in her behavior. It would never do to show affection to Henry until I was very sure that he was enamoured of me. Many times over the years we have joked together about this. Considering the unrestrained behavior of young people today, we agree that our courtship was far more appealing.

And this book was published in 1938, Emily thought! I wonder what Phyllis Gates would think of *this* generation's courting manners and mores.

In the next pages, when the author reminisced about the summers of 1894 and 1895, and her growing romance with Henry Gates, she frequently mentioned the names of other young people.

Emily jotted all the names in her notebook. These would have been Madeline's contemporaries.

The final entry from the diary was written on April 4, 1896.

A most appalling tragedy. Last week Ellen Swain vanished in Spring Lake. She was walking home after visiting Mrs. Carter, whose always precarious health has alarmingly deteriorated since the suicide of Douglas, who was her only offspring. It is now believed that Letitia was not lost by drowning, but that all three of my friends met with foul play. Mother has canceled our lease on the cottage we usually rent for the season. She said she absolutely will not put me at risk. We are planning to go to Newport this summer. But I shall miss Spring Lake very much.

The author concluded.

The mystery of the disappearances gave rise over the years to many wild rumors. The remains of the body of a young woman washed ashore in Manasquan may have been that of Letitia Gregg. A cousin of the Mallards swore she saw Ellen Swain in New York on the arm of a handsome man. There was credence given to that story by some people, since Ellen did not enjoy a happy home life. Her parents were extremely demanding and critical. Those of us who were her confidants and knew of her affection for Edgar Newman never believed that she had run away with someone to New York.

Henry and I were married in 1896 and ten years later returned to Spring Lake with our three young children to resume the gentle life of summer residents of the now ever-so-fashionable resort.

Emily closed the book and laid it on the ottoman. It's like taking a trip back through time, she thought. She stood up and stretched, aware suddenly of how long she had been sitting without moving. She was surprised to see it was nearly noon.

A breath of fresh air would wake me up, she thought. She went to the front door, opened it, and stepped out on the porch. The effects of the combination of the bright sun and mild breeze seemed to be showing already in the grass and shrubs. They seemed greener, fuller, ready to grow and spread. By the end of next month, I can put everything back on the porch, she thought. It will be great to sit out here.

Twenty-seven pieces of the original wicker furniture were packed away in the loft of the carriage house.

"They're sealed in plastic now," the Kiernans had told her. "But they've been repaired and restored, and have new cushions covered with fabric that we believe is a replica of the original floral print."

The set included couches, chaises, chairs, and tables. Probably some of them had been used for the festive luncheon celebrating Madeline's nineteenth and last birthday, Emily reflected. And Madeline might have been sitting on one of those chairs while she waited for Douglas Carter to bring her an engagement ring.

I feel so close to all of them, she thought. They come to life in that book.

Even from a block away the ocean air was pungent and compelling. Reluctantly she went back inside, then realized she was not ready to start another reading session.

A long walk on the boardwalk, she decided, then a sandwich in town on the way home.

Two hours later, when she returned home refreshed and feeling as though her head had cleared, there were two messages on the answering machine.

The first was from Will Stafford. "Give me a ring, will you, Emily? I've got something to tell you."

The second was from Nicholas Todd. "I need to get together with you, Emily. Hope you can pencil me in for a visit sometime Saturday or Sunday. It's important I have a chance to go over some things with you. My direct line is 212-555-0857."

Stafford was in his office. "I spoke to Mrs. Lawrence, Emily," he said. "She'd like you to join them for the luncheon after the memorial Mass. I told her you planned to attend it."

"That's very kind of her."

"She wants to meet you. Why don't you let me pick you up and we'll go to the service and to the Lawrences' together? I can introduce you to some people from town."

"I'd like that."

"Fine. About twenty of eleven tomorow morning."

"I'll be ready. Thanks."

She dialed Nick Todd's number. I hope they haven't changed their minds about hiring me, she thought apprehensively. The possibility gave her a sinking feeling.

Nick answered on the first ring. "We've been following the news. Not a very pleasant way for you to settle in. Hope it hasn't been too upsetting."

She thought she detected a strain in his voice. "Sad, rather than upsetting," she said. "You left word you needed to see me. Has your father changed his mind about hiring me?"

His laugh was both spontaneous and reassuring. "Nothing could be further from the truth. How's tomorrow lunch or dinner for you? Or is Sunday better?"

Emily considered. Tomorrow was the memorial Mass and then lunch at the Lawrence home. And I want to finish these books and get them back to Dr. Wilcox, she thought. "Sunday lunch would be better," she said. "I'll find out where to go and make a reservation."

At five-thirty a member of the forensic team rang the back doorbell. "We're finished, Ms. Graham. There's nothing else buried out there."

Emily was surprised at how relieved she felt. She realized that she had been expecting the remains of Letitia Gregg and Ellen Swain to be unearthed.

The veteran police officer's face and hands and clothing were caked with mud. He looked tired and cold. "A nasty business, all this," he said. "But now maybe some of this talk about a reincarnated serial killer will die down."

"I certainly hope so." But why do I have a feeling it's only going to get worse? Emily thought, as she thanked the police officer, then closed and locked the door against the rapidly encroaching darkness.

twenty-five _____

A SENSE OF DANGER surrounds me. It is similiar to what I felt when Ellen Swain first began to link me to Letitia's death.

At that time I moved swiftly.

It was rash and foolish of me to have consulted Dr. Lillian Madden five years ago. What was I thinking? Of course I could not have allowed her to hypnotize me. Who knows what I might have divulged involuntarily when I opened my mind to her?

It was simply the enticing possibility of being placed directly into my previous incarnation that tempted me to visit her.

Will she remember that five years ago a client asked to be regressed to 1891?

It *is* possible, he decided, with a chill.

Would she consider a conversation that took place in her office, client to psychologist, to be privileged?

Maybe.

Or will she consider it her higher duty to make a telephone call to the police and say, "Five years ago I was asked if I could regress a man from Spring Lake to the year 1891. He was very specific about the date. I explained to him that unless he had been incarnated at that time it would not be possible to bring him back to it."

He could visualize Dr. Madden, her intelligent eyes looking directly at him. She had been challenged by him, but also curious.

Curiosity had been the reason Ellen Swain died, he reflected.

"Then," Dr. Madden might tell the police, "I tried to put my patient into a hypnotic state. He became quite agitated and left my office abruptly. This may not be of great importance, but I felt I should pass this information on to you. His name is . . ."

Dr. Lillian Madden must *not* be allowed to make that call! It was a risk he could not afford to take.

Like Ellen Swain, she will soon learn that *any* knowledge of me is dangerous, he thought—even fatal.

Saturday, March 24 ════════════

twenty-six

"I HAVE NEVER READ such unbridled nonsense in my life." Disdainfully, Rachel Wilcox placed the morning paper on the breakfast table and pushed it away from her. "A reincarnated serial killer! In the name of God, do these media people think we'll swallow anything?"

For many years Clayton and Rachel Wilcox had been having two copies of both *The Asbury Park Press* and *The New York Times* delivered daily.

Like her, he was reading *The Asbury Park Press*. "I think the newspaper is clearly saying that the question of a reincarnated serial killer was asked of the prosecutor Thursday. I do not read anywhere a suggestion that *The Asbury Park Press* gives credence to such a possibility."

She did not answer him. Not surprising, Clayton thought. Rachel's mood had been absolutely foul since Detective Duggan had phoned Thursday afternoon. She had been on her way out, and he had been assembling books for Emily Graham. Rachel had been outraged at the suggestion that the people at the Lawrence home the night before Martha disappeared were going to be brought together as a group, then questioned by the police. Again.

"The absolute *gall* of that man!" she had raged. "Does

he think that suddenly one of you will blurt out a confession, or point a finger at someone else?"

It wryly amused Clayton Wilcox that it apparently did not occur to Rachel that anybody would ever consider *her* a possible suspect in Martha's death.

He was tempted to point that out to her and say, "Rachel, you're a very strong woman. You carry anger in you, and it's always waiting to be unleashed. You have an instinctive dislike for beautiful young women with long blond hair, and I don't have to tell you why."

After twenty-seven years she still occasionally taunted him about that early affair with Helene. Rachel was right that at that time she alone had been responsible for saving his academic career. When the rumors started flying around the campus, he could have lost tenure. Rachel had tonguelashed the teacher who started the rumor, and she lied to cover her husband when someone else claimed that she had seen him in a hotel with Helene.

He had enjoyed his academic career. He still published regularly in academic journals and savored the respect of the academic world.

Thank God neither Rachel nor anyone from Enoch College ever knew why he had taken early retirement from the presidency there.

Clayton pushed back his chair and rose. "I'm confident the Mass will be well attended," he said. "I suggest we leave by ten-thirty to be sure of getting seats."

"I thought we agreed on that last night."

"I suppose we did." He turned to escape into his study but was stopped by the question she flung at him.

"Where did you *go* last night?" she asked.

He turned back to her slowly. "After we watched the news, I tried to work on my novel again, but I had a headache. I went for a long walk, which I'm sure you'll be glad to know did the trick. I came back to the house feeling much better."

"You *do* seem to get these headaches at odd hours, don't you, Clayton?" Rachel asked as she opened her copy of *The New York Times*.

twenty-seven

WILL STAFFORD genuinely meant it when, upon awakening, he resolved to have oatmeal for breakfast instead of bacon and eggs, or sausages and waffles.

Why do I keep that stuff in the refrigerator? he asked himself an hour later, when after being on the bike and treadmill in his exercise room, he was now in his sweat suit in the kitchen, preparing scrambled eggs and sausages.

While he ate, he read the *New York Post*. Their writers had consulted a parapsychologist who taught at the New School about the possibility that a serial killer from the late nineteenth century had been reincarnated.

The parapsychologist said that he did not believe that anyone came back with *exactly* the same personality—criminal or otherwise. Sometimes physical characteristics were carried through, he explained. Sometimes an inherent, almost mystical, fullblown talent arrives with the new person. Mozart, for example, was a musical genius at the age of three. Most certainly, emotional baggage from other incarnations may be the reason some people have to deal with seemingly inexplicable emotional problems or obsessions.

Another article raised the possibility that the murder of Madeline Shapley in 1891 might have been the deed of Jack the Ripper. The time frame was right. He had never been caught, but his brutal crimes had suddenly stopped in England, and there had always been a theory that he had migrated to New York.

A third article carefully reminded readers that although two other young women had disappeared from Spring Lake in the 1890s, there was no definite proof that either had been murdered.

Shaking his head, Will got up and, as second nature, carried his dishes to the sink and began to tidy the kitchen. He looked into the refrigerator and checked to be sure he had a good supply of cheese.

This afternoon, when Duggan got them all together here, it certainly wouldn't be a social event, he thought, but he'd put out some cheese and crackers, and offer everyone a glass of wine or a cup of coffee.

He debated about asking Emily Graham to have dinner with him. Of course, he was escorting her to the church and to the Lawrences' for the luncheon, but he realized that he very much wanted to have some real one-on-one time with her.

A very interesting and attractive lady.

Maybe he would offer to cook dinner here. Show off, he thought with a half smile. Thursday, at lunch, Natalie joked that people around here begged for an invitation to his dinner table.

I *am* a hell of a good cook, he admitted to himself. No—make that a hell of good chef!

He went into the living room to make sure there was nothing out of place. On the wall leading to the sunporch there was a picture of the house as it had looked when he bought it, with the shingles broken, the porch sagging, the shutters peeling. The inside had been just as bad, or worse.

He had hired a contractor for the structural work. The rest he did himself. It had taken years, but it had been an absolutely satisfying job.

It was one of the smaller places, one that had been labeled an "early, unpretentious year-round dwelling." It amused him that the pretentious mansions were gone. Houses like his were in constant demand on the local real estate market.

The phone rang. Will answered with a cheerful greeting, but when he realized who was calling, his grip on the receiver tightened.

"I'm all right, Dad," he said. "How are you?"

Would he *never* get the message? he wondered, as he listened to the halting voice of his father saying he was recovering pretty well from the last bout of chemo, and looking forward to getting together soon. "It's been too long, Will," his father said. "Far too long."

He finally had relented and had dinner with him in Princeton last year. His father had tried to apologize for the years he hadn't called even once. "I wasn't there for you when you needed me, son," he said. "So worried about the job, so busy; you know how it is."

"I'm pretty busy myself, Dad," he said now.

"Oh, that's a disappointment. In a month or so, maybe? I'd like to see your house. We used to have some nice times in Spring Lake, when your mother and you and I stayed at the Essex and Sussex."

"I have to be running, Dad. Good-bye."

As always happened after a call from his father, the stinging pain of the past washed over Will. He waited quietly, willing it to leave, then walked slowly up the stairs to dress for Martha Lawrence's memorial service.

twenty-eight _____

WHEN ROBERT FRIEZE returned home after an early morning jog, he found his wife already in the kitchen, eating her usual sparse breakfast: juice, black coffee, and a single slice of un-buttered toast.

"*You're* up early," he commented.

"I heard you moving around and couldn't get back to sleep. Honestly, Bob, you had a couple of nightmares last night. I had to wake you up. Do you remember that?"

Remember. The word that was beginning to frighten him. It had been happening again lately. Those blank periods when he had not been able to account for a couple of hours, or even a whole afternoon. Like last night. He had started to drive home from the restaurant at 11:30. He didn't get home until one. Where had he been that extra hour? he wondered.

Last week he had been wearing something he didn't even remember putting on.

These disturbing occurrences began when he was a teenager. First he started sleepwalking, then having periods when he would find time gaps in his activities, and not be able to explain to himself where he'd been.

He had never told anyone about it. He didn't want anyone to think of him as a nut case. It wasn't hard to conceal it. His mother and father had always been wrapped up in themselves and their careers. They demanded that he look good, have good manners, and get good marks in school. Otherwise they didn't give a damn what he did.

He had always been an insomniac. Three hours sleep was enough. Sometimes he sat up and read late into the night, at other times he'd go to bed, then get up and go down to the library. If he was lucky he would doze over a book.

The episodes had let up after college, then for years stopped completely. But for the last five years they had been happening again, and now they were becoming frequent.

He *knew* what was causing them: the restaurant—the most colossal mistake of his life. It was hemorrhaging money. It was the stress that was driving him into the blank periods again.

That *had* to be it, he decided.

He hadn't even told Natalie that three months ago he had put the restaurant up for sale. He knew she would have been hounding him every day to see if anyone had shown interest. And if not, why not? And then she would go through the litany of the craziness of buying it in the first place.

The real estate agent called yesterday afternoon. They were getting a nibble from Dom Bonetti who once ran The Fin and Claw, a four-star place in northern New Jersey. Bonetti had sold it, moved to Bay Head, and now had too much time on his hands. Actually, it was more than a nibble. He was bringing an offer to the table.

I'll be fine as soon as I sell it, Frieze promised himself.

"Do you intend to pour that coffee or just stand there holding the cup, Bobby?" Natalie's tone was amused.

"Pour it, I guess."

He knew Natalie was getting sick of his moods, but for the most part she'd been uncomplaining. She looked gorgeous, even with her hair tousled around her shoulders and no makeup and wearing that old chenille robe he hated.

He leaned down and kissed the top of her head.

"Spontaneous gesture of affection. Something that's been lacking for a long time," she said.

"I know. It's just that I've been under a lot of pressure." He decided to tell her about the prospective offer. "I've put The Seasoner up for sale. We may have a buyer."

"Bobby, *fantastic!*" She jumped up and hugged him. "Will you get your money back?"

"Most of it, even allowing for some bargaining on the price." As he said these words, Bob Frieze knew he was whistling in the dark.

"Then promise me once that's done you'll sell this house and we'll move to Manhattan."

"I promise." I want to get out of here too, he thought. I *have* to get out of here.

"I think we should leave early for the memorial Mass. You didn't forget about that, did you?"

"Hardly."

And after that, he thought, we go back to the Lawrence house, where I haven't been since that night I spent so much time talking to Martha.

Then we go to Stafford's place to get grilled by Duggan about what we were doing early the morning after the party.

He dreaded both sessions. The problem was, he remembered the party, but not what followed. Early that next morning he'd had one of his episodes. He hadn't come out of it until he found himself showering in the bathroom. His hands were grimy and his jeans and tee shirt had patches of dirt on them, he remembered.

He had planned to work in the garden that morning. It was his one hobby and always calmed him down.

I'm sure I worked in the garden that morning, he told himself, as he went up to dress for the memorial Mass for Martha Lawrence, and that's certainly what I'm going to tell Duggan.

twenty-nine

As HE HAD PROMISED, Will Stafford arrived at 10:40 on the dot on Saturday morning, to pick up Emily. She was waiting for him downstairs, her purse and gloves ready on the table in the foyer.

She decided that it had been a stroke of luck that she had brought her new black-and-white houndstooth check suit with her to Spring Lake, since most of the clothes she had here were distinctly casual.

Will obviously shared her feeling about how to dress. At the closing last Wednesday, he had been wearing a sports jacket; today, a dark blue suit, white shirt, and subdued blue tie were his choice of suitable garb for the occasion.

"You look lovely," he said quietly. "I just wish we were dressed up to go to a different kind of gathering."

"So do I."

He gestured toward the back of the house. "I see the contractor is filling in the hole out there. Are they satisfied there's nothing else to be found?"

"Yes, they are."

"That's good. We'd better be on our way." As Emily picked up her purse and set the alarm, Will Stafford smiled. "Why do I get the feeling that I'm always rushing you? The other day it was to get over here from breakfast for the final inspection. If you had known what was going to happen, would you have backed out on the purchase?"

"Believe it or not, that hasn't even occurred to me."

"That's good."

He put his hand under her elbow as they went down the steps, and Emily realized it gave her a sense of emotional and physical security to feel it there.

It has been a rough few days, she thought. Maybe it's taken more out of me than I realized.

It's even more than that, she decided, as Will opened the door of the car and she slipped into the passenger seat. In a crazy way, I feel as if this memorial Mass isn't just for Martha Lawrence. *It's for Madeline too.*

As Will began to drive, she told him how she felt, then added, "I had been wrestling with the idea that to go to this Mass for a girl I never knew might seem like being a voyeur. I was honestly troubled about it, but now it seems different."

"Different in what way?"

"I believe in eternal life, that heaven exists. I'd like to think that those two young girls—who must have been so frightened in the last moments of their life; who were murdered a hundred years apart and their bodies dumped in my backyard—are still together now. I want to believe that they're now in 'a place of refreshment, light, and peace,' as Scripture says."

"Where do you think their murderer is now?" Will asked as he started the car. "And what will be his fate someday?"

Startled, Emily turned and stared at him. "Will, surely you mean murderers! Two separate people."

He glanced at her as he laughed. "Good God, Emily, I'm starting to sound like the nutty tabloid writers. Of course I mean *murderers*. Two. Plural. One long-since dead. The other probably out there somewhere."

They were silent for the few minutes it took them to drive around the lake and for St. Catherine's Church to come into view. It was an exquisite domed Romanesque structure. Emily knew it had been built in 1901 by a wealthy man as a memorial to his deceased seventeen-year-old daughter. It seemed to her to be a particularly appropriate place for this service.

They could see a steady stream of cars approaching the church and parking around it. "I wonder if Martha's murderer is in one of those cars, Will?" Emily said.

"If he is from Spring Lake, as the cops seem to think, I doubt very much that he'd have the nerve to stay away. It would be too conspicuous not to be here, grieving with the family."

Grieving with the family, Emily thought. I wonder which of Madeline's friends, with blood on his hands, grieved with our family one hundred and ten years ago.

thirty

AT ELEVEN O'CLOCK on Saturday morning, Joan Hodges was on her way to the beauty salon to have her hair frosted when the phone rang. It was Dr. Madden's sister Esther, phoning from Connecticut.

Her voice was troubled. "Joan, was Lillian going away this weekend?"

"No."

"I tried to call her last night at about eleven-thirty. When she didn't answer, I thought she might have gone out with friends after her class, but I've phoned twice this morning and I still can't reach her."

"Sometimes she turns off the phone. With all the pestering from the media over this murder investigation, she probably did just that. I'll go over and just make sure everything's fine with her." Joan tried to sound reassuring, in spite of her own misgivings.

"I don't like to put you out."

"You're not putting me out. It's a fifteen-minute drive."

Her hair appointment completely forgotten, Joan drove as fast as she dared. The sinking feeling in her stomach and the lump in her throat betrayed the panic that she was trying to keep in check. Something was terribly wrong. She *knew* it.

Dr. Madden's house was on a half-acre lot on Laurel Street, three blocks from the ocean. It's such a beautiful day, Joan thought as she pulled into the driveway. Please, God, let her have gone for a long walk. Or let her have forgotten to turn up the ringer on the phone.

As Joan approached the house, she saw that the bedroom shades were down, and the newspaper was on the front porch. Her hands trembling now, she fumbled for the key to the office door. She knew that if Dr. Madden had locked the connecting door from the office to the rest of the house, there was a spare key hidden in her desk.

She stepped into the small vestibule. In the bright sunshine she did not notice that the lights in the office were on. Her hands soaked with perspiration, her breath shallow, she went into her own office. The file drawers were open. Files had been pulled out, emptied, and tossed aside, the contents strewn all over the floor.

Her legs resisting her attempt to run, Joan entered Lillian Madden's office.

The shriek that ripped from within her was only an agonized moan when it left her lips. The body of Dr. Madden was slumped over her desk, her head turned to one side, her hand still clenched, as if it had been holding something. Her eyes were open and bulging, her lips drawn apart, as if still gasping for air.

A cord was twisted tightly around her neck.

Joan did not remember running out of the office, down the porch steps, across the lawn to the sidewalk screaming all the way. When she became aware again, she was surrounded by Lillian Madden's neighbors, who had rushed out of their homes, drawn by her hysterical cries.

As her knees crumpled and merciful darkness blotted out the gruesome image of her murdered friend and employer, a thought flickered through Joan's mind: *Dr. Madden be-lieved that people who die a violent death return very quickly in a new incarnation. If that's true, I wonder how soon she'll be back?*

thirty-one

THEY ARE BEING simply magnificent, Emily thought. She and Will Stafford had just arrived at the Lawrence home, where an informal receiving line had formed in the spacious living room. Martha's grandparents, the senior Lawrences, silver-haired and straight-backed octogenarians; Martha's parents, George and Amanda Lawrence, a patrician couple in their late fifties; and their other daughter, Christine, a younger ver-sion of her mother, and Christine's husband, were standing together, greeting their guests and accepting condolences.

The dignity and serenity with which they had con-ducted themselves during the memorial Mass had filled Emily with admiration.

She and Will had been in a pew at a right angle to where the family was seated, and she had been able to see them clearly. Although tears had welled in their eyes, they had all sat composed and attentive throughout the service, Chris-tine sitting next to her parents, her new baby, Martha's name-sake, in her arms.

When one of Martha's friends broke down weeping as she eulogized her, Emily had felt her own eyes fill with tears. At that point she saw Amanda Lawrence reach over and take the baby from Christine. She had held her close, the little baby's head tucked gently under her chin.

"I kissed her and she kissing back could not know, that my kiss was given to her sister folded close under deepen-ing snow."

The poignant lines from the James Russell Lowell

poem had run through Emily's mind as she watched Amanda Lawrence taking comfort from her newborn granddaughter even as her murdered daughter was eulogized.

Will introduced her to them. They realized who she was immediately. "This happened in your own family four generations ago," Martha's father said. "We only pray that whoever took our daughter's life will be brought to justice."

"Ignoring the reincarnation nonsense, do you think that Martha's death may have been intended to copy what happened to Madeline Shapley?" Amanda Lawrence asked.

"Yes, I do," Emily said. "And I even believe that a written confession or statement may exist that the present-day killer has found. I'm digging into old records and books, trying to piece together a picture of Madeline and her friends. I'm looking for any references to her, or maybe impressions that other people had of her at that time."

George and Amanda Lawrence exchanged glances, then he turned to his parents. "Mother, don't you have quite a few photograph albums and other memorabilia from your grandmother's time?"

"Oh, yes, dear. All packed away in that cabinet in the attic. My maternal grandmother, Julia Gordon, was *very* meticulous. She wrote captions under all the pictures, listing the date, place, event, and the names of the people and she kept extensive diaries." The senior Mrs. Lawrence looked inquiringly at Emily.

Julia Gordon's name had been sprinkled throughout the diary excerpts in the book *Reflections of a Girlhood*. She had been Madeline's contemporary.

"Would you consider letting me look through the contents of that cabinet?" Emily asked quietly. "You may think it farfetched, but I believe we may learn something from the past that will help now."

Before his mother could answer, George Lawrence spoke firmly and without hesitation. "We will do *anything* that will help in any way to expose our daughter's killer."

"Emily." Will Stafford pressed her arm and indicated the people waiting behind them to speak to the Lawrences.

"I can't hold you any longer," Emily said hastily. "May I call you tomorrow morning?"

"Will has the number. He'll give it to you."

The buffet table was in the dining room. Tables and chairs had been set on the enclosed back porch, which extended the length of the house.

Plates in hand, they went out to the porch. "Over here, Will," a voice called. "We've saved a place for you."

"That's Natalie Frieze," Will said as they walked across the room.

"Join the other suspects," Natalie said gaily when they reached the table. "We're trying to get our stories straight before Duggan gives us the third degree."

Emily winced at the remark, agreeing with the stern-faced woman sitting opposite Natalie, who said sharply, "There are some things that ought not to be joked about, Natalie."

The reproof did not seem to faze Natalie Frieze for a moment. "'Brighten the corner where you are,' Rachel," she quoted briskly. "That's all I'm trying to do. No offense intended."

Dr. Wilcox was at the table and greeted her warmly. His wife, Rachel, was introduced, as were Bob and Natalie Frieze. A May and December romance, Emily thought. I wonder how long the lady will stay. That's one marriage that I wouldn't bet on lasting. On the other hand, you never know, she reminded herself. I certainly would have bet on *mine* hanging in for the long haul!

"Have you found any of the books helpful?" Dr. Wilcox was asking.

"Very much so."

"I understand you're a criminal defense attorney, Emily," Natalie Frieze said.

"Yes, I am."

"I've been wondering—if someone in this room is indicted for Martha's murder, would you consider defending him?"

She likes to make waves, Emily thought, but she noticed that the atmosphere at the table changed instantly. Someone—or perhaps even everyone—is not finding that question amusing, she thought.

She tried to pass off the question lightly. "Well, I *am* a member of the New Jersey bar, but since I'm sure that won't happen, I don't think I'll look for a retainer here."

As they were leaving, Will introduced her to a number of people, most of them year-round or summer residents of the town. Emily immediately felt comfortable with them, as if, like many of the others, her family had retained a place in Spring Lake for generations. The Lawrence home went back to the 1880s. Had the Shapleys been guests in this house? she wondered.

They chatted for a few minutes with John and Carolyn Taylor, Will's close friends, who asked if she played tennis.

A quick image of standing at Gary's side, accepting the tennis doubles cup at their club in Albany, flashed through Emily's mind. "Yes, I do."

"We're members of the Bath and Tennis Club," Carolyn Taylor said. "When it opens in May, join us for lunch there, and bring your racket."

"I'd like that."

In the general conversation she learned that Carolyn ran a nursery school in nearby Tinton Falls, while John was a surgeon in North Jersey Shore Hospital. She could tell immediately that they were people she would enjoy knowing better.

As they were about to leave, Carolyn Taylor hesitated, then said, "I hope you realize that everyone in this room—make that everyone in this *community*—feels sorry that you've had so much on your plate these last few days. I just wanted to say that for *all* of us."

Then she added, "We're fourth generation Spring Lake people. In fact, a distant cousin of mine, Phyllis Gates, wrote a book about life here in the 1880s and 1890s. She was very close to Madeline Shapley."

Emily stared at her. "I read her book cover-to-cover last night," she said.

"Phyllis died in the mid-1940s, when my mother was a teenager. Despite the age difference, they were very fond of each other. Phyllis used to take Mother on trips with her."

"Did she ever talk to your mother about Madeline?"

"Yes, she did. In fact Mom and I were on the phone this morning. Naturally we've been discussing everything that has happened here these last few days. Mom said that Phyllis didn't want to put it in her book, but she was always sure that it was Douglas Carter who killed Madeline. Wasn't he the fiancé, or have I got that wrong?"

thirty-two _____

TOMMY DUGGAN attended the Mass at St. Catherine's with Pete Walsh. The entire time there he had been infuriated by the certainty that Martha's killer was somewhere in the church, though his expression remained composed and suitably grave as he joined in the prayers being offered for her and raised his voice in the final hymn.

> *We shall dwell in the City of God*
> *Where our tears shall be turned into dancing . . .*

When I find *you*, I'll dry your crocodile tears for you, Tommy vowed, his mind on the murderer.

Following the Mass, he had planned to go to his office and stay there until it was time to meet the group at Will Stafford's house, but when he and Pete got back to the car and checked their messages, he learned about the death of Dr. Lillian Madden.

Fifteen minutes later he was at the crime scene, with

Pete at his heels. The body was still there, the forensic team efficiently at work, the local police guarding the scene.

"They figure death occurred sometime between ten and eleven last night," Frank Willette, the Belmar police chief told him. "It wasn't a burglary that went sour, I'll tell you that much. There's jewelry and money in the bedroom, so whoever did this was only interested in finding something here, in her office."

"Did Dr. Madden keep drugs here?"

"No drugs. She was a psychologist, a Ph.D., not a medical doctor. Of course, the person who did it may not have known that, but . . ." He shrugged.

"The secretary, Joan Hodges, found her," Willette continued. "Hodges ran outside and collapsed on the street. She's being treated in there." He nodded toward the open door that led to the living quarters on the other side of the vestibule. "Why don't you talk to her?"

"I intend to."

Joan Hodges was propped up on pillows on the bed in the guest bedroom, a medic from the ambulance team at her side. A Belmar policeman standing at the foot of the bed was about to put away his notebook.

"I do *not* want to go to the hospital," she was saying as Duggan and Walsh entered the room. "I'll be all right. It was just the shock of finding her . . ." Her voice trailed off, and tears began to run down her cheeks. "It's *so* awful," she whispered. "Why would *anyone* do that to her?"

Tommy Duggan looked at the Belmar cop, whom he knew slightly. "I've already talked to Ms. Hodges," the cop said. "I guess you have some questions for her too."

"I do." Tommy pulled up a chair, sat down by the bed, and introduced himself.

His voice sympathetic and understanding, he expressed sorrow and shock, then began to question Joan gently.

It was immediately clear that Joan Hodges had a very definite opinion about the reason for Lillian Madden's murder.

Her voice growing firmer as anger mingled with grief, Joan said, "There *is* a serial killer out there, and I'm beginning to think he *is* a reincarnation of the one who lived in the 1890s. The media kept calling Dr. Madden and asking her about that on Thursday and all day yesterday. They all wanted her opinion about him."

"Do you mean she might have *known* him?" Tommy Duggan asked.

"I don't know *what* I mean, frankly. Maybe she could have told them something that would have helped the police find him. I had a bad feeling about Dr. Madden going to her class last night. I told her I thought she ought to cancel it. Maybe somebody followed her home."

Hodges had a point, Tommy thought. The killer could easily have attended the lecture.

"Joan, you saw the way the office records were thrown around. The killer was obviously looking for something, maybe even his own file. Can you think of any of the doctor's patients who might have threatened her? Or is one of them perhaps psychotic enough to have turned on her for some reason?"

Joan Hodges brushed back hair from her forehead. I was going to have it frosted, she thought. With all her being she wished that the clock could be turned back, that the day could unfold as it had been planned, that right now she was out shopping for the new dress she needed for her best friend's second wedding.

Dr. Madden, she thought. Her patients loved her. She was so kind, so understanding. Oh sure, there'd been a few who had stopped coming, but that happens with any psychologist. Dr. Madden used to say that some people just want reinforcement of their inappropriate behavior, not insight into how to change it.

"I don't know of a single patient who would ever have wanted to harm Dr. Madden," she told Tom. "It's that serial killer. I *know* it is. He's afraid that she figured out something about him."

That makes sense, *if* he'd been a patient of hers at some

time, Tom thought. "Joan, where else would a patient's name appear, besides in his own file?"

"In the appointment book I keep, and in the computer."

Tommy Duggan stood up. "Joan, we're going to find this guy. I promise you that. Your job is to start concentrating on the patients. I don't care how insignificant you may think it is, if anything at all odd about any one of them occurs to you, call me up right away, okay?"

He put his card on the night table beside the bed.

When he and Pete returned to the doctor's office, the body bag holding the remains of Lillian Madden was being carried out.

"We're finished here," the head of the forensic team told him. "I doubt that we have anything useful for you guys. My guess is that this guy was smart enough to wear gloves."

"Whatever he was looking for in the files, he probably found," Chief Willette said. "The cabinets with the patients' files are in the doctor's private office, and the key was in the master lock. Either the guy found it in the top drawer of Dr. Madden's desk, or it was already in the lock."

"Do you know if she often worked at night?" Pete Walsh asked.

"Dr. Madden lectured last night at the community college. Looks like she came back from the college, then went straight to her office. Her coat and briefcase are in the reception area. I wonder what was so important? She was obviously at her desk working when she was killed. Probably never heard the intruder."

"How'd he enter?"

"Nothing forced. Maybe an unlocked window? We found three or four of them. The alarm was turned off."

"He was a patient," Tommy said positively. "Maybe someone who said too much under hypnosis and was worried. Otherwise, why go through the files? Joan Hodges said that if he *was* a patient, his name will be listed in the appointment books."

"He tried to smash the computers," Willette said.

Tommy nodded. He was not surprised. "Unless the hard drive is broken, we may be able to bring them up," he said.

"I'm going to help you." Joan Hodges, still ghostly pale, but determined, had followed them.

An hour later a frustrated Tommy Duggan was certain of only one fact: the murderer of Lillian Madden had been a patient sometime in the last five years. All the appointment books covering that time period were missing, both Dr. Madden's personal copies and the ones Joan Hodges kept.

Joan looked ready to cave in.

"We have to leave, and *you* should go home," Tommy told her. "Let Pete drive your car." An uneasy feeling had been settling over him. "How long have you been with Dr. Madden, Joan?" he asked.

"Six years next week."

"Did Dr. Madden discuss her patients with you? "

"Never."

As he drove through Belmar, following Joan's car to her condominium in Wall Township, Tommy wondered if Dr. Madden's killer might begin to worry that her secretary might also have been her confidante.

I'll tell the local guys to keep an eye on her place, he decided. He tightened his hands on the steering wheel as he felt a primitive need to lash out, to punch something with his fists. "I've been with the killer," he said aloud, spitting out the words. "I've sensed his presence. I just don't know who the hell he is."

thirty-three

MARTY BROWSKI of Albany, New York, did not know Tommy Duggan of Monmouth County, New Jersey, but they were kindred spirits, detectives to the core, with the absolute tenacity of bulldogs when they set out to solve a crime.

They had something else in common. When they got that almost mystical feeling that there was something wrong about a crime—one that apparently had been satisfactorily solved—they could not rest until they had reexamined every aspect of it, looking for a miscarriage of justice.

Since the phone call from Emily Graham about the photograph that had been slipped under her door in Spring Lake, Marty Browski had been deeply disturbed.

He had been convinced that Ned Koehler was the stalker and that they'd caught him just in time, before he had a chance to kill Emily. But now he wasn't so sure.

On Saturday afternoon, Marty talked it over with his wife, Janey, as they took their Labrador, Ranger, for a long walk through the park near their home in Troy. "When we arrested Koehler, he was outside Emily Graham's townhouse. He claimed that he'd only planned to frighten her. He said he had no intention of going inside."

"You believed him, Marty. Everyone did. He was convicted of stalking her," Janey observed.

"He changed his story when I talked to him yesterday. He added to it, saying he wanted Emily to experience how frightened his mother was before *she* died."

"Nice guy."

"Spring's coming," Marty observed, sniffing the air. "Be good to get the boat out." He grimaced. "Janey, Ned Koehler supposedly arrived home and found his mother dead, the knife in her chest. He went crazy: picked her up, carried her body out of the apartment, yelling for help. Joel Lake had been in that apartment, had burglarized it. It's a miracle Emily Graham got him acquitted of the murder charge."

"As I remember, the jury believed Ruth Koehler's sister when she testified that she'd spoken to Ruth after Joel Lake was seen leaving the building."

"I didn't think they'd buy that story at the time. I thought that old lady was as reliable as a weather report."

Janey Browski smiled. She and Marty had been childhood sweethearts and were married the week after they graduated from high school. At age forty-nine, she had three grown children and four grandchildren, a fact belied by her disarmingly youthful appearance. She was a sophomore at Sienna College now, working for a bachelor's degree, the same as Marty had earned when he attended evening classes during the first five years of their marriage.

She knew that Marty's ultimate expression of disbelief was to compare sworn testimony to a weather report.

"Are you saying that Ruth Koehler may have surprised Joel Lake while he was burglarizing her apartment and that he was the killer?"

"I was sure he was. We collared him a couple of blocks away. He had the stuff he'd taken from the apartment on him. The fact that he had no bloodstains didn't mean anything because the knife had been thrown at Ruth Koehler and caught her in the chest."

"Fingerprints?"

"Joel Lake wore gloves during the burglary. Anyhow, Ned Koehler compromised the crime scene by pulling the knife out of his mother's body and carrying her out of the apartment into the hall. We all bought his story that he had found her and become hysterical."

Janey Browski bent down and picked up a stick to throw to Ranger, who was clearly looking for them to play games with him.

She wound up and tossed the stick. It sailed high and clear and well beyond Ranger, who raced to catch it with a happy bark.

"The Mets could use you," Marty said admiringly.

"Sure they could. You had pegged Ned Koehler as a weirdo but also a grieving son who stalked the lawyer who got his mother's killer acquitted."

"Right."

"Is the know-it-all detective about to face the fact that he might have rushed to an erroneous conclusion?"

Ranger was loping back to them, the stick in his teeth.

Marty Browski sighed. "Janey, why didn't your mother teach you to respect your husband? Ned Koehler is a weirdo and a liar. After seeing him yesterday, I now believe he is also a murderer, his mother's murderer. And—"

"What else?" Janey asked.

"I also think that he may not be the stalker who was making Emily Graham's life hell. I think that whoever shoved a picture of her under her door the other night was the real stalker. I've talked to the Spring Lake police. Think about it. If somebody from around here followed her down to Spring Lake, found out where she was staying, even what room she was in, then stood on the beach hoping to catch her at the window, got her picture, developed it, and shoved it under her door the next night while a policeman was on the premises— what does that say to you?"

"Obsession. Recklessness. Cunning."

"Exactly."

"So whoever stalked her up here didn't mind making the drive to Spring Lake. If you eliminate Ned Koehler, where do you start looking for him?"

"Maybe Joel Lake? He's the one she got acquitted. He's slime. He got a light sentence for the burglary and was out on the streets when the stalking started. Then I'm taking a good look at Gary White."

"Oh, come on, Marty! Emily Graham and Gary White have been divorced for over three years. I heard he broke up with Barbara what's-her-name and is playing the field. He's just a minor-league Don Juan."

"He sued Emily Graham for five million dollars, half of what she made when she sold her dot-com stock. Which incidentally was the smartest thing she ever did in her life," Marty added. "It's really taken a beating lately."

They had reached the T junction in the park, where they always turned around and started back home. In an instinctive gesture, they each reached for the other's hand.

"And your next stop is . . . ? " Janey asked.

"To look at the files on Ruth Koehler's death, with the premise that her son, Ned, may well be the killer. And to re-open the stalking case."

"Sounds sensible to me."

"And to warn Emily Graham," Marty Browski added grimly.

thirty-four

AT THREE O'CLOCK a total of twenty-five people, including the five catering employees, were gathered in Will Stafford's living room. Chairs from the dining room had remedied the need for extra seating. Somewhat ill at ease, and glad to feel useful, the catering staff had rushed to get the chairs and had deliberately set five of them to one side for themselves.

Tommy Duggan stood at the fireplace, the focal point of the room. He looked the group over, the image of Dr. Lillian Madden's body in his mind. There was a good chance that whoever murdered her was in this room right now—a thought that both exhilarated and sickened him.

But he had a tangible clue—the scarf found buried with Martha Lawrence's body. If just *one* person remembered that someone had been wearing a silver scarf with metallic beading on it that night, he would have a link to the killer.

"I appreciate that you all were kind enough to join us," he began, his tone conciliatory. "The reason we are here together is that you were the last people to spend time with Martha Lawrence. You were present at the party at the Lawrence home only hours before she disappeared and, as we now know, was murdered.

"I have talked with all of you individually during these past four and a half years. My hope is that by bringing you together, something you noticed that night, then forgot, may surface in your minds. Perhaps Martha mentioned her plans for meeting someone later that night or the next day.

"What I'd like to do is take you into Will's study, one at a time, and ask you to give me the details of any conversation you had with Martha that night at the party, and any conversation you may have overheard her having with someone else."

He paused. "I then want to go over with each one of you exactly where you were the next morning between the hours of six and nine."

Tommy's eyes scanned the room for reactions. Robert Frieze was obviously furious. The skin over his high cheekbones was turning a deep shade of crimson; his lips were compressed in a thin, angry line. He had claimed he'd been working in his flower beds that morning. His wife had been asleep. With the high hedges around his house, no one else would have been able to see him to verify his alibi. Mr. McGregor in his cabbage patch. Tommy did not know why he always thought of the Beatrix Potter character when he pictured Robert Frieze in his backyard, but there it was. The image was stuck somehow.

Dennis and Isabelle Hughes, the Lawrences' neighbors, were frowning in concentration. Both seemed anxious to help. She was a talker. Maybe seeing everyone together like this would trigger a memory.

One guy on the catering staff, the assistant boss, Reed Turner, had always been something of a question mark. Fortyish, not bad-looking, he considered himself a ladies' man. Tommy noticed he looked worried now. Why?

Dr. Wilcox hid behind a philosophic expression as he had whenever Tommy had questioned him during these past four and a half years. He'd admitted to being out for a long walk that morning, but not on the boardwalk, just around town. Maybe. Maybe not?

Mrs. Wilcox. Brunhilde. I'd hate to get in *her* way, Tommy thought. She appears to be one tough cookie. The look on her face right now would stop a clock. Reminds me of

Mrs. Orbach. Mrs. Orbach had been his fifth-grade teacher. What a battle-ax, he thought.

Will Stafford. Good-looking. A single guy. The women were attracted to him. Natalie Frieze had given him a mighty warm kiss when she came in. Right in front of her husband, too. Had Martha Lawrence been attracted to him? Tommy wondered.

There were four other couples, each wife distinctly remembering that her husband never left the house early that morning. Would they lie rather than let their husbands come under any hint of suspicion? Maybe.

Tommy could visualize any one of these men saying to his wife, "Just because I went out for an early walk for ten minutes doesn't mean I want the whole town to wonder if I might have committed a murder. I didn't run into anybody. Let's just agree that I wasn't out of your sight all morning."

Mrs. Joyce. Late seventies. Longtime friend of the senior Lawrences. After the initial investigation, he'd never had much chance to talk to her. She didn't have a home here anymore. Stayed at The Breakers for a month or so every summer. She'd come up for the memorial Mass.

"Why don't I start with you, Mr. Turner?" Tommy asked, then turned to Pete Walsh. "All set?"

They had decided how they would conduct the sessions. Not quite good cop-bad cop, but Pete would sit behind the person being interviewed, the notes of all the previous statements in his hand, and interrupt whenever he found a discrepancy.

That technique always rattled anyone who was trying to conceal something.

Tommy had two questions to ask each of them. The first was, "Do you remember any of the women at the party that night wearing a silver scarf with metallic beading on the edges?" The second, "Have you ever been a patient of Dr. Lillian Madden's or had a consultation with her?"

As Tommy started to walk across the room to the

study, Robert Frieze stopped him. "I must insist that you ask your questions of me before anyone else. I have a restaurant to run, and Saturday night is very busy. I believe I pointed that out to you on the phone the other day."

"I believe you did." Tommy itched to tell Frieze off, to say, *"This is a* murder *investigation, Mr. Frieze. You have been the most uncooperative person in this room. What have you got to hide?"*

Instead he said, "I will be happy to speak to you first, Mr. Frieze." Then he paused and added, "I cannot order anyone to stay, but it is very important to our investigation that everyone remains until all interviews have taken place. We may want to call different people back in after we have initially spoken to everyone."

The first hour went slowly. Everyone stuck to the stories they'd told for the past four and a half years.

Nobody knew anything about a scarf . . . Martha hadn't mentioned any plans she had for the next day . . . Nobody had seen her use a cell phone.

Then Rachel Wilcox came in, every inch of her formidable body conveying her outrage and distaste for the entire matter. Her answers to their questions were brusque and dismissive.

"I spoke to Martha about graduate school since I knew she was planning to attend. Martha *did* mention that she was having second thoughts about her master's program in business. She had worked as a hostess in Chillingsworth, a very fine restaurant on Cape Cod, and thoroughly enjoyed the experience. She told me she wondered if she should not step back and review her choice."

"You never mentioned that to me before, Mrs. Wilcox," Tommy said.

"If every word that people exchanged at social events were weighed and measured, the world would drown in trivia," Rachel Wilcox told him, and then added, "Is there anything more you require of me?"

"Just one more question. Do you know if anyone was

wearing a silvery-gray chiffon scarf with metallic beading that night?"

"*I* was wearing it. Has it been found?"

Tommy felt his palms begin to sweat. *Clayton Wilcox,* he thought. Was he stupid enough to use his wife's scarf to kill Martha?

"You ask if the scarf was found, Mrs. Wilcox. When were you aware that it was missing?"

"It was rather warm that evening, so I took it off. I asked my husband to put it in his pocket and thought no more about it until the next afternoon, when I asked him to give it to me. He did not have it. Has it been found?"

"It's been mentioned that a scarf had been lost," Tommy said evasively. "Did you or Dr. Wilcox look for it?"

"My husband had understood me to say that I wanted him to put the scarf with my pocketbook. He phoned the Lawrences to ask about it, but it wasn't there."

"I see." Leave it alone, Tommy told himself. Let's get *his* version. Banking on the probability that the news of the murder in Belmar had not yet reached the ears of these people who had left the Lawrence home to come directly to this meeting, he asked, "Mrs. Wilcox, do you know a Dr. Lillian Madden?

"The name is familiar."

"She is a psychologist who lives in Belmar."

"She teaches a course on reincarnation at Monmouth County Community College, does she not?"

"Yes, she does."

"I cannot imagine a greater waste of time."

When she left the study, Tommy Duggan and Pete Walsh exchanged glances. "Get Wilcox in here before she has a chance to talk to him," Duggan said.

"I'm already on my way." Pete disappeared into the foyer that led to the living room.

The demeanor of Dr. Clayton Wilcox, by all outward appearances, was measured and calm, but Tommy wondered if he was at last sniffing the scent he'd been trying to catch all day. *Fear.* It had its own pungent aroma that had nothing to do with the sweat glands. Clayton Wilcox was not only afraid, he was close to outright panic.

"Sit down, Dr. Wilcox. I just have to go over a few of the bases I want to touch with you."

The old ploy, Tommy thought. Leave them stewing in the hot seat, asking themselves the questions they're afraid you'll ask them. Then when you start in on them, their guts are already churned up.

They asked Wilcox about any conversation he might have had with Martha Lawrence at the party.

"We had the usual exchange one has at that sort of affair. She knew my career was in academia, and she asked me if I was friendly with anyone at Tulane University Graduate School of Business in New Orleans, which is where she was enrolled." He paused. "I am sure you and I have discussed this before, Mr. Duggan."

"We did, Dr. Wilcox, more or less. And the next morning you went for a long walk but did *not* go on the boardwalk, nor did you run into Martha at any point?"

"I think I have answered that question repeatedly."

"Dr. Wilcox, did your wife lose a silk scarf the night of the party?"

"Yes, she did."

Tommy Duggan watched as beads of perspiration formed on the forehead of Dr. Clayton Wilcox. "Did your wife ask you to hold that scarf for her?"

Wilcox waited, then said deliberately, "My wife's recollection is that she asked me to put the scarf in my pocket. My recollection is that she asked me to put it with her pocketbook, which was on a table in the foyer. That is exactly what I did, and I thought no more of it."

"Then, the next afternoon when you both realized it was missing, did you call the Lawrence home to inquire about it?"

"No, I did not."

Direct contradiction of his wife's statement, Tommy

thought. "Wouldn't it have been appropriate to have asked the Lawrences if the scarf was still in their home?"

"Mr. Duggan, by the time we realized the scarf was missing, we all knew that Martha had disappeared. Do you seriously believe I would ask that distraught family about a scarf at that time?"

"Did you tell your wife you inquired about it?"

"For the sake of peace I did tell her that, yes."

"One last question. Dr. Wilcox, did you personally know Dr. Lillian Madden?"

"No, I did not."

"Were you ever a patient of hers, or did you ever consult her or have any type of contact with her?"

Wilcox seemed to hesitate. Then, the tension apparent in his voice, he said, "No, I was never a patient, and I don't recall ever having met her."

He's lying, Tommy thought.

Sunday, March 25

thirty-five _____

NICHOLAS TODD PHONED EMILY at 9:15 A.M. on Sunday. "Are we still on for today, I hope?" he asked.

"Absolutely. The Old Mill serves a fabulous brunch, I'm told. I made a reservation for one o'clock."

"Great. I'll be at your house by about 12:30 if that's okay. Incidentally, I hope this wasn't too early to call. Did I wake you up?"

"I've already walked to church and back, and it's over a mile away. Does that answer your question?"

"You're showing off. Now run through the directions to your place for me."

AFTER SHE RANG OFF FROM NICK, Emily decided to treat herself to a leisurely hour or two with the morning newspapers. The day before, when Will Stafford had driven her home after the Lawrence luncheon, she'd spent the rest of the afternoon and the evening with the books Dr. Wilcox had loaned her. She wanted to get them back to him as soon as possible.

The fact that he had given her the Enoch College bag and suggested she keep his books together in it suggested to

Emily that Dr. Wilcox would be uneasy if she did not return them promptly.

Besides, she acknowledged to herself, she wanted to let the information she had accumulated settle down into some kind of orderly pattern. Yesterday she had been told that Phyllis Gates, the author of *Reflections of a Girlhood*, had believed that Douglas Carter was Madeline's murderer.

That *had* to be wrong, she decided. Douglas Carter committed suicide before Letitia Gregg and Ellen Swain disappeared. Had Carolyn Taylor, Phyllis Gates's distant relation, meant to say instead that Phyllis was suspicious of *Alan* Carter? He was the cousin, who "was very smitten with Madeline despite the fact that she was about to become engaged to Douglas."

Smitten enough to kill her, rather than lose her to his cousin? Emily wondered.

Leave it alone this morning, she told herself, as she brought coffee into the study, which was fast becoming her favorite room. It was flooded with sunshine in the morning, and in the evening, with the shades drawn and the gas fire on, it had a cozy, intimate quality.

Settling in the big chair, she opened *The Asbury Park Press* and saw the headline: PSYCHOLOGIST MURDERED IN BELMAR.

The word "reincarnation" in the first paragraph of the article riveted Emily's attention.

"Dr. Lillian Madden, a longtime resident of Belmar and a prominent lecturer on the subject of reincarnation, was found brutally strangled in her office . . ."

With mounting horror she read the rest of the story. The final sentence was: "Police are investigating the possibility of a connection between Dr. Madden's death and the person who has been dubbed 'the reincarnated serial killer of Spring Lake.'"

Emily put down the paper, thinking back to the parapsychology class she had visited at the New School while she was a law student at NYU. The professor had regressed one of his students, a shy twenty-year-old woman, to a former life-time.

The subject clearly had been in a state of deep hypnosis. The professor took her back past her birth and into "a warm tunnel," assuring her that it would be a pleasant journey.

He was trying to place the young woman in another time, Emily remembered. He had said to her, "It is May 1960. Does a picture form in your mind?"

The young woman had whispered, "No," in a soft, almost inaudible voice.

The regression had made such a vivid impact on Emily that, sitting in the chair, the paper on her lap, the murdered doctor's picture looking up at her, she was able to remember clearly every detail of the event.

The professor had continued the questioning. "It is December 1952. Does a picture form in your mind?"

"No."

"It is September 1941. Does a picture form in your mind?"

And then we were all shocked, Emily thought, when a clear, authoritative male voice anwered, *"Yes!"*

In the same voice, the subject had given his name and described what he was wearing. "I am Lieutenant David Richards, United States Navy. I am wearing my naval uniform, sir."

"Where are you from?"

"Near Sioux City, Iowa."

"Sioux City?"

"Near Sioux City, sir."

"Where are you now?"

"In Pearl Harbor, Hawaii, sir."

"Why are you there?"

"We believe there may be a war with Japan."

"It is six months later. Where are you, Lieutenant?"

The arrogance was gone from his voice, Emily remembered. He described being in San Francisco. His ship was there for repairs. The war had started.

Lieutenant David Richards then clearly described his life at war for the next three years—and his death when a Japanese destroyer rammed his PT boat.

"Oh God, they've seen us," he had shouted. "They're turning. They're going to ram us."

"Lieutenant, it is the next day," the professor had interrupted. "Tell me where you are."

The voice was different, Emily thought. Quiet. Resigned. She remembered the answer: "It's dark and gray and cold. I'm in the water. There's wreckage all around me. I'm dead."

Was it possible that during regression in Dr. Madden's office, someone had experienced a total recall of having lived in Spring Lake in the 1890s? Had a hypnosis session been the source of someone's knowledge of the events that took place in that time period?

Was it possible that Lillian Madden's death was necessary to prevent her from going to the police with the record of a hypnosis session, and the patient's name?

Emily threw down the paper and got up.

Don't be *ridiculous,* she told herself. Nobody ever tuned in to the mind of a killer who lived over one hundred years ago.

PROMPTLY AT 12:30 her doorbell rang. When Emily opened the door, she realized that since Nick's call on Friday, she had been looking forward to his visit. His smile was warm, his handclasp firm as he stepped inside. She was glad to see that he was casually dressed in a jacket, slacks, and turtleneck sweater.

As she greeted him, she told him that. "I promised myself that unless it was a case of dire necessity, I wasn't going to put on a skirt or heels until I have to report for work," she explained. She was wearing tan jeans, a tan sweater and a brown tweed jacket that had been a favorite for so long it felt like a second skin.

She had started to twist her hair up, then decided to leave it loose around her collar.

"The casual look is extremely becoming," Nick said. "But bring your I.D. The restaurant may want proof of age before they'll serve you wine. It's good to see you, Emily. It's been at least a month."

"Yes, it has. The last few weeks in Albany were really round-the-clock sessions, trying to wrap up everything. I was so weary for the last seventy miles of the drive here Tuesday evening that I could hardly keep my eyes open."

"And you certainly haven't had a restful time since you took over this house."

"That's putting it mildly. Want to take a quick look around? We have enough time."

"Sure, but I have to tell you I'm already impressed. It's a wonderful house."

In the kitchen, Nick walked to the window and looked out. "Where did they find the remains?" he asked.

She pointed to the right-hand section of the backyard. "Over there."

"You were excavating for a pool?"

"It had already been started. It kind of scares me to think that I was within an inch of having it canceled and paying off the contractor."

"Do you wish you had?"

"No. If I had done that, the remains wouldn't have been found. It's good for the Lawrence family to have closure. And now that I know my ancestor was murdered, I'm going to find out who did it and what his connection might be to Martha Lawrence's killer."

Nick turned from the window. "Emily, whoever took the life of Martha Lawrence and then did something so bizarre as to put the finger bone of your relative in her hand has a dangerous, twisted mind. I hope you're not telling people around here that you're trying to find out who the murderer is."

That's exactly what I'm doing, Emily thought. Sensing Nick's disapproval, she chose her words carefully. "It's always been assumed that Madeline Shapley met with foul play, but until four days ago there was no way of proving it. It was suspected she was the victim of someone known to her, but for all they knew, she might have decided to take a short walk while she was waiting for her fiancé, then been dragged into a passing carriage by a perfect stranger.

"Nick, a stranger didn't bury her in her own backyard. Someone who *knew* Madeline, who was *close* to her, buried her there. I'm trying to put together the names of the people around her to see if I can establish a link between her killer and the man who was responsible for Martha Lawrence's death four and a half years ago. There has to be a written statement about it somewhere, maybe even a detailed confession. It might have been read by someone of this generation whose ancestor was Madeline's killer. It might have been found by someone going through old records. But there *is* a link, and I have the time and the will to dig for it."

The disapproval in his expression softened and was replaced by something else. Concern? Emily thought, but that wasn't it. No, I swear he looks *disappointed*. Why?

"Let's finish the tour and head for the Old Mill," she suggested. "I don't know about you, but I'm hungry. And I'm tired of my own cooking." She smiled and added, "Even though I am a fabulous cook."

"The proof of the pudding is in the eating," Nick Todd suggested mildly as he followed her from the kitchen to the staircase.

THEIR TABLE AT THE OLD MILL overlooked a pond, where swans were sedately gliding through the water. When the bloody marys they'd ordered were served, the waitress offered menus. "We'll wait for a few minutes," Nick told her.

In the three months since she had agreed to accept the position with the law firm, Emily had dined with Nick and Walter Todd, his father, three or four times in Manhattan, but never with Nick alone.

Her first impression of him had been mixed. He and

Walter Todd had come up to Albany and stayed overnight to observe her defense of a prominent politician in a vehicular homicide.

She had gone to lunch with the Todds after the jury acquitted her client of criminally negligent homicide. Walter Todd had been lavish in his praise of the way she handled the case. Nick had been reticent, and the few compliments dragged out of him by his father had been perfunctory at best. She had wondered at the time if there was an insecurity in him, and thought perhaps he perceived her as a potential rival.

But that didn't jibe with the fact that since she had accepted the offer to join them, his attitude had been cordial and friendly.

Today he was sending mixed signals again. He seemed uncomfortable. Did it have anything to do with her, or was it a personal problem? She knew he wasn't married, but undoubtedly there was a girlfriend in the picture.

"I wish I could read your mind, Emily." Nick's voice broke in on her reverie. "You're in what they used to call a 'brown study.'"

"I don't think I've ever heard that one."

"It means being deep in thought."

She decided to be candid. "I'll gladly tell you what I was thinking. There's something about me that troubles you, and I wish you'd just lay it out on the table. Do you *want* me in the firm? Do you think I'm the right person for the job? Something's up. What is it?"

"You don't beat around the bush, do you?" Nick picked the celery stalk out of his glass and bit into it. "Do I want you in the firm? Absolutely! I wish you'd start tomorrow frankly. Which, incidentally, is why I'm here right now." He put his glass down and began to tell her about his decision.

As he told her of his desire to leave the firm, Emily was surprised to realize how dismayed she was to learn Nick's plans. I was looking forward to working with him, she thought.

"Where will you apply for a job?" she asked.

"The U.S. Attorney's office. That's where I'd really like

to go. Failing that, I'm pretty sure that I could go back to Boston. I worked as an assistant DA there. When I left, the DA told me I'd be welcome to come back if I didn't like private practice. I'd prefer to stay in New York. But my guess is that I'm not going to be able to sweet-talk you into starting at the office next week, am I?"

"I'm afraid not. Will your father be very upset?"

"The cold, hard reality that I'm leaving is undoubtedly sinking in, and he's probably hanging me in effigy right now. When I report back to him that you'll be unavailable until May 1st, you'll be right there beside me."

" 'We must all hang together or most assuredly . . . ' " Emily smiled.

" 'We'll hang separately.' Exactly." Nick Todd picked up the menu. "Business concluded," he said. "What's your choice?"

IT WAS NEARLY FOUR O'CLOCK when he dropped her off at home. He walked her to the porch and waited while she put her key in the door. "You do have a good alarm system?" he asked.

"Absolutely. And tomorrow an old friend from Albany is going to install security cameras."

Nick's eyebrows went up. "After that stalker you had in Albany, I can understand why you'd want them."

She opened the door. They saw it at the same time. An envelope on the floor of the foyer, the flap side facing up.

"Looks as if someone left a note for you," Nick said as he bent to pick it up.

"Pick it up by the corner. It may have fingerprints." Emily did not recognize her own voice. It had come out as a strained whisper.

Nick looked at her sharply, but obeyed. As he stood up, the flap of the envelope flew open and a photograph fell out. It was of Emily in church at the memorial Mass.

Scrawled across the bottom were three words: "Pray for yourself."

Monday, March 26

thirty-six _____

I AM EAGERLY LOOKING FORWARD to the activity that I know will ensue later today.

I am very pleased that I changed my mind and made Emily Graham the recipient of my message.

Her mail should be delivered soon.

As I expected, there were questions about the scarf, but I'm sure that no one can prove who finally took possession of it that night.

Martha admired it. I heard her tell Rachel that it was very pretty.

I remember that at that very moment, the thought ran through my head that Martha had just chosen the instrument of her own death.

After all, a scarf, I thought, is not unlike the sash that squeezed the breath from Madeline's throat.

At least I no longer have to be concerned about the psychologist. I do not even have to be concerned if they somehow manage to reconstruct her computer files.

When I consulted Dr. Madden it was in the evening, and the receptionist was not there, so no one else saw me.

And the name and address I gave her will mean nothing to them.

Because they do not—*will* not—ever understand that we are one.

There is only one person who, learning that name and address, might begin to suspect, but it won't matter.

For I have no fears on that score, either. Emily Graham is going to die on Saturday. She will sleep with Ellen Swain.

And after that, I shall live out the rest of my life as I have before, as a respectable and honored citizen of Spring Lake.

thirty-seven

TOMMY DUGGAN had been about to leave the office on Sunday afternoon when the call came in from Emily Graham. He immediately rushed to Spring Lake and took the envelope and photograph from her.

On Monday morning, he and Pete Walsh were in the prosecutor's private office, filling their boss in on the events of the weekend. Osborne had been in Washington since Friday evening.

Tommy briefed him on the Madden murder and his interrogation at Will Stafford's home of the guests at that final Lawrence party.

"It's Mrs. Wilcox's scarf, and she was wearing it that night. She claims she asked her husband to put it in his pocket. He claims she asked him to put it next to her pocketbook."

"The Wilcoxes drove their car to the Lawrences that night, sir," Walsh offered. "It was parked down the block. If Dr. Wilcox stuck the scarf in his pocket, it might have fallen out, either in the house or on the street; then anyone could have picked it up. And if he left it with her pocketbook, again, anyone could have taken it."

Osborne tapped the top of his desk with his index finger. "From what was left of it, that scarf appeared to be fairly long. It would have been pretty bulky to fold up and put in the pocket of a summer jacket."

Tommy nodded. "That's what I thought too. By the time it was used to strangle Martha, part of it had been cut off. But on the other hand, Wilcox lied to his wife about calling the Lawrences to ask if it had been found. His story is that by then everyone knew Martha was missing, and he wasn't going to bother them about a scarf."

"He could have spoken to the housekeeper," Osborne observed.

"Something else," Tommy said. "We think that Wilcox was lying about not knowing Dr. Madden."

"How much do we know about Wilcox? I mean *really* know about him?"

Tommy Duggan looked at Walsh. "Pete, you take over. You checked him out."

Pete Walsh pulled out his notes. "Solid academic career. Ended up president of Enoch College. That's one of those places that are small, but snooty. Retired twelve years ago. Used to come to Spring Lake summers when he was a kid, so settled here. Publishes regularly in academic journals. They don't pay enough to keep a sparrow in breadcrumbs, but it's considered hot stuff to be in them. Since he settled here, he's done a lot of historical writing about New Jersey, particularly Monmouth County. He's considered something of the town historian in Spring Lake."

"Which ties in with Emily Graham's theory that Martha Lawrence's killer had access to records about the women who disappeared in the 1890s," Tommy pointed out. "I swear that guy was lying when he said he didn't know Dr. Madden. I want to start digging a lot deeper with him. My bet is that there's dirt to be found."

"Anything more about the Carla Harper case?" Osborne asked.

"The eyewitness is sticking to her story that she saw Carla at a rest stop in Pennsylvania. At the time, she gave interviews to everyone in the media who would talk to her. The cops in Pennsylvania admit they made a mistake in accepting the eyewitness's story, but when Carla's pocketbook was found near that rest stop a few days later, it gave the witness the credibility she needed. The killer was probably laughing when he tossed it out the window of his car. Now the trail is cold, especially since the Warren Hotel closed last year. That's where Carla Harper was staying the weekend before she disappeared." He shrugged. It was a dead end.

Finally Tommy and Pete filled in Elliot Osborne on the call they had received at 4:00 P.M. on Sunday from Emily Graham.

"She has guts," Tommy said. "White as a sheet, but composed when we got there. She thinks it's a copycat situation, and that's the way the Spring Lake cops are leaning too. I talked to Marty Browski, the guy who handled her stalking case in Albany."

"What does Browski think?" Osborne asked.

"He thinks that the wrong guy is doing time on this one. He's reopened the investigation and says he has two possible suspects: Emily Graham's ex-husband, Gary White, and Joel Lake, a slime she got off on a murder rap."

"What do you think?"

"Best possible scenario: copycat. A teenager or a couple of teenagers found out that Emily was being stalked in Albany and are playing sicko games with her now. Middle scenario: either Gary White or Joel Lake. Worst possible scenario: the guy who killed Martha Lawrence is toying with Graham."

"Which scenario do you buy?"

"Copycat. Dr. Lillian Madden, the psychologist who was murdered in Belmar, was definitely tied to the Lawrence case. I'd stake everything that Martha's killer must have been Dr. Madden's patient and couldn't take a chance on her talking to us about him. But on the other hand, I don't think he would be so dumb as to risk being seen hanging around Emily Graham's house. He has too much at stake."

"Have you any idea where the person who took that picture of Emily Graham in church might have been sitting?"

"Across the aisle. In a pew to the left."

"Suppose Browski—that's the name, isn't it?—is right that Graham's original stalker is on the loose in Spring Lake? I'd say that if he's obsessed enough to come all the way down here from Albany, she's in extreme danger."

"If the original stalker is the one doing this, yes, she's definitely in extreme danger," Tommy Duggan agreed soberly.

Elliot Osborne's secretary's voice came over the intercom. "I'm sorry to interrupt, but Ms. Emily Graham is on the phone. She insists she must speak to Detective Duggan at once."

Tommy Duggan picked up the phone. "Duggan, Ms. Graham."

The prosecutor and Pete Walsh watched as the lines deepened on Duggan's face. "We'll be right over, Ms. Graham."

He hung up and looked at Osborne. "Emily Graham received a troubling postcard in the morning mail."

"The stalker? Another picture of herself?"

"No. This one is a drawing of two tombstones. The name on one is Carla Harper. The name on the other is Letitia Gregg. If this card is on the level, they're buried together in the backyard of 15 Ludlam Avenue in Spring Lake."

thirty-eight

ERIC BAILEY BEGAN MONDAY MORNING EARLY, as a guest on the news hour of the local Albany television channel.

Slight of frame and barely medium height, with rumpled hair and frameless glasses that dominated his narrow face, he was unprepossessing in appearance and manner. When he spoke, his voice had a nervous, high-pitched quality.

The anchorman of the program had not been happy to see Bailey's name on the list of guests. "Whenever that guy is on, the loud clicking sound you hear is all the remote controls in Albany switching to another channel," he complained.

"A lot of people around this area invested money in his company. The stock's been on the skids for the last year and a half. Now Bailey claims he has new software that will revolutionize the computer industry," the financial editor snapped back. "He may sound like a chipmunk, but what he has to say is worth hearing."

"Thank you for the compliment. Thank you both."

Eric Bailey had come on to the set quietly, without either man hearing him approach. Now, with a slight smile, as if enjoying their discomfort, he said, "Perhaps I should wait in the green room until you're ready for me?"

THE STATE-OF-THE-ART security cameras he was going to install around Emily's home were already packed in his van, so immediately after the television interview, Eric Bailey began the drive to Spring Lake.

He knew he had to be careful not to drive too fast. Anger combined with humiliation made him want to press the gas pedal to the floor of the car, to weave in and out of traffic, terrifying the occupants of the vehicles he would cut off.

Fear was his answer to all the rejections in his life, to all the rebuffs, to all the ridicule.

He had learned to use fear as a weapon when he was sixteen. He had invited three girls, one after another, to go to the junior prom with him. They all refused. Then the snickering started, the jokes.

How far would Eric Bailey have to go before he could get a date?

Karen Fowler was the one whose imitation of him fumbling to articulate his invitation to her was considered most hilarious. He had overheard her mimicking him.

"Karen, I'd really like . . . I mean, would you . . . it would be nice if . . ."

"And then he started sneezing," Karen Fowler would tell her audience, laughing so hard she was almost gasping. "The poor dope started sneezing, can you believe it?"

The best student in the school, and she called him "the poor dope."

The night of the prom he had waited with his camera at the local hangout where everyone went after the band quit. When the drinking and pot smoking started, he secretly snapped pictures of a glassy-eyed Karen, hanging all over her date, her lipstick smeared, the strap of her dress falling over her arm.

He showed the pictures to her in school a couple of days later. He could still remember the way she paled. Then she cried and pleaded with him to give them to her. "My father will kill me," she said. "Please, Eric."

He put them back in his pocket. "Want to do your imitation of me now?" he asked coldly.

"I'm sorry. Please, Eric, I'm sorry."

She had been so frightened, never knowing whether or not he would ring the bell some evening and hand those pictures to her father, or if one day they'd be delivered to him in the mail . . .

Thereafter, whenever she passed him in the hall in school, she'd given him a frightened, beseeching glance. And for the first time in his life Eric Bailey had felt *powerful*.

The memory calmed him now. He would find a way to punish the two who had dissed him this morning. It just took a little quiet thinking, that's all.

Depending on traffic, he would be in Spring Lake between one and two.

He knew the route faily well by now. This would be his third round trip since Wednesday.

thirty-nine

REBA ASHBY, investigative reporter for *The National Daily,* had taken a room at The Breakers Hotel in Spring Lake for the week. A small, sharp-featured woman in her late thirties, she planned to milk the story of the reincarnated serial killer for all it was worth.

On Monday morning she was having a leisurely breakfast in the hotel dining room, on the alert for someone with whom she could strike up a conversation. At first she saw only business types at the nearby tables, and she knew it would be useless to interrupt them. She needed to find someone who would talk about the murders.

Her editor shared her chagrin that she had not managed to get an interview with Dr. Lillian Madden before she was murdered. She'd tried to contact Dr. Madden all day Friday, but the secretary wouldn't put her through. Finally she'd managed to get one of the single-session tickets to Dr. Madden's lecture Friday night, but still had no luck in talking to her privately.

Reba no more believed in reincarnation than she believed elephants could fly, but Dr. Madden's lecture had been compelling and thought-provoking, and what was going on in Spring Lake certainly was bizarre enough to make one wonder if there was such a thing as a reincarnated serial killer.

She also had noticed how Chip Lucas from the *New York Daily News* had startled Dr. Madden when he asked her if anyone had ever asked to be regressed to the 1890s. It also had brought an end to the evening's open forum.

Even though she couldn't have gotten home before 10:30 P.M. or so, Madden had been in her office when she died. Had she been looking up the record of a patient, Reba wondered, maybe a patient who had asked to be regressed to the 1890s? If nothing else, it provided a good angle for another story on the Spring Lake serial killer.

Hardened as she was by the nature of her job, Reba nonetheless had been shocked to the core by Dr. Madden's cold-blooded murder. She had heard about it shortly after attending the memorial Mass for Martha Lawrence and she had written extensively on both events for the next issue of *The National Daily*.

What she wanted now was to get an exclusive interview with Emily Graham. She rang the bell of Graham's house on Sunday afternoon, but there was no answer. When she swung by her house again an hour later, she saw a woman on the porch, bending down as if she were slipping something under the door.

Reba looked up hopefully when she saw that the table next to her had been cleared, and the hostess was leading a woman who appeared to be in her late seventies over to it.

"The waitress will be right with you, Mrs. Joyce," the hostess promised.

Five minutes later, Reba and Bernice Joyce were deep in conversation. The fact that Joyce was a friend of the Lawrence family was a bit of serendipity, but the fact that all the people who had been guests at a party at the Lawrence home the night before Martha's disappearance had been questioned in a group that had included Mrs. Joyce was the kind of break tabloid writers pray for.

Under Reba's skillful questioning, Mrs. Joyce explained how each of them was called in, one by one, to talk to the two detectives. The questions were general, except that they were asked if they knew if something had been lost that night.

"*Was* anything lost?" Reba inquired.

"I didn't know of anything being lost. But after we spoke to the detectives individually, we were all questioned together. The detectives asked if anyone had noticed Mrs. Wilcox's scarf. Apparently that's what was lost. I felt sorry for poor Dr. Wilcox. In front of the entire group, Rachel was quite brusque, blaming him for not putting the scarf in his pocket as she'd asked him to."

"Can you describe the scarf?"

"I remember it quite well because I was standing next to Rachel when Martha, poor darling, made a point of admiring it. It was a silvery shade of chiffon, with some beading at the edges. Rather gaudy for Rachel Wilcox, actually. She tends to dress more conservatively. Perhaps that's why she took it off a short time later."

Reba was salivating at the thought of writing her next story. The police had said the cause of Martha's death was strangulation. They wouldn't have asked about the scarf if it hadn't been important.

She was so busy composing her headline, in fact, that she did not notice how quiet her elderly companion at the next table had become.

I am certain that I saw Rachel's pocketbook on the table in the foyer, Bernice thought. From where I was sitting in the living room, I could see it. I wasn't paying enough attention to notice if it was lying on something. But then did I see someone move the purse and pick up whatever was under it?

She was putting a face to the figure.

Or am I getting fanciful because of all the talk about it?

There is no fool like an old fool, Bernice decided. I'm not going to discuss this with anyone because I'm not sure.

forty _____

"I DIDN'T EXPECT TO SEE YOU again quite so soon," Emily told Tommy Duggan and Pete Walsh when she opened the door for them.

"We didn't expect to be back this soon, Ms. Graham," Duggan replied as he observed her closely. "How did you sleep last night."

Emily shrugged. "Meaning that you can tell I didn't sleep much last night. I'm afraid that photograph yesterday got to me. Isn't it true that, in medieval times, if somebody who was being pursued managed to get into a church, he could shout 'Sanctuary!' and he'd be safe so long as he stayed there?"

"Something like that," Duggan said.

"I guess that won't work for me. Even in church I can't feel safe. I am terribly frightened, I have to admit it," she said.

"Since you live alone, it would be much safer—"

She interrupted. "I'm not moving out of the house."

"I have the postcard in the study," she said. She had taken it there from the kitchen where she had sorted the mail, having found it between a flyer for a landscaping service and a request for a charitable donation.

After the shock of the card's message sank in, she had walked to the window and looked out at the backyard. On this overcast day, it looked bleak and dreary, like a graveyard. Like the graveyard it had *been* for over a century.

Still holding the postcard, she had rushed into the study and called the prosecutor's office.

"The only mail that's been delivered since I've been here was either addressed to the Kiernans or to 'Occupant,'" she told the detectives. Then she pointed to the postcard, which she'd placed on the writing desk: "But this is addressed specifically to me."

It was as she had described it to them. A crude drawing of a house and the property surrounding it, the address 15 Ludlam Avenue scrawled between the lines of what was meant to be a sidewalk. Two tombstones were depicted side by side at the extreme left-hand corner of the area behind the house. Each bore a name. One was Letitia Gregg. The other, Carla Harper.

Tommy took a plastic bag from his pocket, picked up the postcard by the edges, and slipped it into the evidence bag. "This time I came prepared," he said. "Ms. Graham, this may be someone's idea of a sick joke, but it also may be on the level. We've checked out 15 Ludlam Avenue. It's owned by an elderly widow who lives there alone. We're hoping that she'll be cooperative when we tell her about this, and will let us dig up her yard, or at least the section indicated in this sketch."

"Do *you* think it's on the level?" Emily asked.

Tommy Duggan looked at her for a long moment before answering. "After what we found out there"—he nodded in the direction of Emily's backyard—"I think that there's a very good chance that it is, yes. But until we know for a certainty, I'd appreciate if you don't say anything to anyone about it."

"There's no one I want to talk to about it," Emily said. I'm certainly not going to call Mother or Dad or Gran and worry them sick, she thought. But if my big brothers lived down the street, you bet I'd yell for them. Unfortunately they're over a thousand miles away.

She thought about Nick Todd. He had phoned just after the mail came, but she hadn't told him about it either. When they found the photograph on the foyer floor after they returned from brunch yesterday, he'd urged her to drive to Manhattan and stay in her apartment there.

But she'd insisted that the cameras Eric was going to install were the best hope of finding out who was doing this to her, explaining how it was the hidden camera Eric put in the townhouse that caught Ned Koehler when he was trying to break in. Once the cameras are in place here, we'll have a shot at identifying whoever is pulling this stuff now, she'd assured him.

Brave words, she thought, as she walked Tommy Duggan and Pete Walsh to the door and closed and locked it behind them, but the fact is I'm scared to death.

The little sleep she'd gotten had been filled with nightmares. In one of them, she was being chased. In another, she was at the window, trying to open it, but someone was holding it down on the other side.

Stop it! Emily ordered herself. Get busy! Call Dr. Wilcox and ask if you can drop off his books. Then go to the museum and do some research. See if you can figure out where those people lived in the 1890s in relation to one another.

She wanted to identify the residences of the friends of Phyllis Gates and Madeline Shapley, the friends Gates had repeatedly mentioned in her book.

Phyllis Gates made reference to her own family renting a cottage for the summer season, but seemed to infer that the other families owned their own houses. There had to be records showing where they lived, she thought.

There has to be a map of the town as it was then, too. I need some art supplies. And I should be able to buy a Monopoly game somewhere. The small houses that are part of that game would be perfect for my needs.

On a three-foot-by-three-foot sheet of cardboard, the kind that art students use, she would draw a plan of the town as it had looked in the 1890s, put in the street names, then place the tiny houses on the properties where Madeline Shapley's friends had lived.

Then I'll get the history of the ownership of those properties since that time at the town clerk's office, Emily decided.

It's probably an exercise in futility, she told herself as she went to the closet to get her Burberry, *but the closer she was to entering Madeline's world, the better chance she had of learning what happened to her—and to Letitia Gregg and Ellen Swain.*

forty-one

THE PIERCING RING of the doorbell was an intrusion. Rachel had driven to Rumson to have lunch with friends, and Clayton Wilcox had booted up his computer, looking forward to several hours of uninterrupted work on his novel.

Since the meeting at Will Stafford's house on Saturday afternoon, Rachel had been alternately resentful of the questions they'd been asked and increasingly suspicious of Detective Duggan's motive for inquiring about her lost scarf.

"You don't think it has anything to do with Martha's death, do you, Clayton?" she had asked several times. Then answering her own question, she had brusquely dismissed that possibility as ridiculous.

Clayton had not contradicted her. It had been on the tip of his tongue to say, "Your lost scarf obviously has *everything* to do with Martha's death, and you implicated me by making sure that everyone knew you had asked me to put it in my pocket," but he had restrained himself.

When he opened the door, he realized that he had half expected to see Detective Duggan standing on the porch. Instead, it was a stranger, a small woman with pursed lips and inquisitive gray eyes.

Even before she spoke he was certain that she was from the media. Still her question stunned him: "Dr. Wilcox, your wife's scarf has been missing since the party at the Lawrence home the night before Martha Lawrence vanished. Why are the police asking so many questions about it?"

Clayton Wilcox gripped the doorknob with convulsive force and began to close the door.

The woman spoke hastily. "Dr. Wilcox, my name is Reba Ashby. I'm with *The National Daily,* and before I write my article on the missing scarf, it might well be to your advantage to answer a few questions."

Wilcox considered for a moment, then opened the door a little wider, but still did not invite her into the house. "I have no idea why the police inquired about my wife's scarf," he said deliberately. "To be more accurate, they inquired to see if anything was missing the night of the party. My wife had taken off her scarf and asked me to put it with her purse, which was on a side table in the foyer."

"I understand your wife told the police that she asked you to put it in your pocket," Ashby said.

"My wife asked me to put it with her pocketbook, and that is what I did." Wilcox could feel the beads of perspiration forming on his forehead. "It was there in plain sight, and anyone could have picked it up during the course of the evening."

It was the opening Reba wanted. "But why *would* anyone pick it up? Are you suggesting that it was stolen?"

"I am suggesting nothing. Perhaps someone moved it from under my wife's purse."

"Why would anyone do that unless they planned to take it?"

"I have no idea. Now if you'll excuse me . . ." This time Clayton Wilcox closed the door, ignoring Reba Ashby's raised voice.

"Dr. Wilcox, did you know Dr. Lillian Madden?" she shouted through the door.

SETTLED AGAIN AT HIS DESK, Wilcox stared at the screen. None of the words he had just written any longer made sense to him. He had no doubt that Reba Ashby would write a sensational article about the scarf. Inevitably, he would be the subject of glaring publicity. How far would that rag she wrote for dig into his background? How deeply were the police investigating his past right now?

According to the newspapers, the records in Dr. Madden's office had been destroyed.

All of them?

Should he have admitted to consulting her?

The telephone rang. Be calm, Wilcox told himself, you must be perceived as being calm.

It was Emily Graham, asking if she might drop by and return his books.

"Of course," he said smoothly. "It will be a pleasure to see you again. Come right over."

When he replaced the receiver, he leaned back in his chair. An image of Emily Graham swam through his mind.

A cloud of midnight-brown hair caught up by a clip at the back of her head, the tendrils escaping on her forehead and neck . . .

Sculpted aquiline nose . . .

Full, sooty eyelashes, framing wide, questioning eyes . . .

Clayton Wilcox sighed and put his hands on the keyboard and began to type. *"His need was so great that even the unspeakable consequences of what he was about to do could not deter him."*

forty-two

ON MONDAY MORNING, Robert Frieze started the week by quarreling with Natalie. The fact that he had a meeting scheduled with Dominic Bonetti, the potential buyer of The Seasoner, precipitated the bitter exchange.

Sleepless as usual, he had gone jogging at 6:30, wanting to work out the tension building up in him. He knew he needed to be at his most confident best when he met Bonetti.

On the way back from the North Pavilion, he spotted Susan, his ex-wife, jogging toward him, and left the boardwalk to avoid her. Her semi-annual alimony payment was due at the end of the month, and this wasn't the day to worry about how to squeeze out the cash for it, he decided.

He returned home, the tension if anything increased, and to his dismay he found Natalie at the table in the kitchen. He'd hoped to have a quiet cup of coffee and go over the figures he'd compiled during the night.

"Is this the new regimen?" he asked snappishly. "For the last three days you've been up with the birds. What happened to the beauty sleep you claim you need?"

He was annoyed to see that the financial statements he

had been working on in the predawn hours were spread out on the table.

"It's pretty hard to sleep when there's no reason to be tired," she snapped back. The remark was Natalie's way of reminding him that since he had started opening the restaurant for dinner on Sundays, she spent Sunday evenings alone.

Then she started in on him. "Bob," she said, "will you please tell me what these figures *mean?* Particularly the ones on the last page? You wouldn't sell the restaurant for that little, would you? You might as well *give* it away."

"It might be better to give it away than to go bankrupt," Bob said coldly. "Please, Natalie, I'm trying to prepare myself for a meeting today in which, with any luck, I'll close a deal and get this albatross off my back. Dom Bonetti has me between a rock and a hard place, and he has to know it. I've got to have a bottom-line position that he can't refuse."

"Well, unless I can't either add or *subtract,* it looks to me like your bottom-line position leaves us damn near strapped. I told you when you got involved in living out your innkeeper fantasy that you should have *sold* those stocks, instead of borrowing against them. Now, unless you get a high price for the restaurant, which from a quick look at these calculations you don't expect to, you'll have to sell the stocks to pay back the loans."

Natalie paused, then continued, her voice even more angry and scornful: "I hope I don't have to point out that those stocks are now worth half as much as they were when you started borrowing against them."

Bob felt his stomach cramp and his chest begin to burn. He held out his hand. "*Give* me those papers."

"Get them yourself." Natalie swept the papers off the table and onto the floor, then deliberately stepped on them as she stalked out of the room.

FIVE HOURS LATER, Bob shook his head and looked down at the papers he was holding. There was a narrow oval-shaped hole in one of them. Then he remembered—the stiletto heel of Natalie's bedroom slipper had torn through that paper as she walked on it.

It was the *last* thing he remembered—their quarreling as he stood in the kitchen in his jogging suit, and hearing her slam the door of the bedroom overhead. He closed his eyes for a moment.

Opening them, he looked around slowly. He was in his second-floor office in the restaurant now, wearing his dark-blue jacket and gray slacks.

He looked at his watch. It was almost one o'clock. One o'clock! The potential buyer, Dominic Bonetti, was due any minute. They were going to discuss the sale over lunch.

Frantically, Bob tried to focus on the figures he had compiled. His phone rang. It was the maître d'. "Mr. Bonetti is here. Shall I seat him at your table?"

"Yes. I'm on the way down."

He went into his private bathroom and splashed cold water over his face. At Natalie's insistence, he'd had some work done on his eyes last year, by a plastic surgeon her friends were raving about. Now his lids were tighter and the pouches that had started to form under his eyes were gone, but he knew the results didn't flatter him. As he looked in the mirror, it seemed to him that the upper half of his face was out of sync with the bottom half, something he found disconcerting, even alarming. He had always prided himself on his good looks. Not any more.

A hell of a thing to be worried about now, he thought as he ran a comb through his hair. Then he hurried downstairs.

He knew they didn't have many Monday lunch reservations, but he had counted on the drop-in crowd to make the place look at least reasonably busy. He felt his palms begin to sweat when he walked into the dining room to see that only six tables were occupied. Dominic Bonetti was waiting for him, a notebook open at the table.

Was that a good sign?

He'd met Bonetti once before, at a golf outing. The

man was powerfully built, not very tall, with a thick head of dark hair and shrewd dark eyes. He had a hearty, outgoing manner, and when he was not speaking, he exuded an air of quiet confidence.

They did not begin discussing business until after they finished the broiled salmon, which had been dry and unappetizing. Bob had managed to keep up his half of the conversation, but it had been a real effort.

As espresso was served, Bonetti came to the point. "You want *out* of this place. I want *in*. Don't ask why. I don't need it. I'm fifty-nine years old, and I have as much money as I'll ever want to spend. But I miss having a restaurant. It's in the blood, I guess. And you've got a great location here."

But then, in the next half hour, Bob learned what The Seasoner did *not* have, which turned out to be almost everything.

The decor: "I know you spent a fortune on it, but it doesn't invite you in. It's cold and uncomfortable because . . . The kitchen is inefficient . . ."

Natalie had picked the pricey interior designer. The first chef he hired, that hotshot from Madison Avenue, dictated the way the kitchen would be laid out.

The price Dominic Bonetti offered was a half million dollars less than the absolute bottom price Bob Frieze thought he could accept.

"That's your initial offer," he said with a dismissive smile. "I'll be happy to counter it."

Bonetti's easygoing manner vanished. "If I buy this place, I'm going to spend big bucks to make it look the way I want it and to staff it with top-quality people," he said quietly. "I've given you my price. I won't consider a counteroffer."

He stood up, a warm smile on his face again. "Think it over, Bob. It's actually a very fair price, considering what needs to be done and undone. If you decide not to accept it, no hard feelings. My wife will be thrilled."

He extended his hand. "Let me know."

Bob waited until Bonetti left the dining room, then caught the waiter's eye and held up his empty wineglass.

A moment later the waiter returned with the wine and a cell phone. "Urgent call from Mrs. Frieze, sir."

To Bob's surprise, Natalie did not ask him about the meeting with Bonetti. Instead she said, "I just heard that there's a backhoe digging up the yard at 15 Ludlam Avenue. The rumor is that they're looking for the body of Carla Harper, that girl who disappeared two years ago. My God, Bob, 15 Ludlam Avenue! Isn't that the house your family lived in when you were growing up?"

forty-three

"YOUR FATHER IS HERE TO SEE YOU, Mr. Stafford." The receptionist's voice sounded puzzled. It was almost as if she were saying, "I didn't know your father was alive."

"My father!" Will Stafford threw down the pen he was holding. Angered and dismayed, he waited until he was sure his voice was calm. "Send him in."

He watched as the door handle turned slowly. Afraid to face me, he thought. Afraid I'll throw him out. He did not get up, but remained seated rigidly at his desk, willing every inch of his body to convey his displeasure at the intrusion.

The door opened slowly. The man who came in was a shadow of the one he had seen a year ago. Since then his father had lost at least fifty pounds. His complexion was now waxy yellow, the cheekbones prominent under tightly drawn skin. The full head of graying sandy hair that Will remembered, and had himself inherited, was now reduced to loose strands of dingy gray.

Sixty-four and he looks eighty-four, Will thought. Am I supposed to feel sorry for him, to throw my arms around him? "Close that door," he ordered.

Willard Stafford, Sr., nodded and obeyed. Neither man noticed that the door had not completely shut and then had drifted open several inches.

Will stood up slowly. His voice rising, spitting out the words, he demanded, "Why won't you leave me alone? Can't you understand that I want no part of you? You want me to forgive you? Fine. I forgive you. Now get out."

"Will, I made mistakes. I admit it. I haven't got long. I want to make it up to you."

"You can't. Now go and don't come back."

"I should have understood. You were an adolescent . . ." The older man's voice began to rise.

"Shut up!" In two strides, Will Stafford was around his desk and in front of his father. His strong hands gripped the other man's thin, shaking shoulders.

"I paid for what someone else did. You didn't believe me. You could have afforded a team of lawyers to defend me properly. Instead you washed your hands of me, your only son. You publicly disowned me. But now the juvenile record is sealed. I don't need you coming in here and destroying everything I've built up for the past twenty-three years. Just get *out* of here. Get back in your car. Drive back to Princeton and stay there."

Willard Stafford, Sr., nodded. His eyes moist, he turned around and groped for the handle of the door. Then he stopped. "I promise I won't be back. I wanted to see you face to face for the last time and ask your forgiveness. I know I failed you. I just thought that maybe you could see . . ." His words trailed off into silence.

Will did not respond.

His father sighed and opened the door. "It's just"—he mumbled more to himself than to Will—"it's just that reading about what's been going on in this town. I mean that girl whose body was found. I got worried. You understand . . ."

"You have the nerve to come here and say *that* to me? Get out! Do you hear me! Get out!"

It did not matter to Will Stafford that he was shouting, that Pat, the receptionist, was surely overhearing him. It only mattered that he get control over his blinding rage before he put his hands around the scrawny throat of the man who had sired him, and squeezed it until the neck snapped.

forty-four

NED KOEHLER'S LAWYER, Hal Davis, was not pleased to meet Marty Browski at Gray Manor again at three o'clock on Monday afternoon.

"The state doesn't pay me enough to help you with a witch hunt," he complained as they waited together for Koehler to be brought into the conference room.

"The state pays me to make sure that people pay for their crimes," Browski shot back. "As I told you this morning, we've reopened the Ruth Koehler investigation, and your client is under suspicion of murder."

Davis looked incredulous. "You've got to be kidding. You couldn't prove your case against Ruth Koehler's killer, Joel Lake, he went free, and now you're trying to make yourselves look good by making that poor dope Koehler the fall guy? I rushed here and spoke to Ned after you called me and advised him not to speak to you. But he is adamant that he is innocent and is insisting that he be permitted to talk to you."

"Maybe he's smarter than you think," Browski said. "We all thought Koehler compromised the crime scene because of his shock and grief. Another way to look at it though, is that he was cunning enough to make sure that there was a reason his fingerprints were all over that knife and there was blood on his clothes."

"He picked her up. He didn't know she was dead. He ran for help."

"Maybe."

The door opened. Ned Koehler was escorted to a seat by the guard. "Ned's a little agitated today," the guard said. "I'm right outside if you need me."

"Why are you doing this to me?" Koehler demanded of Marty. "I loved my mother. I miss her."

"I just have a few questions," Browski said soothingly. "But I must specifically inform you that you are a suspect in the death of your mother, so anything you say can be used against you." He rattled off the rest of the Miranda warnings by rote.

"Ned, you understand that you don't have to answer any questions." Hal Davis leaned forward as though by getting closer to Koehler he could get through to him better.

"Ned, I talked to your aunt," Marty said quietly. "She wasn't mistaken. She *did* talk to your mother after Joel Lake was seen leaving the building."

"My aunt is crazy. If my mother talked to her after that guy left, she would have told her that she'd been robbed."

"Maybe she didn't know it yet. Ned, did your mother ever get angry at you?"

"My mother loved me. Very much."

"I'm sure she did but she used to get angry at you sometimes, didn't she?"

"No. Never."

"She was especially angry because you were so careless about pulling the door closed tight when you went out so that the lock would engage. Isn't that right?"

"I always locked that door when I went out."

"Always? Joel Lake says the door wasn't even fully closed. That's why he went into your apartment."

Ned Koehler's eyes had narrowed to slits. His mouth was working convulsively.

"Isn't it a fact, Ned, that the week before your mother died, the same thing happened? Didn't she shout at you and say that someone could come in and put a knife through her? Your neighbors told me that was what she always said to you when you didn't make sure the lock had caught."

"Ned, I don't want you to talk anymore," Davis urged.

Ned shook his head at his lawyer. "Leave me alone, Hal. I want to talk."

"Ned, how do you know how frightened your mother was when she saw the knife and knew she was going to die?" Marty hammered the question across the table at Ned Koehler.

He did not wait for an answer. "Did she beg you not to hurt her? Did she say she was sorry for picking on you? She was sitting at the kitchen table. She had just realized the apartment had been burglarized. She must have been very angry. The knife was right there on that rack on the wall. Did she point to it and *tell you* that whoever came in could have used it on her, and that it would have been your fault?"

Something between a wail and a scream burst out of Ned Koehler's throat, startling the two men. The door opened, and the guard rushed in.

Ned Koehler buried his face in his hands. "She said, 'Don't, Ned, I'm sorry, Ned, don't Ned, please.' But it was too late. I didn't know I was holding the knife, and then it was in her chest."

Great racking sobs shook his body as he shouted, "I'm sorry, Mommy! I'm sorry, Mommy!"

forty-five

ERIC BAILEY WAS WAITING on Emily's porch when she arrived home, back from delivering the books to Dr. Wilcox, visiting the museum, and buying the supplies she needed for the project she planned to begin.

He waved away her apologies. "Don't worry. I made good time, but I am hungry. What have you got to eat?"

She brought in sandwich makings—ham and Swiss

cheese, lettuce and tomatoes, and fresh Italian bread—and while she prepared lunch, he began to unpack the camera equipment.

They ate in the kitchen. "I added some leftover chicken soup to the menu," she told him. "I made it the other night and froze what was left over. It's good, I promise."

"This reminds me of when we were in those dumpy offices in Albany," Eric said as he scraped the last drop of soup from the bowl. "I'd go down and get sandwiches from the deli, and you'd heat up your homemade soup."

"It was fun," Emily said.

"It was fun, and I wouldn't have had a company if you hadn't defended me against that lawsuit."

"And *you* made *me* rich. Fair's fair."

They smiled at each other across the table. Eric's three days older than I am, Emily thought, but I always feel as if he's my little brother.

"I was concerned when I saw that the company stock had gone down," she told him.

He shrugged. "It will come back. You made your money, but you'll still be sorry you sold when you did."

"I was raised on hearing how my grandfather lost all his money in 1929, when the market went kaput. I guess I just wasn't comfortable holding onto the stock. I'd have been worried that something would go wrong. This way, I can live the rest of my life without a financial care, thanks to you."

"Anytime you need taking care of . . ." Eric left the sentence unfinished, as Emily smilingly shook her head.

"Why spoil a beautiful friendship?" she asked.

He helped to load the dishwasher. "That's my job," she protested.

"I like helping you."

"Since you say that you absolutely have to make the drive back to Albany tonight, I'd rather you got started on installing the cameras."

A few minutes later she closed the dishwasher with a decisive snap. "Okay. All set. If you work at one end of the dining room table, I'll set up at the other end." She explained what she was planning to do with the copies of the maps and town records.

"I want to enter these people's lives," she said. "I want to see where Madeline's circle of friends lived. I'm convinced it was someone she knew who killed her, then buried her here. But how did he get away with it? There must have been police activity around the house, at least for the first few days, when she was reported missing. Where was she being held? Or where was her body being kept? Or did the killer bury her here that same day after dark? The holly tree blocked off that section of the yard."

"You're sure you're not becoming obsessed with this crime, Emily?"

She looked at him sharply. "I'm obsessed with finding the link between the crimes of the 1890s and the recent ones in this town. Right now the police are digging up someone else's backyard a few blocks from here, and they think they may find the remains of a young woman who has been missing two years."

"Emily, don't stay here alone. You tell me you've had two incidents of stalking in the five days you've been here. You wanted a break, a vacation. From the looks of you, you certainly aren't getting it."

The sudden ringing of the phone caused Emily to gasp and grab Eric's arm. She managed a shaky laugh as she ran to the study to answer the call.

It was Detective Browski. He did not waste time greeting her. "Emily, your client in the Koehler case is a louse and a bum, but you may be glad to hear he's not a murderer. I just left Ned Koehler. Wait till you hear . . ."

Fifteen minutes later she returned to the dining room.

"That was quite a conversation," Eric commented, his tone light. "New boyfriend?"

"Detective Browski. You've met him. He's been saying nice things about you."

"Let's hear. Don't leave out a detail."

"According to him, you probably saved my life, Eric. If

the camera you installed hadn't caught Ned Koehler, we wouldn't have known who was stalking me."

"Your neighbor heard something and called the cops."

"Yes, but Koehler figured out how to disable the alarm system. And he got away before the cops came. If we didn't have him on-camera, thanks to you, we wouldn't have known who had tried to get in. The next time might have been very different for me."

Emily heard the quiver in her voice. "He admitted today that he was planning to kill me. Marty Browski said that in Koehler's twisted mind, Joel Lake, the guy I defended, caused his mother's death. He told Browski that if Joel hadn't burglarized the apartment, his mother would be alive today, that Joel was the real killer."

"Pretty crazy logic, I would say." Eric Bailey's hands worked effortlessly as he assembled the equipment needed to install the cameras that he had brought to Spring Lake.

"Crazy, but in another way understandable. I'm sure he didn't mean to kill his mother, and I know he can't bear to think that he's the cause of her death. If Joel Lake had been found guilty, he would have been able to transfer his own guilt to him. Then I got Joel off, so *I* became the villain."

"You're not a villain," Eric Bailey said emphatically. "What worries me is that from what you say Browski is worried about this renewed stalker business. Who does he think is doing it?"

"He's checked out my ex. Whatever Gary is, he's not a stalker. He has airtight alibis for Tuesday night and Saturday morning, when these last pictures were taken. Browski hasn't been able to locate Joel Lake yet."

"Are you worried about Lake?"

"You'll be surprised to hear that on one level I'm *relieved* about him. Remember how Ned Koehler flew at me after the jury acquitted Lake?"

"You bet I do. I was there."

"When the guards pulled Koehler off me, Joel Lake helped me up. He was right next to me, because we had stood up to hear the verdict. Eric, do you know what he whispered to me?"

The tone of Emily's voice made Eric Bailey stop what he was doing and look intently at her.

"He said to me, 'Maybe Koehler's right, Emily. Maybe I *did* kill the old lady. How does that make you feel?'

"I haven't told that to anyone, but it's been haunting me ever since. And yet I didn't *believe* he had killed her. Can you understand that reasoning? He's just a despicable human being, who, instead of being grateful that he wasn't going to prison for life, needed to taunt me."

"You know what I think, Emily? I think he was attracted to you and knew it wouldn't do him any good. Rejection can do terrible things to some people."

"Well, if he *is* the stalker, I hope to God that one of your cameras catches him for me."

When Eric left shortly before 7:00 P.M., the cameras were in place on all sides of the house. What he did not tell Emily was that he had installed others inside the house, and attached a line-of-sight antenna on an attic window. Now, within a half-mile radius, with the television set in his van, he would be able to follow her movements and hear her conversations in her living room, kitchen, and study.

As he left her with a friendly kiss on the cheek and began the return trip to Albany, he was already planning his next visit to Spring Lake.

He smiled, thinking of how she had jumped when the phone rang. She was far more unnerved than she wanted to admit, even to herself.

Fear was the ultimate weapon of revenge. She had sold her stock at peak value. Shortly after that other sell-offs had started, leading to a chain of them. Now his whole company was on the verge of bankruptcy.

He could even forgive her for that if she had not rejected him as a man. "If you will not love me, Emily," he said aloud, "you will live your life in fear, waiting for that moment when someone steps out of the dark and you can't get away."

Tuesday, March 27

forty-six _____

ON MONDAY AFTERNOON the backhoe that had been delivered to 15 Ludlam Avenue had turned over only one shovelful of dirt before malfunctioning. To their chagrin, the forensics experts were told that a replacement would not be available until Tuesday morning.

Bowing to the inevitable, they taped off the backyard and left a police officer to guard the premises.

At eight o'clock on Tuesday morning, even before the new backhoe arrived, the media were present. Vans displaying the logos of television channels lined the quiet streets. Helicopters hovered above the area as cameramen began to shoot aerial views of the search site. Reporters with mikes waited to see the forensic team sift through every shovelful of dirt.

Emily, in a jogging suit and sunglasses, mingled with the people standing on the sidewalk in quiet, somber groups and listened to their comments.

Everyone knew the searchers had to be looking for another body. But whose? It almost had to be Carla Harper, that young girl who vanished two years ago, they whispered among themselves. People had heard that the police now seriously doubted that Carla had ever left Spring Lake.

Two questions were on everyone's lips: "Why did they

decide to search here?" and "Was it because someone has confessed to the crime?"

Emily listened, as a young-looking grandmother pushing a stroller said grimly, "We'd better all pray that they have the killer in custody. It is too frightening to think that a murderer is on the loose in this town. My daughter, this baby's mother, is only a few years older than Martha Lawrence and Carla Harper were."

Emily remembered what she had read in Phyllis Gates's book: *"Mother has become a fierce guardian, unwilling to have me even stroll down the street unless I am accompanied."*

Mother was right, Phyllis, she thought. She had spent Monday evening until well past midnight preparing her model of the town and marking in the streets as they had been at the time of the earlier murder. On her cardboard plan she had Monopoly houses in place, indicating where the Shapleys, the Carters, the Greggs, and the Swains had lived.

She recognized the columnist from *The National Daily,* standing not far from her, and turned away quickly, deciding to go home. I don't want *her* to collar me, Emily thought. And after last week, I certainly don't want to be here if they do uncover bodies. I already have what I need to know about 15 Ludlam Avenue.

But she still didn't see a pattern emerging that would point the finger of guilt at the nineteenth-century killer.

REBA ASHBY had been on the scene on Monday, and was back on Tuesday, furiously scribbling her impressions. This was the hottest story of her entire career, and she intended to milk it dry.

Near her, Irene Cornell of CBS radio was on-air with her report: "Shock and disbelief are on the faces of the residents of this quiet Victorian town as they wait to see if the body of yet another missing young woman will be found," she began dramatically.

At 9:30, nearly an hour and a half after the excavation

began, the onlookers saw the backhoe abruptly stop digging and the forensic crew rush to look down into the hole from which the last shovelful of dirt had been taken.

"They've found something!" one person cried.

Reporters standing on the lawn, their backs to the house, their cameras focused on the backhoe, began talking urgently into their mikes.

The local spectators, some grasping a friend's hand, waited silently. The arrival of the hearse from the morgue confirmed to all of them that human remains had been found. The prosecutor arrived in a squad car and promised to make a statement shortly.

A half hour later, Elliot Osborne stepped up to the microphones. He confirmed that a full skeleton wrapped in the same heavy plastic that had contained the remains of Martha Lawrence had been uncovered. A human skull and several loose bones had been found only inches farther down. There would be no further statements until the medical examiner had had the opportunity to complete a thorough examination and give his report on the findings.

Osborne refused to answer the dozens of questions shouted at him, the loudest of which was, "Doesn't this absolutely *prove* you have a reincarnated killer stalking this town?"

TOMMY DUGGAN and Pete Walsh had planned to follow the hearse from the crime scene to the morgue, but delayed to speak to Margo Thaler, the eighty-two-year-old present owner of the house.

Visibly upset, she was sitting in her living room, sipping a cup of tea a neighbor had prepared for her.

"I don't know if I'll ever be able to go out in my backyard again," she told Tommy. "I had rose bushes where they found that skeleton. I used to be out there on my knees, weeding right above that very spot."

"Mrs. Thaler, we'll make very sure that any remains have been removed," Tommy said soothingly. "Your rose bushes can be replanted. I'd just like to ask you a few questions, and then we'll get out of your way. How long have you lived here?"

"Forty years. I'm the third owner of the house. I bought it from Robert Frieze, Senior. He owned it for thirty years."

"Would he be the father of Robert Frieze, the owner of The Seasoner?"

A look of disdain came over Margo Thaler's face. "Yes, but Bob's nothing like his father. Divorced his lovely wife and married that Natalie woman! Then he opened that restaurant. My friends and I tried it out once. High prices and bad food."

Bob Frieze certainly doesn't have many fans in this town, Tommy thought, as he began to do some arithmetic.

Frieze was about sixty years old. Mrs. Thaler had owned the house for the past forty years, and the Frieze family owned it for thirty years before that. That meant that Bob Frieze was born ten years after his father bought the house and lived in it for the first twenty years of his life. Tommy filed the information in his head for further consideration.

"Mrs. Thaler, we believe that the skeleton will prove to be the remains of a young woman who disappeared about two years ago, on August 5th. It seems to me that you would have noticed if someone had dug up your yard at that time of year."

"I certainly *would* have noticed, yes."

Which means that the remains had to have been kept somewhere else until they could safely be buried here, Tommy thought.

"Mrs. Thaler, I was on the police force here for eight years," Pete Walsh said.

She looked sharply at him. "Oh, of course. Forgive me. I should have recognized you."

"I seem to remember that it was your habit to leave for Florida in October and not return until May. Do you still do that?" Pete asked.

"Yes, I do."

That explains it, Tommy thought. Whoever murdered Carla kept her body somewhere else, maybe in a freezer, until he could safely bury it here.

He stood up. "You've been very cooperative and also very kind to let us talk to you now, Mrs. Thaler."

The elderly woman nodded, then after a pause said, "I realize how selfish it sounds for me to be concerned that I was in essence kneeling on a grave. It won't be too terribly long, I'm sure, before my children and grandchildren will be kneeling at mine. The roses were beautiful. If they don't recover from being uprooted, I'll replace them. In a way maybe it wasn't so bad that they were decorating that poor girl's grave."

Tommy was on his way out when another question occurred to him. "Mrs. Thaler, how old is this house?"

"It was built in 1874."

"Do you know who owned it then?"

"The Alan Carter family. They owned it for some fifty years before selling it to Robert Frieze, Senior."

DR. O'BRIEN WAS STILL conducting his examination of the remains when Tommy Duggan and Pete Walsh arrived at the morgue.

An assistant was taking down the information as O'Brien dictated it.

As Tommy Duggan listened to the statistics, he visualized the description of Carla Harper that lay on top of his desk: *Five feet four inches tall, one hundred and two pounds, blue eyes, dark hair.*

The picture in the file showed an appealing, vivacious young woman with shoulder-length hair. Now, as he listened to the stark description of the weight of her bones and the size of her teeth, Tommy thought, I'll never be tough enough to get used to this part of it.

The sum of the findings was nearly identical to the

ones they had heard on Thursday. The skeleton was that of a young female. The cause of death was strangulation.

"Look at this," O'Brien said to Duggan and Walsh. With his gloved hands he held up threads of material. "See those metal beads? This is a piece of the same scarf that we found around Martha Lawrence's neck."

"You mean that when someone stole that scarf at the party—assuming that's what happened—he not only killed Martha with it, but cut it up so that he could use it again?" Pete Walsh sounded disbelieving.

Duggan looked at him sharply. "Go outside and get some air. I don't want you to pass out on me."

Walsh nodded, gagging as he hurried out of the morgue.

"I don't blame him for getting sick," Tommy Duggan said angrily. "You see what this means, Doc? This killer *is* following the 1890s timetable. There may not even have been anything personal about killing either Martha Lawrence or"—he looked at the figure on the table—"or Carla Harper, if this is her. The only reason they would have been chosen is that both Martha and Carla were around the age of the women who vanished in the 1890s."

"A comparison of dental records will establish if this is Carla Harper." Dr. O'Brien adjusted his glasses. "The separate skull we found had been in the ground much longer than the full skeleton. My estimate is it's been there at least one hundred years. We can reconstruct the features on the skull, but that will take time. My educated guess, though, is that it was part of the body of a young woman not more than twenty years old."

"Carla Harper and Letitia Gregg," Tommy Duggan said softly.

"Judging from the names printed on that postcard, it would seem likely," Dr. O'Brien agreed. "There's something else here you'll be interested in."

He was holding up a small plastic bag for Duggan to see.

"It looks to me to be a pair of old-fashioned earrings," O'Brien explained. "Garnets set in silver, with a pearl teardrop. My wife's grandmother had a pair something like that."

"Where did you find them?"

"Same as before. Folded in the hand of the skeleton. Guess the killer couldn't find a finger bone but wanted you to get the connection between the two sets of remains."

"Do you think he found those earrings in the ground?"

"I don't think anyone can answer that. My guess is he'd be mighty lucky to find both of them. Even though, if she had been wearing them, they'd still be intact, they'd have been fastened to the earlobes, and those are long gone, of course. When in the 1890s did you say the third girl disappeared?"

"Ellen Swain disappeared on March 31st, thirty-one months and twenty-six days after Letitia Gregg vanished on August 5th. Carla Harper disappeared on August 5th. Thirty-one months and twenty-six days this Saturday, March 31st." Tommy knew he was not so much responding to the question as thinking aloud.

"Madeline and Martha on September 7th, Letitia and Carla on August 5th, and now you have the next anniversary coming up this Saturday," Dr. O'Brien said slowly. "Do you think that this killer plans to choose another victim and bury her with Ellen Swain?"

Tommy Duggan felt overwhelmingly weary. He knew that this question was exactly the one the media would ask. "Doctor O'Brien, I hope and pray that *isn't* the scenario, but I promise you that everyone connected with law enforcement in this area is going to act on the premise that a psycho is planning to choose and kill another young woman from this town four days from now."

"In your boots, I would assume that too," the medical examiner said crisply, as he stripped off his gloves. "And with all due respect to our law-enforcement people, I'm sending *my* two daughters to visit their grandmother in Connecticut over the weekend."

"I don't blame you, Doctor," Tommy agreed. "I completely understand."

And *I'll* be talking to Dr. Clayton Wilcox, whose own wife admits she gave him the scarf the night of the Lawrences' party, he thought, as he felt anger building up within him.

Pete and I both sensed Wilcox was lying to us the other day at Will Stafford's house, he told himself. Now it's time to sweat the truth out of him.

Wednesday, March 28

forty-seven _____

THEY HAVE BEGUN TO BELIEVE IN ME, he realized. This morning the highlight of the *Today* show was an interview with Dr. Nehru Patel, prominent philosopher and writer on the subject of psychical research. *He* firmly believes that I am the reincarnation of the serial killer of the late nineteenth century!

What puzzles the good Dr. Patel, as he explained to the interviewer, Katie Couric, is that I am acting against the laws of karma.

Patel said that some may choose to return near to where they had lived in a previous lifetime because they need to meet again people whom they knew in a previous incarnation. They wish to repay the karmic debts they may owe to these people. On the other hand, these karmic actions are supposed to be good, not evil, which was very puzzling.

It is possible, he continued, that in a previous lifetime Martha Lawrence had been Madeline Shapeley, and Carla Harper had been Letitia Gregg.

That's not true, but it's an interesting concept.

Dr. Patel voiced the thought that by repeating the crimes of the nineteenth century, I am flying in the face of karma and will have much to atone for in my next incarnations.

Maybe. Maybe not.

Finally he was asked whether it is possible that Ellen Swain is now alive in a different body and that I have recognized her and will seek her out on Saturday.

Well, I have chosen my next victim. She is *not* Ellen, but she will sleep with Ellen.

And I have conceived of a novel plan to throw the police off the track.

It is quite *delicious* and pleases me very much.

forty-eight _____

WHEN THE PHONE RANG AT 9:30, Clayton Wilcox was in his study with the door closed. Rachel had been intolerable at breakfast. A friend who had bought a copy of that sensationalist rag *The National Daily,* had phoned and warned her that it contained a lurid front-page story about her lost scarf.

He picked up the receiver, filled with dread, sure that it was the police wanting to question him again.

"Dr. Wilcox?" The voice was silky.

Even though it had been more than twelve years since he had heard it, Clayton Wilcox recognized it immediately. "How are you, Gina?" he asked quietly.

"I'm fine, Doctor, but I've been reading a lot about Spring Lake and everything that's going on there. I was sorry to hear that it was your wife's scarf that was used to strangle that poor girl Martha Lawrence."

"What are you talking about?"

"I'm talking about Reba Ashby's column this morning in *The National Daily.* Have you read it?"

"I have heard about it. It is rubbish. There is no official verification that it was my wife's scarf that was used by the killer."

"In the column it says that your wife swears she gave it to you to put in your pocket."

"Gina, what do you want?"

"Doctor, I've been feeling for a long time that it wasn't right for me to have settled for so little money, after what you did to me."

Clayton Wilcox tried to swallow, but the muscles in his throat did not respond. "Gina what I 'did to you,' as you put it, was to respond to your overture."

"*Doctor . . .*" The teasing note was still in her voice. Then it disappeared. "I could have sued both you and the college and gotten a very big settlement. Instead, I let you talk me into a paltry one hundred thousand dollars. I could use more money right now. What do you think Reba Ashby's tabloid would pay for *my* story?"

"You wouldn't do that!"

"Yes, I would. I have a seven-year-old child now. I'm divorced, and I think my marriage failed because I was still psychologically damaged by what happened to me at Enoch. After all, I was only twenty years old then. I know it's too late to sue the college now."

"How much do you want, Gina?"

"Oh, I think another hundred thousand will do it nicely."

"I can't put my hands on that much money."

"You could last time. You can this time. I'm planning to come to Spring Lake on Saturday, to see either you or the police. If you don't pay me, my next step is to find out how much *The National Daily* is willing to pay for a juicy story about the revered former president of Enoch College who just *happened* to lose his wife's scarf before it was used to kill a young woman. Remember, Doctor, *I* have long blond hair too."

"At Enoch College, did you ever learn the meaning of the word 'blackmail,' Gina?"

"Yes, but I also learned the meaning of some terms like 'sexual harassment' and 'unwanted personal overtures.' I'll call you Saturday morning. 'Bye, Doctor."

forty-nine _____

NICK TODD HAD PICKED UP the phone a dozen times on both Monday and Tuesday, intending to call Emily, and each time he put it down. He knew that before leaving her on Sunday night he had overdone his insistence that she stay in her Manhattan apartment until whoever was stalking her had been exposed and arrested.

She had finally shown a flash of anger and said, "Look, Nick, I know you mean well, but I'm staying here, and that's final. Let's talk about something else."

Mean well, Nick thought. Surely there is nothing worse than to be the kind of pain in the neck who "means well."

It did not please his father, either, when he relayed the message that Emily had firmly refused to start work before May 1st—unless, of course, she solved the mystery of her ancestor's murder before then.

"Does she *really* think that she's going to solve a crime, or a series of crimes, that occurred in the 1890s?" Walter Todd had asked incredulously. "Maybe I should take a second look at hiring that young woman. That has to be the single flakiest proposition I've heard in the last fifty years."

After that, Nick decided not to tell his father that either the stalker who had haunted Emily in Albany or a copycat was now shadowing her in Spring Lake. He knew his father's reaction would be exactly like his own: *Get out of that house. You're not safe there.*

On Wednesday, after reading stories in the morning papers about the grisly discovery of two more victims, one from the present, one from the past, Nick was not surprised to see his father barge into his office, his face set in the angry and frustrated expression that sent chills down the spines of new associates in the firm.

"Nick," he snapped, "there's a psycho on the loose down there, and if he knows that Emily Graham is trying to establish a link between himself and the killer of the 1890s, she could be in danger."

"That has occurred to me," Nick replied calmly. "In fact I discussed it with Emily."

"How did they know where to start digging for those remains yesterday?"

"The prosecutor would only say that it was an anonymous tip."

"Emily had better be careful, that's all I can say. She's a smart woman. Maybe she's onto something with that link she's investigating. Nick, call her. Offer her a bodyguard. I have a couple of guys who'd watch out for her. Or maybe you want me to call her."

"No, that's fine. I was planning to give her a ring." As his father left the office, Nick thought of Lindy, the fashion editor he'd dated on and off for several years. Six months ago, when he was dropping her off at her home, he had said, "I'll give you a ring."

She'd replied, "Good. I hope you mean the one I want."

Seeing the startled look on his face, Lindy had laughed. "Nick, I think it's time for both of us to move on. As a couple, we're not going anywhere, and I'm not getting any younger. Ciao."

I don't know whether Emily will want even a ring of the *telephone* from me, Nick thought as he dialed her number.

fifty

ON WEDNESDAY MORNING, Emily got up at six o'clock, and with the inevitable cup of coffee in her hand went straight into the dining room to work on her project.

The discovery of the skeleton and the skull on Ludlam Avenue had added fresh impetus to her search for a link that would tie together the two killers, old and new.

She had the same feeling that she experienced when she was working on a defense—the sense of being on the right path, the certain knowledge that somehow she would find what she needed to prove her theory.

She was also absolutely certain that, unless he was stopped, the copycat killer would take another life on Saturday, the 31st.

At nine o'clock, George Lawrence phoned. "Emily, my mother and I went through all those photograph albums and memorabilia that she has stashed away in the attic. We didn't want you to have to wade through any more of this stuff than necessary, so we culled anything that wasn't relevant. If it's all right with you, I'll drop off the rest of it in a half hour or so."

"That would be wonderful." Emily rushed upstairs to shower and had just finished dressing when the doorbell rang.

George Lawrence entered with two heavy boxes. He was wearing a windbreaker and slacks, and Emily's immediate impression was that he appeared far more vulnerable today than his composed exterior had suggested when she met him on Saturday.

He carried the boxes into the dining room and set them on the floor. "You can go through them at your convenience," he said.

He looked around the dining room, taking in the piles of papers on the chairs, the drawing board on the table. "You look pretty busy. Don't feel rushed to return this stuff. Mother hasn't looked at it for at least twenty years. When you're ready, give her a call. The housekeeper's husband will pick it up."

"That's perfect. Now let me show you what I'm trying to do here," Emily offered.

George Lawrence bent attentively over the table as she showed how she was recreating the layout of the town in the 1890s.

"There were a lot fewer houses then, as you would know better than I," Emily told him, "and the records aren't complete. I'm sure I'll learn something from your material that I don't have yet."

"This is your home?" he asked, touching the top of one of the Monopoly houses.

"Yes."

"And this is ours?"

"Yes."

"What exactly are you trying to do?"

"Figure out how three young women could have vanished without a trace. I'm looking for a house of one of their friends—one of the young male friends, perhaps—where they might have been enticed inside. For example, I met Carolyn Taylor at your luncheon the other day. She told me that her relative Phyllis Gates, who was a friend of my ancestor Madeline and your ancestor Julia Gordon, thought Madeline's fiancé Douglas Carter killed her."

Emily pointed. "Think about this. Here's the Shapley house, and here, right across the street, is the Carter house. Supposedly, Douglas missed the early train home the day Madeline vanished. But did he?"

"Surely that was checked out at the time?"

"I've been promised a look at the police records. I'll be very interested to see what they show. Visualize that day. Madeline was sitting on the porch, waiting for Douglas. I don't think she would have just gotten up and gone for a walk without calling in to tell her mother. But suppose Douglas suddenly appeared, on his porch, and she ran down to greet him?"

"And he pulled her into the house, killed her, and hid her body until he could find a way to bury it in her own backyard?" George Lawrence looked skeptical. "What would his motive be?"

"I don't know, and admittedly it *is* a farfetched theory. On the other hand, I've found indications that his cousin Alan Carter was in love with Madeline as well. His family lived in the house on Ludlam Avenue where the bodies were found yesterday. Suppose *he* came by in a closed carriage and, perhaps, told Madeline that Douglas had been in an accident?"

"We heard about the discovery yesterday, of course. Now the Harper family has to face what we faced last week. They're from the Philadelphia area. We don't know them personally, but we do have mutual friends."

The stark pain George Lawrence was experiencing was evident to Emily as, in a tone that was both bitter and sad, he said, "Maybe the Harpers and Amanda and I will end up in the same support group."

"How is Amanda doing?" Emily asked. "I admired her so much on Saturday. It must have been so terribly difficult for her, for all of you."

"It was, and as you saw, Amanda was wonderful. Having the baby here was a big help. But Christine and Tom and the baby went home on Sunday. We visited the cemetery yesterday, and Amanda absolutely fell apart. I think that was probably good. She needed to let it out. Well, I'm on my way. We're starting home this afternoon. Mother said to call her if you have any questions."

As she closed the door behind George Lawrence, the phone rang. It was Nick Todd.

Emily was somewhat chagrined to realize that her emotions on hearing his voice were mixed. On the one hand, she was glad that he called. On the other, she was disappointed that he had not bothered to phone since the weekend to ask if she had had any more problems with the stalker.

But then his shy explanation pleased her: "Emily, I realize I had a hell of a nerve to try to practically drag you out of your house the other night. It's just that I was terribly troubled when I realized that the stalker had left that photograph. I would have called before, but I didn't want to become a public nuisance to you."

"You mean a private nuisance. Trust me, that's the last thing I'd ever consider you to be."

"No more incidents with your stalker, I hope?"

"Not a one. And Monday, my friend Eric Bailey came down from Albany and installed security cameras around the outside of the house. The next time someone tries to slip something under the door, he'll soon see his own picture on a mug sheet."

"And you turn your security system on when you're alone in the house?"

It's not on now, Emily thought. "Always at night."

"It wouldn't be a bad idea to have it on during the day as well."

"I guess it wouldn't. But I don't want to live my life in a cage. I don't want to step out on the porch for a breath of air and have that banshee wail go off because I forgot the alarm was on." A slight edge had crept into her voice.

"Emily, I'm sorry. I don't know what makes me think I have the right to act like some kind of damn monitor."

"You don't need to apologize. You sound like a very nice, concerned friend. I intend to be very careful, but there is a point where I begin to feel as if whoever is doing this is winning. I'm trying not to let that happen."

"Believe it or not, I do understand. The papers are full of what happened in Spring Lake yesterday."

"Yes, it's become quite a sensation in the media. I was out jogging and taking a few mental notes for that project I mentioned I was starting when I saw them digging in that yard."

"The stories say the police got an anonymous tip. Have you any idea where it came from?"

As soon as they were spoken, Emily would have taken back her next two words if it were possible: "From me," she said, then immediately had to explain about the postcard.

From the shocked silence at the other end of the phone, she realized that Nick Todd had the reaction to that information that she would have expected from her parents.

Finally he said, "Emily, do you think there is even the *slightest* chance that this Spring Lake killer is also the guy who stalked you in Albany?"

"No, I don't. And neither does Detective Browski."

Mentioning the name of the Albany policeman meant filling Nick in on Ned Koehler's confession.

When the conversation ended, she had firmly refused Walter Todd's offer of a bodyguard, and accepted Nick's invitation to have a return brunch at the Old Mill on Sunday.

"I only hope we won't be talking about another murder," she said.

Long after they had said good-bye, Nick Todd sat at his desk, his hands folded. Emily, he thought, why are you so smart and still so dense? Has it never occurred to you that *you* might be targeted as the next victim?

fifty-one

TOMMY DUGGAN and Pete Walsh began the morning in Elliot Osborne's office, where the desk was covered in newspapers. "You're not very photogenic, Tommy," Osborne commented.

"I hadn't seen that one," Tommy muttered. The picture had been taken yesterday and showed him leaving the Ludlam Avenue house. Studying it, he began to consider paying more attention to his diet.

Walsh, of course, photographed like the all-American jock. "Too bad you didn't try out for *Law & Order*," Tommy observed tartly, looking at a photo of his partner.

"I should have. I was Joe Fish in the fourth-grade school play, *Joe Fish and His Toy Store*," Pete told him. "That was the lead."

"All right, let's leave it at that," Osborne decided.

The moment of levity vanished. Osborne nodded to Duggan. "You first."

Tommy had his notebook open. "As you know, we now have a positive ID on the skeleton we found yesterday.

The dental records confirm it to be the remains of Carla Harper. The section of scarf apparently used to strangle her is part of the same scarf that was used to strangle Martha Lawrence. The killer used one end piece on Martha, and the center piece on Carla. The third piece is missing."

"Meaning that if the killer follows what seems to be his plan, he'll use the scarf again on Saturday." Osborne frowned and tilted back his chair. "No matter how many cops we have patrolling Spring Lake, we can't be on every street, in every backyard. How's the background check on Wilcox progressing?"

"So far there's nothing much more than we had before. To go over it quickly, he was an only child, raised in Long Island. Father died when he was a baby. Very close to his mother, a schoolteacher, who helped him with his homework, I guess. Anyway, he was always at the head of his class.

"His father's sister lived in Spring Lake, which is his connection here. He visited her every summer, for years. His mother died when he was thirty-eight, and a couple of years later, he married Rachel." Tommy paused. "Chief, if she were my wife, I'd get a job as a traveling salesman.

"He went up the usual academic ladder and was finally offered the presidency of Enoch College in Ohio. Retired twelve years ago at age fifty-five. He writes for academic journals and has done considerable research on the history of this area and written articles about it for the local papers. He recently told the Spring Lake librarian that he's writing a novel with the old Monmouth Hotel as the setting."

"No smoking guns there," Osborne observed.

"If Emily Graham is right, there may be. She thinks we have a copycat killer who found explicit details of the 1890s murders and is basing his actions on them. Something else. We've learned that Wilcox abruptly resigned his presidency of Enoch College. At the time, he'd just had his contract renewed and had all kinds of plans for further expansion, lecture series with major speakers, all that stuff."

"Any explanation?"

"Ill health was the official reason. Apparently a serious heart condition. Got a big, tearful send-off. They named a building after him."

Tommy smiled grimly. "Guess what?"

Elliot Osborne waited. He knew Tommy Duggan liked to present juicy information with a flair. Like pulling a rabbit from a hat, he thought.

"Let's have it, Tommy," he said crisply. "You're on to something."

"Well maybe. It's more of a hunch than anything concrete. I'd bet the ranch that he has no more heart trouble than you or me or Pete. My guess is that either he was told to resign, or resigned on his own because he had a big problem that he didn't want made public. Now our job is to squeeze out of him what it was."

"We're seeing him at three o'clock," Pete Walsh volunteered. "We thought it would be a good idea to let him squirm a little while waiting for us."

"It is a good idea." Osborne made a move to get up, but Pete Walsh had more to say.

"Just to keep you posted, sir, I spent last evening going through the records of the police investigation about the disappearance of those three girls in the 1890s."

It was obvious to Osborne that the newest detective on his staff wanted to impress him. "Did you find anything at all useful?"

"Not that I could see. It's like what's been happening now. The girls seem to have vanished off the face of the earth."

"You're giving a copy of those records to Emily Graham?" Osborne asked.

Pete looked worried. "I cleared it with the first assistant."

"I know you did. I'm generally not in favor of any records, even if they're over one hundred years old, being made available outside the usual channels, but if you've promised them to her, I'll let it happen."

Elliot Osborne stood up decisively, a signal that the meeting was over.

Duggan and Walsh got to their feet. "One piece of good news," Tommy added as he headed to the door. "Dr. Madden's killer is better at strangling people than at whacking computers. Our research people were afraid the hard drive had been damaged, but they've been able to get it going. With any luck we'll retrieve Madden's files—and maybe find out that a guest at the Lawrence party that night four and a half years ago also spent some of his time with a shrink who specialized in regression therapy."

fifty-two

"BOB, WHAT ARE YOU TRYING TO PULL ON ME?"

"I wasn't aware that I was trying to pull anything on you."

"Where did you *go* last night?"

"When I couldn't sleep, I went downstairs as usual, and read. I came up about five o'clock, took a sleeping pill, and for once it worked."

It was nearly noon. Robert Frieze had come downstairs to find Natalie, his wife, sitting in the living room, obviously waiting for him.

"You look very nice," he observed. "Are you going somewhere?"

"I have a lunch date."

"I was thinking of inviting you to lunch."

"Don't bother. Go over and gladhand your customers at The Four Seasons. If you can find any, that is."

"The name of my restaurant is The Seasoner. It is not The Four Seasons."

"No, it sure isn't. No argument about that."

Bob Frieze looked at his beautiful wife, taking in her shimmering blond hair, her near-perfect features, her catlike turquoise eyes. Remembering how exciting he had once found her, he was amazed at how detached he had begun to feel about her now.

More than detached, he realized. Fed up. *Sick to death of her.*

Natalie was wearing a tailored dark green pantsuit that he had never seen before. Obviously new. Obviously pricey. He wondered how she found room for it in her closet.

"Since I'm not to have the honor of your company, I'll be on my way," he said.

"Not yet, you won't." Natalie got to her feet swiftly. "Believe it or not, I'm not sleeping very well myself. I came down here at two this morning. You weren't here, Bobby. And your car was gone. Now will you please explain to me where you were?"

She wouldn't tell me that unless it's true, Frieze thought frantically. I don't know where I was. "Natalie, I was so tired I forgot. I did go out for a spin. Wanted to get some fresh air and do some heavy thinking." He groped for words. "It's going to be a setback, but I've decided to take Bonetti's offer, even though he's low-balled me. We'll sell this house and move to Manhattan, maybe take a smaller apartment than we'd planned, and—"

Natalie interrupted. "When you were taking your spin last night to clear your head, you apparently thought that a drink would clear it more. A drink with a friend, I mean. Here's what I found in your pocket." She tossed a piece of paper at him.

He read what was written on it. "Hi, handsome. My number is 555-1974. Don't forget to call. Peggy."

"I don't know how that got there, Natalie," he said.

"I do, Bobby. Someone named Peggy put it there. I have news for you. Get rid of that restaurant. Sell this house. Pay off your stock loans and cash out your holdings. And then figure out what you were worth the day I became your blushing bride."

She stood up and walked over to him, brought her face to within inches of his.

"Let me explain why. It's because half of what you were worth that day is what I intend to take out of this marriage."

"You're out of your mind, Natalie."

"Am I? Bobby, I've been doing a lot of thinking about the night at the Lawrence party. You were wearing that boxy jacket that you think is straight from the pages of *Gentleman's Quarterly*. You could have hidden that sash under it. And the next morning when I got up, you were digging in the garden. Any chance you were getting rid of Martha's body until you could move it to the backyard of the Shapley house?"

"You can't believe that!"

"Maybe I can. And maybe I can't. You're a strange man, Bob. There are times when you look at me as if you don't know me. You have a way of just disappearing without telling me where you're going. Maybe it's my civic duty to tell Detective Duggan that I've become concerned about your behavior and, for your own sake as well as for the safety of the young women in this community, feel I have to report it."

The veins in Robert Frieze's forehead began to bulge. He grasped Natalie's wrist and tightened his grip on it till she cried out in pain. His face was flushed with rage.

Between clenched teeth he spat out, "You tell Duggan, or anyone, a story like that, and you'd better start being concerned for *yourself!* Got it?"

fifty-three

At 3:00 A.M. on Wednesday morning, the missing Joel Lake was found. He was in the process of burglarizing a house in Troy when the police arrived, summoned by the silent alarm.

Seven hours later, Marty Browski went to the jail where Lake was being detained to interview him.

"In your natural habitat again, I see, Joel. You never learn, do you?"

The permanent sneer on Joel Lake's face hardened. "I *do* learn, Browski. I stay out of houses with old ladies in them. Too much trouble."

"It could have been a lot more trouble if Emily Graham hadn't gotten you off on the murder charge. We all thought you did the hit on Ruth Koehler."

"You *thought* I did it? You changed your mind?" Lake looked surprised.

The bad seed, Browski thought, as he looked intently at Lake. Twenty-eight years old and in trouble since he was twelve. A juvenile rap sheet an arm long. Probably attractive to some women, though, in a cheap kind of macho way, with his powerful build, dark curly hair, narrow eyes, and full mouth.

Emily had told Browski that Lake had tried to come on to *her* a couple of times. He's the kind who won't tolerate rejection, Browski decided now as his hopes began to build that he was face to face with the stalker.

The time frame was right. Joel Lake had broken parole and dropped out of sight right about the time the stalking began.

"We've missed you, Joel," Browski said pleasantly. "Now let me get your Miranda warnings out of the way before we get down to business. It's a waste of words, of course. You know it by heart."

"I told the guys who arrested me that I happened to be passing by, saw the door was open, and thought I should look in and just make sure no one was in trouble."

Marty Browski laughed heartily. "Oh come on, you can do better than that. Joel, I don't give a damn about your burglary. That's up to the cops here in Troy. I want to talk about where you've been lately. And I want to know about your interest in Emily Graham."

"What about Graham? The last time I saw her was in court." Joel Lake grinned. "I really got her attention. I told her that maybe I *did* kill the old lady. You should have seen the look on her face. Bet that's been eating her, wondering if maybe I wasn't kidding and knowing I couldn't be tried for it again."

Marty felt an urge to punch the insolent face, to wipe the nasty, satisfied smile from the felon's lips.

"Ever been to Spring Lake, Joel?" he snapped.

"Spring Lake? Where's that?"

"In New Jersey."

"Why would I go there?"

"You tell me."

"Okay, I'll tell you. Never been there in my life."

"Where were you last Saturday morning?"

"I don't remember. Probably in church." As he spoke, Lake wore an expression of mock sincerity, and a sneer curled at his lips.

"That's just where I think you were. I think you were in St. Catherine's church, in Spring Lake, New Jersey."

"Listen, are you trying to pin something on me? Because if it has to do with last Saturday, you're wasting your time. I was in Buffalo where I've been for the last year and a half—and where I should have stayed."

"Can you prove it?"

"You bet I can. What time are you talking about?"

"Around noon."

"Couldn't be better. I was having a sub and a couple of beers with some buddies in the Sunrise Café, on Coogan Street. They know me as Joey Pond. Get it? I figured if I can't be a Lake, I'll be a Pond. Pretty good, huh?"

Marty pushed his chair back and got up. That had been the name on the ID Lake had been carrying when he was arrested. No doubt the alibi would check out, and anyhow, when you came right down to it, this guy just didn't seem either subtle or sophisticated enough to carry out the kind of stalking campaign Emily Graham was enduring.

No, Marty thought, this bum got his revenge on Emily for rejecting him by hinting he was guilty of Ruth Koehler's murder, and letting her blame herself for helping him to walk out of the courtroom a free man.

"No more questions, Browski?" Lake looked surprised. "I kind of enjoy your company. What happened in Spring Lake that you wanted to pin on me?"

Browski leaned on the table that separated him from Lake. "Somebody's been bothering Emily Graham down there."

"Bothering? You mean stalking. Hey, that's not my thing," Joel told him.

His tone low and menacing, Browski said, "You had some pretty scummy friends rooting for you at your trial. If any one of them got a fixation on Emily Graham after seeing her in court and you know about it, you'd better come clean now. Because if anything happens to her, I warn you that your butt will never see the outside of Attica again."

"You don't scare me, Browski," Joel Lake sneered. "I thought old lady Koehler's son was supposed to be the stalker. Gee, Browski, you're batting zero. You were wrong about me, and you're wrong about him. You better take a brush-up course on how to be a detective."

WHEN HE GOT BACK to the office, Marty called Emily to tell her that Joel Lake had been located and was definitely not the stalker. "Something else," he said. "He brought up the fact that he'd hinted to you that he might actually have killed Ruth Koehler. Just in case you have even the most lingering doubt that you got a killer off, he admitted he just did it to upset you."

"When you told me that Ned Koehler had confessed, any lingering doubt I had about Lake was gone. But I'm still glad to hear it from his lips."

"Nothing more from the stalker, Emily?"

"No, not so far. The alarm system is state of the art, although I admit that in the middle of the night I think about how Ned Koehler disarmed the one in the townhouse. But I do feel that the cameras Eric Bailey put in are added security. In a way, I'm sorry Joel hasn't turned out to be the stalker. At least I'd have the comfort of knowing he's behind bars again."

Browski could hear the nervous tremor that occasionally surfaced in Emily Graham's voice. He felt angry and frustrated that he was again completely without a stalking suspect. He admitted to himself that he was also deathly afraid that Emily was in very real danger.

"Emily, last year we checked out as many as possible of the people who might have been upset at some of the not guilty verdicts you got for your clients. They all seem to be clean. How about that building where you had your office? Was there anyone who might have had big eyes for you or become jealous after you came into all that money?"

Emily had just gone into the kitchen to make a sandwich for lunch when Marty's call came. When she answered, she had picked up the phone and walked to the window.

After the cloudy morning, the day had turned sunny, and there was a pinkish haze around the trees. I always watch for that haze, she thought. It's the first sign of spring.

Marty Browski was desperate to find another suspect who might be the stalker. She understood why. Like Eric and Nick, he was afraid that at some point the stalker, whoever he is, might make an overt move to harm her.

"Marty, I have an idea," she said. "You know that Eric Bailey worked in the office next to mine for several years. Maybe he could come up with the name of someone in our building or even one of the deliverymen that he thought was a little strange. I know he'd be glad to talk to you. He calls every few days to make sure I'm okay."

It would probably be another dead end, Marty thought, but then you never know. "I'll do that, Emily," he said, then added, "I've been reading about Spring Lake. Pretty nasty business, finding two more bodies there yesterday. Papers are saying that if that psycho follows the pattern, there might be another murder on Saturday. It might be a good idea if—"

"If I leave Spring Lake and hole up in the apartment in

Manhattan?" Emily said. "Marty, thanks for the concern, but I have some new documents I'm studying, and I honestly think I'm making progress on my own investigation. You're a doll, but here I stay."

Cutting off his continuing protest, she said firmly, " 'Bye, Marty."

THE TELEVISION RECEPTION in the van parked six blocks away was excellent. Eric sat in the small but comfortable chair he had placed in front of the television set. Very good, Emily, he thought in silent approval. Thank you for the vote of confidence. I'd hoped to stay another day, but now I'll have to get back to see Mr. Browski tomorrow. Too bad.

He had an excellent shot of Emily opening the door for George Lawrence, but it would be unwise to send it to her now. He would return on Friday night.

fifty-four

"MR. STAFFORD ASKED if you'd mind waiting for a few minutes, Mrs. Frieze. He has to finish writing up a contract."

Twenty-three-year-old Pat Glynn, Will Stafford's receptionist, smiled nervously at Natalie Frieze, who thoroughly intimidated her.

She's so glamorous, Pat thought. Every time she walks through that door I feel as if everything about me is wrong.

When she'd gotten dressed that morning, she'd been pleased with her new red wool pantsuit, but now she wasn't so sure. It didn't hold a candle to the cut and fabric of the dark green pantsuit that Natalie Frieze was wearing.

And she had just had her hair drastically styled into a cap cut that barely covered her ears, something that two days ago had seemed to her the height of fashion. But now, when she looked at Natalie's long, silky blond hair, Pat was sure she'd made a dreadful mistake.

Natalie Frieze appeared to have on no makeup, but no one could look that good without some help, could they? Pat thought hopefully. "You look gorgeous, Mrs. Frieze," she said shyly.

"Why, how nice of you." Natalie smiled. She was always amused by the awe she knew she inspired in Will's plain young secretary, but realized that it gave her an unexpected lift to hear a compliment. "It's good to hear a kind word, Pat."

"Don't you feel well, Mrs. Frieze?"

"Not really. My wrist is terribly sore." She held up her arm, causing her sleeve to slide back and reveal an ugly purple bruise.

Will Stafford emerged from his office. "Sorry to keep you waiting. What's with your wrist?"

Natalie kissed him. "I'll tell you all about it over lunch. Let's go." She turned toward the door, then glanced over her shoulder and gave Pat Glynn a perfunctory smile.

"Back in an hour, Pat," Will said.

"Make that an hour and a half," Natalie corrected him.

As they exited, Will pulled the door closed behind them, but not before Pat Glynn heard Natalie say, "Will, I was scared to death of Bobby this morning. I think he's going crazy."

It was apparent she genuinely was on the verge of tears. "Calm down," he said sympathetically as they got into his car. "We'll talk over lunch."

They had a reservation at Rob's tavern two miles away, in the neighboring town of Sea Girt.

When they were seated and their orders taken, Will looked at Natalie, a quizzical expression on his face. "You do realize that Pat probably overheard what you said about Bob, and that she is something of a gossip? She's probably on the phone right now, filling in her mother."

Natalie shrugged. "At this point I really don't care. Thanks for agreeing to go out with me, Will. I think you're my only real friend in town."

"There are plenty of nice people in town, Natalie. Oh, sure, some of them didn't like it when Bob dumped Susan for you, but on the other hand, these are fair people. They all know it wasn't much of a marriage, even though Susan kept trying to make it one. I think everyone feels she's better off without him."

"That's really good news. I'm so happy for her. I've given five years of my life to Bob Frieze. Five important years, I might add. Now he's not only going to hell in a handbasket financially, but he's getting weird."

Will raised his eyebrows. "Weird? What's that supposed to mean?"

"I'll give you an example, something that happened just last night. I know Bobby has told you that he's an insomniac and often reads half the night?"

Will smiled. "Looking at you, I'd say that's a bit of a waste."

Natalie smiled wryly. "See why I made you come out to lunch with me. I needed to hear that silver tongue of yours."

"I wasn't aware I had one."

"You do. But about last night—Will, I went downstairs at 2:00 A.M. and looked into Bobby's study. There was no sign of him. I looked in the garage, and his car was gone. I don't know where he went, but this morning I found a note in his pocket from some woman, saying she wanted him to call her. When I confronted him about it, he was shocked. I honestly don't think he *remembered* meeting her! He tried to make some lame excuse, but I believe he may have blacked out. In fact, I think he's been having intervals of blacking out for some time."

Natalie's voice was rising. Will noticed that the elderly women at the next table were openly listening to the conversation.

"Best keep it down, Natalie," he suggested.

"I don't know if I want to," she retorted, but then, her voice slightly lower, she went on. "Will, I keep thinking back to that night at the Lawrences' party. I mean the night before Martha vanished."

"And?"

"It's funny, but you know how when you really concentrate, you do remember little things? I mean I hadn't thought about the fact that Bobby was wearing that stupid boxy jacket he seems to think makes him look younger—"

"Boy, when you're down on someone, you don't quit."

Natalie flashed a worried smile across the table, as the waitress placed steins of beer in front of them. "I really got to him today," she admitted, then asked, "Why did I order beer?"

"Because it goes well with a corned-beef sandwich."

"I swear, if Bobby had this kind of restaurant instead of that Seasoner mausoleum, maybe he'd have made a buck."

"Forget that, Natalie. Are you suggesting that Bobby stole Rachel Wilcox's scarf?"

"I'm saying that when I went into the powder room, I noticed it on a side table, but when I came back, it was gone."

"Did you see Bobby anywhere near it?"

A shade of uncertainty flickered over her face. "I'm pretty sure I did."

"Why didn't you tell this to the police?"

"Because until the other night nobody knew they were asking about the scarf. Right?"

"Right."

"I'll just keep concentrating on trying to remember that night; maybe something more will come to me," Natalie concluded, as she took a healthy bite of her sandwich.

fifty-five _____

"I HAVE SOME OTHER BOOKS you might be interested in see-ing, Emily. May I drop them off in half an hour?"

"Dr. Wilcox, I don't want to inconvenience you. I can pick them up."

"It won't inconvenience me at all. I'm going out now to do a few errands."

When she replaced the receiver and checked the time, Emily was surprised to realize it was four o'clock. After Marty Browski called, she gave herself a short break, then returned to the research materials she'd spread out in the dining room, to continue to try to trace and identify the 1890s serial killer.

There were more Monopoly houses placed on the map she had sketched, all of them neatly marked with the names of people who had lived at that address at that time. She had added houses for the Mayers and Allans and Williamses and Nesbitts. The names of their daughters or sons appeared in the lists of those regularly present at gatherings and parties and picnics and cotillions attended by Madeline Shapley, Letitia Gregg, Ellen Swain, Julia Gordon, and Phyllis Gates.

She had opened one of the boxes George Lawrence brought over and was thrilled to see that it contained diaries and letters. Fascinated, she immediately began to read some of them, then realized she should complete her study of the museum material first.

In the end she compromised and worked with both sources simultaneously. As the collective personal stories began to unfold, she felt as if she was stepping back in time and actually sharing the world of the 1890s.

Sometimes she found herself almost wishing she had

lived then. Life in the 1890s seemed so much more sheltered, so much less demanding than her own life.

Then Emily asked herself abruptly if she was crazy. Sheltered! she thought. Three of those friends who had confided in each other, who had shared gatherings and picnics and dances, died at ages nineteen, eighteen, and twenty. That's not very sheltered.

One bundle of letters that she was sure would be very promising had been written over the years by Julia Gordon to Phyllis Gates, when the Gates family returned to Philadelphia after the summer ended. Obviously Phyllis Gates kept them and then returned them to the Lawrence family.

Julia became engaged to George Henry Lawrence in the fall of 1894. That winter he traveled to Europe on business with his father, and when he returned Julia wrote to her friend:

> *Dear Phyllis,*
>
> *After these three long months, George has returned, and I am so very happy. The best way I can make you understand the depth of my emotion is to quote from the collection of letters I have recently read.*
>
> To attempt to describe my joy and feelings at meeting and greeting my dear one must prove a failure. We spent the evening very sweetly and pleasantly.
>
> *And now we plan our wedding, which will take place in the spring. If only Madeline and Letitia were here to be my bridesmaids along with you. What has become of our dear friends? Madeline's family has moved away. Douglas Carter has taken his own life. Edgar Newman continues to be very low in spirits—I do believe he loved Letitia very dearly. We must continue to keep all of them, the missing and the dead, in our thoughts and prayers.*
>
> *Your loving friend,*
> *Julia*

Her eyes moist, Emily reread that letter. She doesn't mention Ellen Swain, she thought, then realized that Ellen did not vanish until over a year later.

I wonder what Julia would have thought if she could have looked into the future and known that her great-great granddaughter, Martha, would be found buried with Madeline.

She laid the letter down on her lap and sat quietly. Madeline and Martha, she thought, Letitia and Carla, Ellen and . . . ?

Unless something happened, there would be another victim on Saturday; she was now convinced of the inevitability of that. Oh, dear God, help us to find a way to stop him, she prayed.

She had intended to close off the dining room before Clayton Wilcox arrived, but she was so deeply absorbed in reading the letters that when the doorbell rang, she ran to answer it, forgetting either to turn off the light or close the door.

For a moment after she opened the front door, the sight of Dr. Clayton Wilcox's hulking figure standing on the porch caused a sensation of pure fright to rush through her. What is *happening* to me? she asked herself, as she stepped aside to let him in and murmured a greeting.

She had been hoping that he would hand her the bag of books and leave, but instead Wilcox walked past her and stood well inside the foyer.

"It's gotten quite chilly," he said pointedly.

"Of course." Emily knew she had no option but to close the door. She realized her palms were drenched with perspiration.

He was holding the bag of books and glancing around the foyer. The arched entrance to the living room was to the right, revealing a room already filled with shadows.

There was also an entrance to the dining room from the foyer, and in that room she had turned on the chandelier over the table, and it starkly illuminated the drawing board with the Monopoly houses. The table and dining room chairs piled with books and papers were plainly visible to Wilcox.

"I see you're working in here," he said. "Why don't I put these books with the others?"

Before she could find a way to stop him, he was in the dining room, had placed the Enoch College book bag on the floor, and was carefully studying the drawing board.

"I could help you with this," he offered. "I don't know if I mentioned that I am attempting to write a novel set in Spring Lake during the last twenty-five years of the nineteenth century." He pointed to the house at 15 Ludlam Avenue that she had labeled with Alan Carter's name.

"You are correct," he said. "This is where the Carter family lived for many years, beginning in 1893. Before that, *this* was their home." He picked a house out of the box and placed it directly behind her own home.

"Alan lived right behind this house?" Emily said in shock.

"At that time the house was in the name of his maternal grandmother. The family lived with her. When she died, they sold her home and moved to Ludlam Avenue."

"You *have* done a great deal of research on the town, Dr. Wilcox." Emily's mouth was dry.

"Yes, I have. For my book, of course. May I sit down, Emily? I have to talk to you."

"Yes, of course."

She quickly decided she would not invite him into the living room. She did not want to go into that darkened area with him walking behind her. Instead she deliberately took the chair nearest the door to the foyer. I can run if he tries anything, she told herself. I can get outside and scream for help . . .

He sat down and folded his arms. Even seated across the table he conveyed a powerful presence.

His next words stunned her.

"Emily, you are a criminal defense lawyer and from what I understand a very good one. I believe I have become the prime suspect in the deaths of Martha Lawrence and Carla Harper. I want you to represent me."

"Have the police told you that you are a suspect, Dr. Wilcox?" Emily asked, playing for time. Was he toying with her? she wondered. Was he about to confess to her, and then . . . She tried not to complete the thought.

"Not yet, but they will be able to build a substantial case against me. Let me tell you why."

"Please don't, Dr. Wilcox," Emily interrupted. "I must tell you that I absolutely could *never* represent you. I am a witness in any legal hearing involving Martha Lawrence. Don't forget I was here when her body—or I should say, *skeleton*—was discovered. So please don't tell me anything that I might be asked to repeat under oath. Since I can't be your lawyer, there would be no attorney-client privilege."

He nodded. "That had not occurred to me." He got up slowly. "Then, of course, I won't share with you any more of the great difficulty I am facing." He looked down at the board. "Do you believe in reincarnation, Emily?" he asked.

"No, I do not."

"You don't think you might have had a previous life—as Madeline Shapley?"

The image of the finger bone with the sapphire ring flashed through Emily's mind. "No, I don't, Doctor."

"With all that has been said and written about the subject of reincarnation this past week, I find myself beginning to wonder. Did I live here before in one of these houses? Did I *choose* to return here for that reason? What could I possibly have done in an earlier life that I have so many psychic debts to repay now?"

His face became suddenly haunted. "If only one could undo a moment of weakness," he said quietly.

Emily felt that at that moment Dr. Wilcox was not even aware of her presence.

"I have to make a very hard decision," he said, then sighed. "But it is one that must be made."

She shrank back as he passed her. She did not follow

him to the door, but stood ready to escape from the dining room to the porch if he turned on her.

To her relief, he went directly to the front door and opened it. Then he paused. "I think it would be a good idea if you lock and bolt the doors these next few nights, Emily," he warned.

Thursday, March 29 ═══════════

fifty-six

ONE CAN FEEL the increasing nervous apprehension of the residents of Spring Lake.

The police are grim-faced. Already they patrol the streets more frequently.

One seldom sees a woman walking alone, even in the daytime.

Each day the tabloids have become more sensational in their rush to feed the frantic curiosity of their readers.

"The Reincarnated Serial Killer of Spring Lake" has become national, even international, news.

The talk shows vie with each other to present differing views on regression and reincarnation.

This morning, on *Good Morning America,* yet another prominent scholar on the subject soberly explained that while many people believe reincarnation gives them countless new opportunities for continued life, others regard it as a great burden.

The Hindus, the scholar pointed out, are absolutely certain that they will be reincarnated. They desperately wish to *break* the cycle of birth and rebirth, to *halt* the process. For that reason they are willing to endure severe self-inflicted austerities and the most demanding kind of spiritual practices to achieve release.

Do I want release?

In two more days, my task will be finished. I shall again return to a normal state, and live out the remainder of my life in peace and tranquillity.

But I shall continue to write a detailed account of everything that is occurring. In it, as in the other diary, the "who" and "what" and "why" and "when" will be made clear.

Maybe someday a fourteen-year-old boy will again find the diary—the two diaries—and want to relive the cycle.

When that happens, I will know that I have returned to Spring Lake for the third time.

fifty-seven _____

BERNICE JOYCE HAD DECIDED to spend the week in Spring Lake. "As you know, I flew up from Florida for the memorial Mass," she explained to Reba Ashby, as they shared breakfast on Thursday morning.

"I had intended to fly back to Palm Beach Monday afternoon, but then realized that would be quite foolish since I'd be coming north next week. So instead, I extended my stay here."

They were seated at a window table. Bernice glanced out. "It's a real spring day, isn't it?" she asked, her voice wistful. "I walked the boardwalk for over an hour yesterday. It brought back so many wonderful memories. Then I had dinner with the Lawrences at another old friend's home. How we reminisced!"

Reba had not run into Mrs. Joyce at the hotel on either Tuesday or Wednesday and assumed she had checked out as planned. She was delighted to see her in the elevator this morning, both of them on the way to the dining room.

At their first meeting she had said she was a journalist with a national news magazine, careful to avoid mentioning the name of *The National Daily*. Even though I probably could have, she thought now, as she locked a sympathetic expression on her face while listening to an anecdote about Spring Lake in the 1930s. She was positive Bernice Joyce had never read *The National Daily*, if indeed she had ever heard of it.

"Let it not even be mentioned among you," as St. Paul had counseled the Ephesians. Bernice Joyce undoubtedly felt that way about tabloids.

Reba wanted to get a line on the other people who had been at the party the night before Martha Lawrence vanished. She intended to continue to milk the Dr. Wilcox angle for all it was worth, but there was always the possibility that he was telling the truth, that he had placed the scarf with his wife's pocketbook and someone else had taken it.

"Have you gotten together with any of the other people who were questioned by the police last Saturday, Mrs. Joyce?"

"Actually, I have compared notes with two couples who live near the Lawrences. Most of the others I know less well. For example, I am very fond of Robert Frieze's first wife, Susan. His second wife, Natalie, I do not care for. Robert was there with Natalie. Then there was . . ."

By the end of her second cup of coffee, Reba had a list of names to work on. "I want to write a sensitive profile of Martha as people remember her," she explained. "How better than to start with the people who were with her in the last hours of her life."

She scanned the list. "Why don't I read these names back to you and see if I have them all."

As she listened, Bernice Joyce realized that she was visualizing the living room of the Lawrence home. She had been thinking of that night of the party so much this week that it seemed to be coming back to her in ever-sharpening focus.

The scarf *was* on that table in the foyer, she thought. I noticed Natalie Frieze walk down the foyer with her purse in her hand, and I assumed she was in the powder room. I was watching for her to return.

The face of another guest came into her mind. I am becoming increasingly certain that I saw him move Rachel's pocketbook. The scarf was under it.

Should I discuss this with Detective Duggan? she wondered. Do I have the right to even mention a name in a police investigation if I am not absolutely sure that my impression was accurate?

She focused again on the woman seated across from her. Reba Ashby was such a nice person. She seemed like an old friend. And as a journalist, surely she understood ethical problems.

"Ms. Ashby," Bernice Joyce began, "may I share with you a problem I'm having? It seems to me I may have observed that scarf being taken from the table that evening of the party. In fact I am almost certain that I did."

"You may have *what?*" Reba Ashby was so shocked that for an instant she lost her professional you-can-trust-me-I'm-your-friend demeanor.

Bernice was again looking out the window at the ocean. If only I could be one thousand percent sure, she thought.

"Who did you see take the scarf that night, Bernice, I mean Mrs. Joyce?"

Bernice turned her head and looked at Reba Ashby. The woman's eyes were glistening. Her body language suggested a tiger ready to spring.

Bernice suddenly realized that she had made a terrible mistake—Reba Ashby was *not* to be trusted.

"I think I'd best say no more about it," she said firmly as she signaled the waiter to bring her check.

fifty-eight _____

WHEN MARTY BROWSKI got to his office on Thursday morning, he saw that at seven o'clock on Wednesday evening Eric Bailey had returned his phone call in which he had requested an appointment.

"I love playing phone tag," Marty said aloud, as he dialed Bailey's number. When Bailey's secretary answered, Marty was put through to him immediately.

"Sorry to have missed you yesterday," Eric said pleasantly. "I played hookey. I took an afternoon off to brush up on my golf game."

He readily agreed to a meeting. "This morning, if you want. I happen to be free at eleven o'clock."

The office was located just outside the Albany city limits. As Marty drove there, he reflected that he had actually only met Bailey face to face once, and that had been in the courtroom where Ned Koehler was on trial for stalking Emily Graham. Bailey had testified about the cameras he had installed around her townhouse.

He had slumped in the witness stand, Marty remembered, twisting his hands nervously. His voice had been quiet and squeaky. The judge had repeatedly asked him to speak up.

Since then, Marty had seen Bailey's picture in the newspapers from time to time. He was a local celebrity, Albany's miniversion of Bill Gates.

It was grasping at straws to call on Bailey now to see if he could come up with any useful information that might help them find the stalker. Marty, however, knew that extreme measures were called for, even if it meant grasping at straws.

He was driving through an area where a number of company headquarters were located, all of them situated in parklike surroundings. None of the buildings was more than three stories high, he noticed.

Observing the descending street numbers, Marty slowed the car. The next turnoff had to be Bailey's, he figured.

A long driveway led to a handsome two-story red-brick structure with floor-to-ceiling tinted windows. Very nice, Marty thought, as he pulled into a visitors' parking space.

Inside, the receptionist's desk was in the center of the front-to-back lobby. Expensive red leather sofas and chairs trimmed with brass nail heads were placed around Persian carpets in defined seating areas. Paintings that looked to be of very fine quality were hanging in tasteful groupings on the walls. The overall effect was soothing, low key and expensive.

Browski was reminded of something he had read, a remark the theatrical producer George Abbott had made to playwright Moss Hart on viewing Hart's Bucks County estate: "Shows what God could do if He only had money."

The receptionist had been told to expect him. "Mr. Bailey's suite is on the second floor. Turn right and go to the end," she directed.

Ignoring the elevator, Browski climbed up the winding staircase. As he walked down the long corridor on the second floor, he glanced into the offices he was passing. Many of them seemed to be empty. He had heard rumors that Bailey's dot-com was losing money hand over fist, and that the technology that had built the company and made it a hot stock had already been surpassed by others. He also heard that some experts were skeptical about Bailey's claim that he was about to introduce a new kind of wireless transmitter.

The carved mahogany double doors at the end of the corridor signaled that he had arrived at Eric Bailey's private domain.

Should I knock or yell yoo-hoo? Marty wondered, but settled instead for slowly pushing open the door.

"Come in, Mr. Browski," a voice called. As he stepped

inside, a sleek, stylish woman of about forty got up from behind her desk. Introducing herself as Louise Cauldwell, Mr. Bailey's personal assistant, she ushered Marty into the private office.

Eric was standing at the front window and turned when he heard them approaching.

Browski had forgotten that Eric Bailey was so slight. It wasn't that he was that *short,* he thought as he walked across the room to him. He was of average height, really. It was the way he carried himself. Bad posture, Marty decided, remembering how his father used to order him to "stand up straight, and don't slouch!"

The problem was that because of his round-shouldered stance, the obviously expensive tan cashmere jacket and dark slacks that Bailey was wearing appeared to be too large and ill-fitting.

For all his money, Eric Bailey still looks kind of *nerdy,* Marty thought, as he extended his hand. To see this guy, you'd never guess he was a genius.

"Detective Browski. It's good to see you again."

"Good to see you, Mr. Bailey."

Eric Bailey gestured toward the couch and chairs by the bank of windows overlooking the rear of the property. "It's quite comfortable here," he said. He looked expectantly at Louise Caldwell.

"I'll send for coffee, right away, Mr. Bailey," she said.

"Thank you, Louise."

As he settled on the butter-soft leather couch, Marty compared this setup with his own office. He had a two-by-four unit with one small window overlooking the parking lot. Janey was convinced that his desk had been made with wood from Noah's ark. His filing cabinet was practically bursting, and the overflow of files was stacked on his one extra chair, or heaped on the floor.

"This is a beautiful office in a beautiful building, Mr. Bailey," he said sincerely.

A smile flickered across Eric's lips, then disappeared.

"Did you ever see my *old* office?" he asked. "It was the one next to Emily's."

" 'I saw Emily's office a few times. Fairly small, but pleasant, I would say."

"Envision one a third of that size and you have my former workplace."

"Then you must have had my present digs before I inherited them, Mr. Bailey."

This time Bailey's smile seemed real. "Since I don't believe you are here to give me a Miranda warning, and since we're both friends of Emily, why don't we drop the formalities. My name is Eric."

"Marty."

"I visited Emily in her new home on Monday. She may have told you I installed cameras there for her," Eric began.

"Yes, she did tell me," Marty said.

"I'm terribly concerned that this stalker seems to have followed her to Spring Lake. Or do you think he's a copycat?"

"I don't know," Marty said frankly. "But I *can* tell you this. Any stalker is a potential time bomb. If this *is* the same guy who hounded her up here, he's getting ready to put a match to the powder keg. She showed you some of the photographs he took of her in Albany?"

"Yes, she did. The same ones I believe she turned over to you."

"Yes, and here's what worries me: Most of the Albany pictures were shot when she was outside jogging or getting in or out of her car or going into a restaurant. The ones in Spring Lake are taking on a different character. Someone had to find out where she was staying that first night, then stand on the beach in cold, blustery weather hoping to catch a glimpse of her.

"Here's a copy of the second one, which was taken four days later."

Marty leaned over and handed Eric the photograph of Emily in St. Catherine's church on Saturday morning. "That guy was nervy enough to follow Emily into the memorial

Mass for the murder victim who had been found buried in Emily's backyard."

"I've been puzzling over that," Eric said. "To me it suggests that the stalker is somebody she has never met. I mean even in a crowded church you can get a glimpse of a familiar face. I think that argues for a copycat stalker."

"You may be right," Marty admitted unwillingly. "But if you are, it means that we may be dealing with two stalkers, not one. The reason I wanted to see you, Eric, is to ask you to concentrate on the people in the building where you and Emily both had offices. Is there *anyone* who you think might have focused on her? It could be one of the maintenance staff, or a deliveryman, or it could be some nice, amiable, nondescript guy who has a wife and kids, and who looks as if butter wouldn't melt in his mouth."

"Don't forget, I've been out of that building for three years," Eric warned. "Emily closed her office there for good only last week. She insisted on completing all the cases she'd begun herself rather than give them to other lawyers."

"She did that because that's the kind of person she is, and none of us wants to think that anything might happen to her." Marty picked up the pictures and put them back in his breast pocket.

"Eric, I hope you'll rack your brain to think of anyone who might have become obsessed with Emily Graham."

"I'll certainly try."

"Something else. Is there any device that you can install that will help to further insure Emily's safety, at least when she's alone in her home?"

"I wish there were. My only suggestions would be to have panic buttons installed in every room and tell her to carry Mace. I get the feeling that for all her brave front, Emily is terribly frightened, don't you?"

"Frightened? She *has* to be. She's human. And of course it's wearing her down. I can hear it in her voice. Too bad she hasn't got a boyfriend to help take care of her, preferably one who's also a linebacker for the Giants."

Marty expected Eric Bailey to agree with him. Then he saw the change in Bailey's face and recognized it for what it was, an expression of pain and anger. *This guy's in love with Emily,* he thought. Oh, brother.

Louise Cauldwell returned, followed by a maid carrying a tray.

Marty sipped his coffee quickly. "You're a busy man, Eric. I am not going to take any more of your time," he said, putting down the cup and standing.

But you're going to start taking a *lot* of mine, he thought, as he said good-bye and started back down the long hallway to the staircase.

A little chat with the receptionist might be in order, he decided.

Joel Lake's mocking words ran through his head. *I thought old lady Koehler's son was supposed to be the stalker . . . You were wrong about me, and you're wrong about him.*

I may be wrong again, Marty thought, but all of a sudden I think that Eric Bailey may be the guy we're looking for.

You were wrong about me, and . . .

But wait a minute—surely Eric Bailey would never take a chance on going into the church last Saturday? Emily would have seen him.

Maybe I *should* take a course on how to be a detective, Marty thought with disgust, as he descended the staircase and passed the receptionist without stopping to chat with her.

fifty-nine

"THERE IS NOTHING on Wilcox we can dig up at Enoch College," Tommy Duggan snapped as he put down the phone. "Not a hint of any scandal. Nothing. The investigator who checked for us is smart. We've worked together before. He spoke to people who were on the board of trustees when

Wilcox resigned. Every one of them was indignant at the suggestion that Wilcox had been forced out."

"Then why did he resign so suddenly?" Pete Walsh asked practically. "Want to know what I think?"

"I'd be thrilled."

"I think Wilcox might have faked a heart condition because he had something hanging over his head and didn't want the college to be involved if it became public. The people there may not know the actual reason he resigned."

They were in Tommy's office, where they had been waiting for the call from their investigator in Cleveland. Now that it had come, they got up and headed for the car. They were going to stop at Emily Graham's house with the copies of the 1890s police reports, then have another talk with Dr. Clayton Wilcox.

"You thought he might have had his hand in the till there," Pete reminded Tommy. "Suppose it's the other way round. Why don't we try to get a look at his income tax records for the year he resigned from Enoch and see if he liquidated any assets?"

"It might be worth a try." This big galoot is smarter than he looks, Tommy thought, as they walked through the parking lot to the car.

On the way to Emily Graham's house, he placed another phone call to the investigator in Cleveland.

sixty _____

"TO WHAT DO I OWE the pleasure of your visit?" Bob Frieze asked as he joined Natalie at his table at The Seasoner. He had been both surprised and displeased to receive a call from the maître d', informing him that his wife had joined him for lunch.

"Neutral territory, Bobby," Natalie said quietly. "You

237

look terrible. After you did *this* to me"—she indicated her bruised wrist—"I slept in the guest room last night, with the door locked. I see you didn't make it home at all. Maybe you were with Peggy."

"I stayed here last night and slept on the couch in my office. I thought after yesterday's scene, it might be a good idea to have a cooling-off period."

Natalie shrugged. "Neutral territory. Cooling-off period. Listen, we're both saying the same thing. We're sick of each other, and quite frankly, I'm physically afraid of you."

"That's ridiculous!"

"Is it?" She opened her purse and took out a cigarette.

"You can't smoke in here. You know that."

"Then let's move to the bar where I can smoke; we'll have lunch there."

"When did you start smoking again? You've been off cigarettes since right after we got married, and that's nearly five years ago."

"To be precise, I promised you I'd give them up right after Labor Day that summer four and a half years ago. I've always missed them. No need to miss them now."

As she ground out the cigarette in the serving plate, Natalie was seized with a sudden awareness.

That's what I've been trying to remember, she thought. The last time I smoked prior to yesterday was at that party the Lawrences gave for Martha. That was September 6th. I went out on the front porch because, of course, you weren't allowed to smoke in that house.

He had something in his hand and was walking to the car.

"What's the matter with you?" Bob snapped. "You look as though you've seen a ghost."

"Let's skip lunch. I thought I owed it to you to tell you face to face that I'm leaving you. I'm going home to pack now. Connie's letting me use her apartment in the city until I find a place. I told you yesterday what I want for a settlement."

"There's no way any judge will give you that ridiculous amount. Get real, Natalie."

"*You* get real, Bobby," she snapped. "You *find* a way to make it happen! And keep in mind that your income tax statements don't bear scrutiny, especially the one where you got the big payoff from the company when you retired. The IRS loves to reward whistle-blowers."

She pushed her chair back and almost ran to the door.

The maître d' waited a tactful ten minutes before he approached the table. "Would you like to order now, sir?" he asked.

Bob Frieze looked up at him blankly. Then, without responding, he got up and walked out of the restaurant.

You'd swear he didn't know I was talking to him, the maître d' muttered to himself, as he hurried over to greet the rare and welcome party of six.

sixty-one

THE MAP on the dining room table was dotted with a dozen more tiny houses. All roads lead to Rome, Emily thought, but it still doesn't make sense. There *has* to be another answer.

The photograph albums George Lawrence had brought over with the rest of the memorabilia were putting faces to many of the names. She found herself going back and forth between references to people and the pages of the album.

She had found one group picture with the names of the participants inscribed on the back. It was faded, and too small to see the faces clearly, so when the detectives came by later she planned to ask them if the police lab could make an enlarged copy, with the features enhanced.

It was a large group. All three victims, Madeline, Letitia, and Ellen, were listed on the back of the photo as being present in it, as were both Douglas and Alan Carter and some of their parents, including Richard Carter.

The back of her house and the back of the house where Alan Carter had lived at the time of the murders faced each other. The holly tree that had sheltered the grave had been practically at the border of the two properties.

Douglas Carter had lived directly across Hayes Avenue.

In reviewing what she'd learned about Letitia Gregg, she decided that the young woman may well have been planning to have a swim when she disappeared. Her bathing dress was missing when she vanished. Her house had been on Hayes Avenue between Second and Third. She would have had to pass the homes of both Alan and Douglas Carter to get to the beach. Had she been waylaid along the way?

But Douglas Carter committed suicide *before* Letitia disappeared.

Alan Carter's family later bought the property where Letitia's body was buried. There seemed to be many connections.

Ellen Swain, however, did not fit into that scenario. She lived in one of the houses on the lake.

Emily was still pondering the street map when Detectives Duggan and Walsh arrived. She gave them the group picture, which they promised to take care of for her. "Our guys are good," Tommy Duggan told Emily. "They'll be able to enlarge it and bring it up."

Walsh was studying the cardboard map. "Nice job," he said admiringly. "You getting anywhere with this?"

"Maybe," Emily said.

"Ms. Graham, can we help you out?" Tommy Duggan asked. "Or maybe let me put it another way. Can you help us out? Is there anything you're finding that may be useful in giving us something to work with?"

"No," Emily said honestly. "Not yet. But thanks for bringing over the copies of the old records."

"I don't think the boss was too pleased," Pete told her, "so I hope they're useful. I have a feeling we're still going to get some flak about copying them for you."

· · ·

AFTER THE DETECTIVES LEFT, Emily made a sandwich and a cup of tea, put them on a tray and carried it to the study. She put the tray on the ottoman, settled her body into the comfortable chair and began to read the police reports, starting with the first page of the file on Madeline Shapley.

"Sept. 7, 1891: Alarmed phone call received from Mr. Louis Shapley, of 100 Hayes Avenue, Spring Lake, at 7:30 P.M., reporting that his nineteen-year-old daughter, Madeline, is missing. Miss Shapley had been on the porch of the family home, awaiting the arrival from New York City of her fiancé, Mr. Douglas Carter, of 101 Hayes Avenue.

"Sept. 8, 1891: Foul play is suspected in the mysterious disappearance . . . family questioned closely . . . mother and younger sister had been at home . . . under Mrs. Kathleen Shapley's supervision, eleven-year-old Catherine Shapley had been taking a piano lesson with teacher, Miss Johanna Story. Theorized that the sound of the piano may have kept any cry Miss Madeline Shapley may have uttered from being heard.

"Sept. 22, 1891: Mr. Douglas Carter was questioned again in the disappearance of his fiancée, Miss Madeline Shapley, on Sept. 7 last. Mr. Carter continues to claim that he missed the train he had intended to take from Manhattan by moments, and was obliged to wait two hours for the next one.

"His response to the claim of a witness who says he spoke to him in the station just before the first train began to board is that he was in a somewhat nervous state because he intended to give an engagement ring to Miss Shapley that day and had felt suddenly nauseated. He said he rushed to the gentlemen's lavatory for a moment and emerged to find the train pulling out of the station.

"The later train was quite crowded, and Mr. Douglas states he did not recognize anyone on board. Neither the conductor on the early train nor on the later one remembers having punched his ticket."

No wonder he was a suspect, Emily thought. Is it possible he was nervous because he didn't want to go through with the engagement? And here I had the idea it was a great love match!

For an instant she had a mental image of her own wedding reception and dancing the first dance with Gary. At the time, *he* had seemed very much in love as well.

And I thought I was, Emily told herself. Looking back, though, I always knew there was something lacking.

Like a husband who would forsake all others.

The ringing of the phone came as a welcome intrusion to these depressing thoughts. It was Will Stafford.

"I've been wanting to call you," he said, "but it's been an awfully busy week. Look, this is absolutely no notice, but would you like to have dinner tonight? Whispers is a fine restaurant, right here in town."

"I would love to," Emily said sincerely. "I feel as if it's time to take a break and join the present world. I've been living in the 1890s all week."

"How do you like it back there?"

"In a lot of ways, I'm enchanted by it."

"I can envision you in a hoopskirt."

"You're about forty years too late. The hoops were in style during the Civil War."

"What do I know? I help people get—or get rid of—the roof that's over their heads. Seven o'clock good for you?"

"It's fine."

"See you then."

Emily hung up the phone, and then, realizing how stiff she felt from sitting so long, did a few quick stretches to limber up.

The camera noiselessly recorded her every move.

sixty-two

JOAN HODGES had spent the last four days trying to put the patients' files back in order. For her, it was a labor of love. As far as she was able, she was determined to see that Dr. Madden's patients, already reeling from the shock of her death, not suffer because their records were unavailable to her replacement.

It was a tedious task. The killer had done a thorough job of trashing the records—clinical information and Dr. Madden's observations and notes had been totally scattered and mixed. At times, Joan felt overwhelmed and was sure it was hopeless. When that happened, she took a walk along the boardwalk for half an hour, then went back to the task somewhat refreshed.

It had been arranged that Dr. Wallace Coleman, a colleague and close friend of Dr. Madden's, would take over her practice. Now he was spending as much time as he could spare from his appointments to help Joan with the task.

On Thursday a police technician came back with the rebuilt computer. "That guy did his best to wreck this one," he said, "but you got lucky. He didn't get to the hard drive."

"That means that all the records can be retrieved?" Joan asked.

"Yes, it does. Detective Duggan wants you to look for one name right away, Dr. Clayton Wilcox. Does that sound familiar to you?"

"Isn't he the one I've been reading about? The one whose wife's scarf . . . ?"

"That's Wilcox."

"That may be the reason his name rings a bell. I don't get to meet. . . ." Joan paused. "I mean I didn't get to meet all of Doctor Madden's patients, the ones who came in when she had evening hours. She'd just leave the billing information on my desk."

Joan was at the computer, her fingers flying. If the police were asking her to look up a name, it had to be because that person was a suspect. With every fiber of her being she wanted the person who had killed Dr. Madden to be found and punished. *If only I could be on the jury when he goes to trial,* she thought grimly.

Dr. Clayton Wilcox.

His file was on the screen. Joan began clicking the mouse to retrieve the file's contents. Then she reported triumphantly, "He was a patient for a brief time in September four and a half years ago, and again in August, two and a half years ago. He came in the evening, so I never met him."

The police technician was on his cell phone. "I need to get in touch with Duggan right now," he snapped. "I have some information he needs to have immediately."

sixty-three

REBA ASHBY KNEW that when her story appeared Friday morning in *The National Daily* all hell would break loose. EYEWITNESS TO THEFT OF MURDER WEAPON SCARF HESITATES TO COME FORWARD.

In the front-page story she was writing, Reba described her breakfast meeting at The Breakers Hotel on Ocean Avenue in Spring Lake with "Bernice Joyce, the elderly and fragile dowager who dismissed the missing scarf as 'showy,' then confided to this writer that she was having an ethical problem: 'I am sure that I observed the scarf being taken from the table. I am almost certain that I did.'

"*Police take note!*

"Someone in attendance at the party in the Lawrence

home that fatal night stole that scarf and the next day used it to snuff out the life of Martha Lawrence.

"Who is he?

"As Bernice Joyce described them, here are the possibilites:

"Several elderly couples who were neighbors of the Lawrences.

"Dr. Clayton Wilcox and his formidable wife, Rachel. *He's* a retired college president. *She's* the one who wore the scarf to the party. Rachel heads a lot of committees, gets things done, but isn't much liked. She says she asked her henpecked hubby to put the scarf in his pocket.

"Bob and Natalie Frieze. Bernice Joyce is very fond of Susan, the first Mrs. Frieze, but definitely does *not* care for the glamorous second one.

"Will Stafford, real estate lawyer. Good-looking, one of the few single men in Spring Lake. Watch out, Will—Bernice Joyce thinks you're a doll."

That was as far as Reba had gone with the article. She wanted to get a look at Will Stafford herself and form her own impressions of him. After that she would go over to The Seasoner and see if Bob Frieze was around.

She located Will Stafford's office on Third Avenue, in the center of town. As Reba opened the door of the outer office, she spotted the receptionist and said a silent prayer that Stafford was either out or busy.

He was out, Pat Glynn told her, but expected back soon. Would Miss Ashby care to wait?

You *bet* I would, baby, Reba thought.

She settled in the chair nearest the receptionist's desk and turned to Glynn, her manner warm and confiding. "Tell me about your boss, Will Stafford."

The telltale blush on Glynn's cheeks and the sudden brightening of her eyes, told Reba what she'd half expected. The receptionist-secretary had a huge crush on the boss.

"He's the nicest person in the world," Pat Glynn said fiercely. "*Everybody* looks to him for help. And he's so fair.

He'll tell people not to rush into buying a house, or if he thinks they're really not happy with the one they put a deposit on, he does everything to get them their money back. And he . . ."

The key phrase Reba had heard was "everyone looks to him for help." She knew that was where the story would be.

"I guess you're saying that he's a shoulder to cry on for lots of people," she suggested. "Or the kind of guy who gives you that spot loan when you need a few bucks, or cuts his fee for—"

"Oh, he's definitely a shoulder to cry on," Pat Glynn said with a misty smile. Then the smile vanished. "People take advantage of that."

"I know," Reba sympathized. "Is there anyone who's been overdoing it lately?"

"Natalie Frieze certainly is."

Natalie Frieze. She's the wife of Bob Frieze, the owner of The Seasoner, Reba recalled. They had been guests at the Lawrence home the night before Martha disappeared.

Pat Glynn warmed to the subject. For the last twenty-four hours, since she had seen Natalie Frieze kiss Will Stafford so warmly, and then go out to lunch with him for the second time in a week, Pat's moods had been alternating between fury and misery.

Absolutely, totally in love with her boss, her earlier admiration for Natalie Frieze had completely disappeared and changed into intense dislike.

"*Nobody* around here likes her. She's a big show-off, marching around town all dressed up every day as if she's on her way to Cirque 2000. Yesterday she was playing up to Mr. Stafford, trying to get sympathy. She showed him how her husband had bruised her wrist."

"He *bruised* it? Deliberately?"

"I don't know. Could be. It was swollen and purple. She told me how much it was hurting her." Looking into Reba's sympathetic eyes was like going to confession. Pat

Glynn took a deep breath and plunged ahead. "Yesterday, as they were leaving here, Mr. Stafford told me he'd be back in an hour. Natalie Frieze smirked and said, 'Make that an hour and a half.' And he was *really* busy, too. He had a lot of work on his desk."

"Does he have a girlfriend?" Reba asked mildly.

"Oh, no. He's been divorced forever. He was married when he was just out of law school in California. His mother died around that time. He keeps her picture on his desk. I thought his father was dead too, but then he showed up here last week, and Mr. Stafford got real angry and upset . . ." Glynn's voice trailed off.

Don't let *anyone* come in, Reba prayed. Don't let her stop.

"Maybe his father had neglected his mother, and he won't forgive him," Reba suggested, hoping to keep the conversation going. She could see that Pat Glynn was beginning to look uncomfortable, perhaps sensing that she had said too much.

It was the same expression that Reba had seen on the face of Bernice Joyce.

But Pat overcame whatever misgivings she had and picked up the bait. "No, it was between them. Mr. Stafford practically threw his father out of the office. In the two years I've been here, I've never *once* heard him raise his voice, but he shouted at his father—he told him to get in his car and drive back to Princeton and stay there. He said, 'You didn't believe me, you disowned me, your only son, you could have paid to have me defended.' The father was crying when he came out, and you can tell he's very sick, but I didn't feel sorry for him. He obviously had been just terrible to Mr. Stafford when he was a kid."

Pat Glynn paused for breath, then looked at Reba. "You're just too nice and too easy to talk to. I shouldn't be telling you all this. It's just between us, all right?"

Reba stood up. "Absolutely," she replied firmly. "I don't think I can wait any longer to see him, though. I'll phone for an appointment. Nice to meet you, Pat." She pushed open the door, exited, and began to walk rapidly down the street. The last thing she wanted was to confront Will Stafford now. If he saw her and realized who she was, he would undoubtedly get his gossipy secretary to admit how much she'd had to say.

Tomorrow's paper would headline Bernice Joyce's eye-witness story.

The next day, Saturday, her story would concentrate on Natalie Frieze, a battered wife, taking comfort in the arms of Will Stafford, one of the other potential suspects in the murders of Martha Lawrence and Carla Harper.

Sunday, if *The National Daily* research team could dig up the dirt fast enough, her angle would be on why Will Stafford, Spring Lake's popular and handsome real estate lawyer, had been disowned by his wealthy father, who wouldn't pay to defend him in court.

Reba, of course, was only guessing. She didn't know yet whether the father was wealthy, but he was from Princeton, which was upscale; besides, it would look good in print.

sixty-four

AFTER THEY LEFT EMILY, Tommy Duggan and Pete Walsh went directly to the home of Dr. Clayton Wilcox. Their interview with him had been frustrating and unsatisfactory.

Wilcox had stuck to his story about laying the scarf under his wife's pocketbook. When asked about Dr. Lillian Madden, he *did* recall that some years ago he was experiencing mild depression and might have consulted her. "Or someone with a similiar name."

"How long ago was that, Dr. Wilcox?" Tommy Duggan had asked.

"It's quite a while ago. I'm really not sure."

"Five years? Three years?"

"I just can't pin it down."

"Give it a shot, Doctor," Pete Walsh suggested.

The only satisfacion the policemen had been able to extract from the meeting was the fact that Wilcox was visibly coming apart at the seams. His eyes were sunken. When he'd talked, he kept folding and unfolding his hands. Beads of perspiration kept forming on his forehead, even though the temperature in his study was cool to the point of discomfort.

"If nothing else, he's getting rattled," Tommy told Pete.

Then, at four o'clock that afternoon, two things happened almost simultaneously. The technician phoned from Dr. Madden's office and gave them the dates Dr. Clayton Wilcox had consulted the psychologist.

"He saw her four weeks running after Martha Lawrence vanished, and three weeks running after Carla Harper vanished," Tommy Duggan repeated, his tone both incredulous and exhilarated. "And he claims he didn't remember! The guy's a world-class liar."

"He told us he saw her for a mild case of depression. If he *did* strangle those girls, it's no wonder he was depressed," Pete Walsh said sarcastically.

"The secretary, Joan Hodges, tells me they still haven't found the private file with the doctor's notes on Wilcox, but even if they can put it together, we'll need a court order to see it." Tommy Duggan's mouth became a thin, angry line. "But no matter what, we're going to get that file."

The second serving of manna from heaven came in the form of a phone call from the investigator in Ohio.

"I have a connection at the brokerage firm where Wilcox has his portfolio. It would cost the guy his job if it were known, but he looked up the Wilcox file. Twelve years ago when Wilcox retired, he took a one-hundred-thousand-dollar loan against his stocks. He took it in the form of a cashier's check made out to himself. However, the check was deposited in a bank in Ann Arbor, Michigan, in a new account opened by one Gina Fielding. On the bottom left of the face of the check someone wrote, 'Antique desk and bureau.' "

"Is Gina Fielding a bona fide antiques dealer?" Tommy asked.

From the smile on Duggan's face as he listened, Pete Walsh knew good things were happening.

"You're gonna love this, Duggan. Gina Fielding was a junior at Enoch College and dropped out of school abruptly, just before Wilcox resigned."

"Where is she now?"

"We're tracing her. She moved to Chicago, got married, then divorced. We'll locate her in the next day or two."

When Tommy Duggan hung up the phone, he looked at Pete Walsh with grim satisfaction. "We may have our smoking gun," he said. "Tomorrow morning we pay another visit to the eminent former president of Enoch College. I wouldn't be surprised if before we're finished they'll be taking his name off that building they dedicated to him out there."

Friday, March 30

sixty-five

IT HAS BEEN a most distressing morning. Just as my final plan was unfolding so beautifully, I had to make a radical and potentially fatal decision.

I have been purchasing *The National Daily* every morning. That insidious columnist, Reba Ashby, has been staying at The Breakers all week and is omnipresent in the community, gathering gossip.

This morning I realized that her conversations with Bernice Joyce would prove to be either my downfall or my salvation.

Mrs. Joyce confided to Ashby that she was virtually certain she knew who had removed the scarf from under the pocketbook that evening.

If she had told that to the police, they would have successfully urged her to reveal my name. At that point, they would have started to investigate every detail of my life. They would no longer accept my unsubstantiated explanation of where I was and what I was doing when Martha disappeared.

They would have arrived at the truth, and this life as I choose to live it would be over.

I had to take the risk. I sat on a boardwalk bench near The Breakers, ostensibly deep in the newspaper, trying desperately to decide how it would be possible to go into the hotel and find Mrs. Joyce's room without being noticed and recognized. Under my hood I wore a wig so that if described it would be as having graying hair falling on my forehead. I also wore dark sunglasses.

I knew it was a pitifully poor attempt at a disguise, but I also knew that if the police had the opportunity to question Mrs. Joyce, she would surely reveal my name.

And then my opportunity came.

It is a beautiful day, sunny, and truly mild.

At 7:30 Mrs. Joyce came out of The Breakers for an early morning stroll. She was alone, and I followed her at a distance, my mind seeking how I could separate her from the other early morning strollers and joggers. Fortunately, the very early ones were already gone, and it was still too early for the people who walk after breakfast.

After several blocks, Mrs. Joyce sat on a bench on one of the boardwalk extensions that are for those who wish to sit and enjoy the ocean without the distraction of people constantly passing in front of them.

A perfect spot for my purpose!

I was about to go to her when Dr. Dermot O'Herlihy, a retired physician who never misses a daily walk, spotted Mrs. Joyce and paused to chat with her. Fortunately, he stayed only a few minutes, then continued on his way. I know he did not give me any heed as he passed the bench where I was seated.

There were people coming from both directions, but none of them was less than a full block away. With the knotted cord in my hand, I sat down quietly beside Mrs. Joyce, whose eyes were closed as she enjoyed the morning sun.

She opened them when she felt the tug on her neck, turned her head, startled and frightened, as I tightened the cord and she understood what was happening.

She recognized me. Her eyes widened.

Her last words before she died were, "I was wrong. I didn't think it was you."

sixty-six

"YOU DIDN'T EXACTLY sleep like a baby last night," Janey Browski told Marty, as she placed a steaming bowl of oatmeal in front of him.

"And I don't *feel* as if I slept like a baby," Browski responded. "I kept dreaming. You know the kind of dreams that make you feel rotten, but then you can't remember them when you wake up? The dreams are gone. The rotten feeling remains."

"Your subconscious is trying to tell you something. If you could remember even a little bit of your dream, I could help you to analyze it."

Janey Browski poured coffee into their cups, sat down at the table, and began to spread strawberry jam on a piece of toast.

"Are you learning how to analyze dreams in your psych course?" Marty asked with a hint of a smile.

"We talk about how they can be made to work for you."

"Well, if I dream tonight, I'll wake you up, tell you about it, and you can start analyzing."

"Keep a pad on your night table and jot down all the details. But don't turn on the light when you do it." Janey's tone became serious. "What's wrong, Marty? Something specific or just the overall worry about the stalker?"

"You were baby-sitting last night, and I went to bed early, so I didn't get a chance to tell you. I saw Eric Bailey yesterday." Marty described the meeting and his sudden suspicion that Bailey might be the stalker.

"Frankly, I think you're reaching," Janey said, "but on the other hand, is there some way you can check him out?"

"Janey, common sense says that he wasn't in St. Catherine's Church at the memorial service last Saturday morning, seated not far from the pew where Emily was sitting. It would have been all over if she'd spotted him. As you know, it's a lot harder for a man to disguise himself than it is for a woman."

He looked at the clock and hastily finished breakfast. "I'm out of here. Don't learn too much. I'd hate to be your intellectual inferior." He paused. "And don't dare tell me I already am," he cautioned as he kissed the top of her head.

Harder for a man to disguise himself than it is for a woman. Like the unsettling dreams that he couldn't remember, the phrase lingered somewhere in Marty's subconscious all day.

He did go so far as to get the license numbers of Eric Bailey's van and Mercedes convertible and check them against EZPass records.

The activity of the vehicles indicated neither of them had been driven more than thirty miles south of Albany in the last week.

Let it go, Marty told himself, but like a chronically aching tooth, the suspicion that Eric Bailey was the stalker would not subside.

sixty-seven

WHEN EMILY WOKE UP on Friday morning and looked at the clock, she was surprised to see that it was already 8:15. Shows what a couple of glasses of wine will do to relax you, she thought, as she pushed back the covers.

But the long, dreamless sleep *did* make her feel a lot more refreshed than she had been feeling all week. And it had been a very pleasant evening, she reflected, as she went through the morning ritual of making coffee, then carrying it up to her room to drink while she showered and dressed.

Will Stafford is a nice guy, she thought, as she opened the doors of the walk-in closet and puzzled for a moment over what to wear. She chose white jeans and a red-and-white checkered long-sleeved cotton shirt, both old favorites.

Last evening she'd worn a silk navy suit with subtle pleating around the sleeves and cuffs. Will Stafford had remarked on it several times.

He had arrived to pick her up almost half an hour early. I was buttoning the suit jacket on the way downstairs, Emily thought. I still hadn't put on lipstick or jewelry.

She had left him in the study, watching the news, and been glad that she'd already closed the doors to the dining room. She did not want anyone else scrutinizing her cardboard map.

This morning, as she slipped into the jeans and blouse and pulled on her sneakers, she thought how funny it was that an outsider's impression of other people's lives can be so different from what actually is going on in them.

Like Will Stafford, Emily thought, as she began to make the bed. From what he told me the day I closed on the house, I'd have thought that his life was always pretty much okay and free of hardship.

Over dinner, however, Will had opened up about himself, and a different picture had emerged. "You know I'm an only child," he told her, "raised in Princeton, and that I moved with my mother to Denver after my parents split when I was twelve. And I guess I told you that until then we used to come to Spring Lake for two weeks every summer and stay at the Essex-Sussex.

"But it's not quite that straightforward," he explained. Within a year of being made chief executive officer of his company, his father divorced his mother and married his secretary, the first of three successive wives.

Will's eyes filled with sadness when he said, "My

mother was absolutely heartbroken. She was never the same after that. He broke her spirit."

Then he had hesitated and said, "Emily, I'm going to tell you something no one in this town knows. It's not a pretty story."

I tried to stop him, Emily remembered, but he wouldn't listen. He told me that after his junior prom in Denver, he and a friend went joyriding. They'd both been drinking a lot of beer. There was an accident, and the car was smashed. The friend, who'd been driving, was eighteen and had begged Will to switch seats with him. "You're not sixteen yet," he'd argued. "They'll go easy on you."

"Emily, I was so out of it I let it happen. What I didn't know was that it hadn't been a simple accident. In my own confused state, I hadn't realized that he'd hit and killed a pedestrian, a fifteen-year-old girl. When I tried to tell the police what really happened, they wouldn't believe me. My friend lied on the witness stand. My mother was a rock and stood by me. She knew I was telling the truth. My father washed his hands of me, though, and I spent a year in juvenile detention."

There was so much raw pain in his face when he talked of that time, Emily thought. But then he shrugged and said, "So there it is. There isn't a soul in this town who knows what I've just told you. I laid it on the line now because I'm going to ask you out for dinner again in a week or two, and if that story upsets you, it's better to know it right away. One thing I'm sure about: I can trust you not to talk about it to anyone."

I reassured him about that, Emily thought, but I also told him to wait a while before he asks me out to dinner again. I don't want to be perceived as going out regularly with anybody, either in Spring Lake or anywhere else.

She started down the stairs, stopping to admire the way the sunlight was streaming through the stained-glass window at the landing.

Next time I get serious about anyone—if there *is* a next

time—I'm going to be very, *very* sure I'm not making another mistake.

One good thing, she thought wryly, as she walked toward the kitchen, I don't have to worry about falling in love as a junior in college anymore. Thank goodness that only happens once in a lifetime!

But how it changed my life, she mused. By marrying Gary right after law school, I ended up living in Albany because he was going into the family business. If I hadn't married him, I would have started out practicing law in Manhattan.

But then if I hadn't been living in Albany, I wouldn't have defended Eric in that lawsuit, and I wouldn't have made ten million dollars by selling the stock he gave me.

And I certainly wouldn't be here in this house, she thought as she stopped in the dining room to pick up a book from the Lawrence collection of memorabilia. It was a diary kept by Julia Gordon Lawrence after her marriage. Emily was eager to see what it might reveal. Over toast and a grapefruit, she opened it and began to read.

In one of the early entries, Julia wrote, "Poor Mrs. Carter continues to decline. She will never recover from the loss of Douglas. We all visit her frequently and bring flowers to brighten her room, or a sweet to tempt her appetite, but nothing seems to help.

"She talks constantly about Douglas. 'My only son,' she sobs when we try to console her.

"Mother Lawrence and I talk about it and agree how very sad life has turned out for Mrs. Carter. She was blessed with great beauty and substantial wealth. But crippling rheumatism set in shortly after Douglas was born. She has been a semi-invalid for years, and now never leaves her bed.

"Mother Lawrence feels that for a long time, in an attempt to alleviate her pain, the doctors have been prescribing daily doses of laudanum that are far too strong. Now Mrs. Carter is in a sedated state that gives her no opportunity to take an interest in life, and with the passage of time perhaps find some measure of surcease. Instead, the only outlet for her grief is to shed copious tears."

Emily closed the book after she had finished reading that entry and went into the dining room. Mrs. Carter was at home the day Madeline disappeared, she remembered. But suppose Douglas actually had been on the early train, arrived home, and Madeline had run across the street to greet him.

If something had gone wrong between Madeline and Douglas, would Mrs. Carter, upstairs in her room, sedated by laudanum, be aware that a tragedy was unfolding downstairs?

Or had Madeline perhaps left the porch and walked into her own backyard and found Alan Carter outside in *his* backyard. He was in love with her, and probably was aware that she was about to receive his cousin's engagement ring. He might have made a pass at her, Emily reflected, and then became enraged when she rebuffed him.

Either possibility was intriguing. I firmly believe, she thought, that Madeline died that afternoon, within sight of this house, and that either Douglas or Alan Carter was involved in her death.

If Douglas was innocent of Madeline's death, then Alan becomes the next most likely suspect, she thought.

Geographically he lived close to Madeline. Letitia had to pass his house to get to the beach. In the diary, Julia had written that she and her friends regularly visited Douglas's invalid mother. Had Ellen Swain been visiting Mrs. Carter the day she disappeared? The old police records might provide some information on that point.

As Emily carefully returned the diary to the collection of Lawrence memorabilia, a new possibility occurred to her.

Did Douglas Carter *really* commit suicide? Or was he murdered because he began to suspect the truth?

sixty-eight

ON FRIDAY MORNING, Bob Frieze was woken by the jarring ring of the telephone on the night table beside his bed. He opened his eyes and groped for the phone. His greeting was raspy and gruff.

"Bob, this is Connie. I expected Natalie to be here in time for dinner last night. She never called and she never showed up. Is she there? Is everything all right?"

Bob Frieze pulled himself up. He was lying on top of the bed. Natalie, he thought, his mind still foggy. We were in the restaurant. She said she didn't want lunch and practically ran out.

"Bob, what's going on?" Irritation was apparent in Connie's voice, but he detected something else as well. There was fear.

Fear? Natalie probably had told Connie all about their fight. He was sure of it. Had she told Connie about her bruised wrist too?

He tried to think. Natalie told me she was leaving. She was going home to pack. She was going to stay at Connie's apartment in New York. She never got there?

It was morning now, and Connie told him that Natalie had been due there last night.

I've lost almost a day, Bob Frieze thought. How long exactly have I been out?

He held his hand over the speaker, cleared his throat and said, "Connie, I saw Natalie at the restaurant at lunchtime yesterday. She told me she was going home to pack and was planning to go to New York to your apartment. I haven't seen her since."

"*Did* she pack? Are her bags there? What about her car?"

"Hang on." Bob Frieze stumbled to his feet, realizing that he had a massive hangover. I don't normally drink much, he thought. How did this happen?

He had bought this house and moved into it while he was waiting for the divorce from Susan to be finalized. Natalie had taken an active interest in decorating it and had insisted on some renovation. In the process, the small bedroom next to theirs had been turned into two side-by-side walk-in closets. He opened hers.

There was a single waist-height shelf at one end of the closet, for convenience in packing suitcases. Natalie's largest suitcase was open on the shelf. Bob looked into it and saw that it was half filled.

Afraid of what he might find, he stumbled into the guest bedroom, remembering that was where Natalie had told him she had spent the night. The bed was made, but when he looked into the bathroom, he saw that her cosmetics were all still on the vanity, unpacked.

There was one more thing he had to do before he figured out what to tell Connie. He ran downstairs into the kitchen and opened the door to the garage. Her car was parked inside.

Where *is* she? he wondered. What had happened to her? Clearly *something* had happened, he was sure of it.

But *why* was he sure of it?

Back in the bedroom, he picked up the phone. "Looks like Natalie changed her mind, Connie. All her stuff is here."

"So where is Natalie?"

"Look, I don't know where she is. We had a disagreement Wednesday evening. She's been sleeping in the guest room. I got home late last night, as I usually do, and went straight to bed. I didn't check on her. I'm sure she's fine. Natalie can be pretty careless about calling people when she makes a sudden change of plans."

The click in his ear told Bob that his wife's best friend had hung up on him.

She was going to call the police. That certainty hit him with the impact of a gun firing in his face. What should he do?

Act normal, he decided. He pulled the spread off the bed, rumpled the blankets, and lay down between the sheets for a minute to give the impression of having slept there.

Where have I been since yesterday noon? he asked himself, straining to remember. What have I been doing? His mind was a complete blank. He rubbed his hand across his face and felt a stubble of beard.

Shower, he thought. Shave. Get dressed. When the police come, *act normal*. You and your wife had a disagreement. When you came home last night, you didn't check on her. She obviously changed her mind about leaving for New York.

When a police officer rang his doorbell thirty minutes later, Bob Frieze was prepared for him. He was calm, but explained he was becoming concerned. "With all that has been going on in town this last week, I am beginning to be deeply worried about my wife's disappearance." His face was set in a worried expression.

Then he added, "I can't bear the thought that anything might have happened to her."

Even to his own ears, *that* statement did not ring true.

sixty-nine _____

PETE WALSH HAD GONE OUT to a convenience store for milk before he left for work at eight o'clock. At his wife's insistence, he had picked up a copy of *The National Daily* for her as well. While he waited for his change, he glanced at the headline. Less than a minute later, he was on the phone with the Spring Lake police station.

"Get someone over to The Breakers," he said. "Tell him to stay with an elderly woman, Bernice Joyce, who's a guest there. She's been fingered as an eyewitness to the theft of the scarf in the Lawrence murder case. She may be in a life-threatening situation."

The milk forgotten, he ran out of the store to his car. On the way to the prosecutor's office, he contacted Duggan, who was on his way to work.

Ten minutes later they had piled into their specially equipped vehicle and were headed for Spring Lake.

Tommy Duggan dialed the desk at The Breakers Hotel. Mrs. Joyce had been seen going out for a walk on the boardwalk, he was told. The police were already looking for her.

DR. DERMOT O'HERLIHY walked to the post office, then decided to return home by way of the boardwalk. He was surprised to see Bernice Joyce still sitting on the bench. Her back was to him, so he could not see her face. She's probably fallen asleep, he decided. But then something about the way her head was leaning forward on her chest made him quicken his step and hurry to check on her.

He walked around to the front of the bench, looked down at her and saw the cord knotted tightly around her neck.

He squatted in front of her, taking in the staring eyes, the open mouth, the flecks of blood on her lips.

He had known Bernice Joyce for over fifty years, all the way back to when she and Charlie Joyce, and he and his wife, Mary, used to come every summer to Spring Lake, bringing their children.

"Ah, Bernice, poor darling, who would do this to you?" he whispered.

The sound of running feet made him look up. Chris Dowling, the newest cop on the town police force, came bounding across the boardwalk extension. In just moments he was at the bench, squatting beside Dermot, staring at the lifeless body.

"You're too late, lad," Dermot told him as he straightened up. "She's been gone for at least an hour."

seventy

ALTHOUGH HE DIDN'T SAY ANYTHING TO HER, Pat Glynn knew that Mr. Stafford was angry at her. She could see it in his eyes and feel it in the way he came into the office on Friday morning and passed her desk with just a brief, unsmiling greeting.

When he had returned to the office yesterday afternoon, she had told him that a Miss Ashby had stopped by.

"Miss Ashby? The gossip columnist from that tabloid? I hope you didn't let her pump you about me, Pat. That woman is *vicious.*"

With a sinking heart, Pat had remembered every single word she had said to Ashby. "I just told her what a wonderful person you are, Mr. Stafford," she said.

"Pat, every word you said to her will be twisted and slanted. You will help me if you tell me absolutely everything you said. I won't be angry, I promise, but I *do* need to be prepared. Do you read *The National Daily?*"

She admitted that she sometimes read it.

"Well, if you read it at all this week, you've seen what this Ashby woman has been doing to Dr. Wilcox. That's what she's going to do with me. So what kind of questions did she ask you, and what did you tell her?"

IT WAS HARD FOR PAT to concentrate on the work on her desk. She had to resist the impulse to go to Mr. Stafford's office and tell him again how terribly sorry she was. But then a phone call from her mother shocked her out of her remorseful state.

"Pat, there's been another murder in town. An older woman, Bernice Joyce, one of the people who was at the party at the Lawrence house the night before Martha's disappearance, has been found strangled on a bench on the boardwalk. She told that columnist from *The National Daily* that she thought she could identify the person who took that scarf that killed Martha, and the columnist printed it, and now Mrs. Joyce is dead. Can you *believe* it?"

"I'll call you back, Mom." Pat hung up the phone, and, walking like a robot, went down the hall. Without knocking, she opened the door of Will Stafford's office. "Mr. Stafford, Mrs. Joyce is dead. I know you knew her. She told that columnist that she thought she saw someone take the scarf at that party, and the columnist printed it. Mr. Stafford, I'm sure I didn't tell Miss Ashby anything that would cause anyone to die."

Pat's voice rose, quivered, and broke in a flood of tears. "I just feel so terrible."

Will got up and came around his desk. He put his hands on her shoulders. "Pat, it's all right. Of *course* you didn't tell Ashby anything that would cause someone's death. Now, what are you talking about? What happened to Mrs. Joyce?"

Pat was aware of the warm, strong hands on her shoulders. She calmed herself and relayed what her mother had just told her.

"I am so very sorry," Will said quietly. "Bernice Joyce was a kind and elegant lady."

We're talking like friends again, Pat thought. Anxious to prolong the intimacy of the moment, she asked, "Mr. Stafford, do you think Dr. Wilcox might have done this to Mrs. Joyce? I mean, according to all the papers, his wife said she gave him the scarf to hold."

"I imagine they're questioning him very closely," Will said briskly.

Pat caught the change of tone. The moment of intimacy was over. It was time for her to go back to her desk. "I'll have all those letters ready for you to sign by noon," she promised. "Will you be going out to lunch?"

"No. You can order in for both of us."

She had to take the chance. "I'll wait until later to order, just in case you change your mind. Mrs. Frieze might drop by like she did the other day."

"Mrs. Frieze is moving to New York, permanently."

Pat Glynn returned to her desk in a state of bliss.

IN HIS OFFICE, Will Stafford was on the phone with the employment agency that had sent him Pat Glynn two years ago. "And for God's sake get me someone mature and sensible, who isn't a gossip and isn't looking for a husband," he implored.

"We have someone who just registered with us this morning. She's winding up her old job. Her name is Joan Hodges and she was with that psychologist who was murdered last week. She's efficient. She's smart. She's a nice person. I think you'd be very happy with her, Mr. Stafford."

"Send over her résumé, in a plain envelope. Mark it personal."

"Of course."

As Will replaced the receiver, Pat announced another call. This one was from Detective Duggan, requesting an appointment with him at his earliest possible convenience.

seventy-one

ON THURSDAY AFTERNOON, not wanting to run into Bernice Joyce again, Reba Ashby had checked out of The Breakers Hotel and moved to the Inn at the Shore in Belmar, a few miles away. She had expected a backlash when the tabloid with her headline about Joyce hit the stands on Friday morning, but was jolted to her soul when she learned from the radio of the woman's death.

Then her natural instinct for self-protection set in. Bernice should have gone to the police, Reba told herself. It was her own fault. God knows how many other people in addition to me she might have told about seeing someone pick up the scarf. Nobody tells just one person anything in confidence. Anyhow, if they can't keep it to themselves, they shouldn't expect others to keep it quiet.

For all I know, Bernice might even have asked the *killer* if he'd picked up the scarf just to look at it, then put it down somewhere else. She was just naïve enough to do that.

Still, Reba immediately called Alvaro Martinez-Fonts, her editor, to agree on how they would handle any flak from the police. Then she told him that she had gone to The Seasoner for dinner Thursday night, but that Bob Frieze hadn't been around at all.

"I laid fifty bucks on the maître d', Alvaro," she said. "That opened *him* up. According to him, Frieze has been acting weird for a long time now. This guy thinks he's in the process of a nervous breakdown or something. Yesterday, Natalie Frieze came in to the restaurant, but she didn't stay long. She and Bob had words at the table, and the maître d' overheard her tell him she was afraid of him."

"That fits in with the battered woman angle."

"There's more. A waiter who was serving the next table heard them talking about breaking up, and he's willing to talk, but he wants big, *big* bucks."

"Pay him and write it up," Alvaro ordered.

"I'm going to try to see Natalie Frieze today."

"Get her to talk. Robert Frieze used to be a hotshot on Wall Street. He's good for some headlines even if he had nothing to do with the murder."

"Well, he's no hotshot in the restaurant business. Food's only so-so. Decor overdone and uncomfortable. Absolutely zero buzz to the place. Trust me. It'll never be the Elaine's of Monmouth County."

"Keep up the good work, Reba."

"You bet. How are you doing on Stafford?"

"So far, nothing. But if there's any dirt to find, we'll dig it up."

seventy-two _____

"NO MORE SITTING IN HIS STUDY letting him run the show," Tommy Duggan told Pete Walsh grimly as they left the crime scene. "We've got to flush him out, and make him show his hand—and we've got to do it soon." The body of Bernice Joyce had been removed. The forensic team had done its work and was wrapping up. As the head investigator had said to Tommy, "With the breeze from the ocean, there isn't the chance of a snowball in hell that we'll get anything we can use. We've dusted for prints, but we all know the killer had to be wearing gloves. He's a pro."

"He's a pro all right," Tommy snapped to Pete as they got in the car. The face of Bernice Joyce filled his mind, as she had looked a week ago when he'd interrogated her at Will Stafford's house.

She was forthcoming when he asked her if she had noticed the scarf, he remembered. She knew Rachel Wilcox had been wearing it. But did she remember then that she had seen someone pick it up? Tommy wondered. I don't think so, he decided. It probably came to her later.

She told me she was going back to Palm Beach on Monday. But even if I'd known she was staying over, it wouldn't have occurred to me to talk to her again.

He felt both disgusted and angry with himself. The killer read that article in the tabloid and got scared, he thought, so scared that he took a chance on killing Mrs. Joyce in broad daylight. And if he still was following a game plan, then there would be someone else tomorrow, Tommy reminded himself. Only this one would be a *young* woman.

"Where to?" Pete asked.

"You called Stafford?"

"Yes. He said anytime we want to stop in is okay. Said he'll be at his desk all day."

"Let's start with him. Check the office first."

That was when they learned that Natalie Frieze was missing.

"Forget Stafford," Tommy said. "The local guys are talking to Frieze. I want to sit in on it."

He hunched back in the seat, pondering the terrible possibility that the serial killer had already elected his next victim: Natalie Frieze.

seventy-three

NICK TODD phoned Emily the moment he heard the news report of the death of Bernice Joyce. "Emily, did you know that woman?" he asked.

"No, I didn't."

"Do you think the article in that rag was the reason she was killed?"

"I have no idea. I haven't seen the article, but I understand it's pretty bad."

"It was a death sentence for that poor woman. This kind of thing makes me itch to get into the U.S. Attorney's office."

"How is that going?"

"I put out feelers to some of his top people. I won an important case against them last year, which could either hurt or help me, who knows?"

There was a subtle change in his voice. "I called last night, but I guess you were out."

"I was out to dinner. You didn't leave a message."

"No, I didn't. How's the project going?"

"I may be kidding myself, but I'm seeing a pattern to all those deaths, and it's horrific. You remember I told you that Douglas Carter, the young man Madeline was engaged to, killed himself?"

"Yes, you told me about that."

"Nick, he was found with a shotgun beside him. He'd been terribly depressed over Madeline's disappearance, but he was also young, good-looking, with family money, and a promising future on Wall Street. Everything that's written about him in all the diaries and other materials I have is positive, and nothing points specifically to his being suicidal. Something else. His mother was very sick, and he apparently was very close to her. He must have known that his death would destroy her. Just think—how would your mother feel if something happened to you?"

"She'd never forgive me," Nick said wryly. "But how would your mother feel if something happened to you?"

"She wouldn't like it, of course."

"Then until both your stalker and this serial killer you're trying to identify are apprehended, please keep your doors locked and the alarm on, especially when you're there alone. Look, I've got a call coming in I have to take. I'll see you on Sunday, if we don't talk before then."

Why does Nick feel the need to sound like the voice of my better judgment? Emily wondered as she hung up the phone. It was 11:30. For the past two and a half hours she had been alternating between the old police reports and the Lawrence memorabilia.

She had also called her mother and father in Chicago and her grandmother in Albany and given all of them a cheerful account of how much she was enjoying the house.

All of which is true enough, she told herself as she thought as well of everything she was withholding from them.

Julia Gordon Lawrence had kept yearly diaries. She had not made daily entries, but she did write in the books frequently. I could enjoy reading every word, Emily thought, and

I will if the Lawrences let me keep them long enough. But for now I need to find information in them that directly ties in to those disappearances and to Douglas's death. With a start, she realized she no longer thought of his death as a suicide, but considered him a likely victim of the same person who had killed the three young women.

Ellen Swain vanished on March 31, 1896.

Of course, Emily thought. Julia must have written about that. She went through the diaries and found the one for that year.

Before she started reading it, however, there was something else she wanted to do. She opened the door that led from the study to the porch, went outside, and looked across the street. The records showed that the old Carter house had been destroyed in a fire in 1950 and replaced by the one that was there now, a loving copy of a turn-of-the-century Victorian home, complete with the wraparound porch.

If Madeline was sitting here and Douglas, or Alan, beckoned to her . . .

Emily wanted to verify in her mind that the scenario she had come up with yesterday was possible.

She walked around on the porch to the back of the house and went down the steps into the backyard. The contractor had smoothed the dirt, but her sneakers immediately gathered mud as she walked the length of the yard to the boxwoods that defined the end of her property.

Deliberately she walked to the site where the remains of the two victims had been found, and she stood there. The massive holly tree with its heavy, low branches would have made it impossible for anyone in the house to know if Alan Carter had seen Madeline come out, and then either deliberately or accidentally harmed her. The sound of Madeline's sister taking her piano lesson would have covered any outcry.

But even if it happened this way, Emily asked herself, how does that tie any of these murders to the present?

She went back inside, picked up the 1896 diary and looked for entries dated after March 31st.

On April 1, 1896, Julia had written, "My hand shakes as I write this. Ellen has disappeared. Yesterday she stopped to see Mrs. Carter to bring her a blancmange to tempt her appetite.

"Mrs. Carter has told the police that she had a pleasant but brief visit. Ellen was quite thoughtful, she said, and seemed to be in a state of excitement. Mrs. Carter was resting in a lounge chair at the window of her bedroom and saw Ellen exit the house and begin walking down Hayes Avenue on her way home. That was the last she saw of her."

Which meant she went past Alan Carter's house, Emily thought.

She turned the next pages quickly, then stopped. The entry dated three months later read, "Dear Mrs. Carter has been called to her heavenly home this morning. We are all so saddened, yet feel that for her this is a great blessing. She has been released from pain and grief and is now reunited with her beloved son, Douglas. Her last days were spent with her mind in a state of confusion. Sometimes she thought Douglas and Madeline were in the room with her. Mr. Carter has endured with grace his wife's long illness and the loss of his son. We all hope that the future will be kinder to him."

What about him, the husband and father? Emily wondered. There isn't very much at all written about him. On the other hand, obviously he and Mrs. Carter weren't attending the parties and festivities. From the few references to him, she had learned his name was Richard.

She kept turning the pages, looking for more references to anyone named Carter. There were many more references to Ellen Swain for the rest of 1896, but nothing that Emily could spot about either Richard or Alan Carter.

The first entry in the 1897 diary had been made on January 5th.

"This afternoon we attended the wedding of Mr. Richard Carter to Lavinia Rowe. It was a quiet affair due to the fact that the late Mrs. Carter is not yet deceased a year. However, no one begrudges Mr. Carter his happiness. He is a strikingly handsome man and still only in his forties. He met Lavinia when she was visiting her cousin and my close friend, Beth Dietrich. Lavinia is a most attractive girl, poised and mature in her ways. At twenty-three, she is half Mr. Carter's age, but we have all seen many May and December romances, and some of them very successful and happy.

"They say they will sell the house on Hayes Avenue, which has known so much pain, and have already purchased a smaller but most charming residence at 20 Brimeley Avenue."

At 20 Brimeley Avenue, Emily thought. Why does that address sound familiar?

And then she remembered. She had been there last week.

It was where Dr. Wilcox lived.

seventy-four

TOMMY DUGGAN AND PETE WALSH arrived at the Frieze home to find a highly agitated Robert Frieze sitting on a couch in his living room, speaking with local police officers.

"My wife has been eager to move to Manhattan, which is something we've been planning to do," he was saying. "I have just sold my restaurant and will put this house on the market immediately.

"She was offered the use of a friend's apartment and planned to go there yesterday. I don't know why she changed her mind. Natalie is impulsive. For all I know, she got on a plane to Palm Beach. She has dozens of friends there."

"Can you tell if any of her warm-weather clothes are missing?" the police officer asked.

"My wife has more clothes than the Queen of Sheba. I've seen her buy exactly the same outfit twice because she forgot the duplicate was hanging in her closet. If Natalie made up her mind to get on a plane to Palm Beach, she would think nothing of going with the clothes on her back and when she got there, spending a couple of hours on Worth Avenue with her credit card in hand."

The more Bob Frieze talked, the more credible the suggestion seemed to him. Just the other day, Natalie had been complaining about the weather. Raw. Cold. Dull. Dreary. Those were just a few of the words she had used to describe this time of year.

"Do you mind if we take a look around, Mr. Frieze?"

"Go ahead. I have nothing to hide."

Tommy knew that Bob Frieze had seen him and Walsh when they came into the room, but he had not bothered to acknowledge them. Now Tommy moved into the seat the police officer had just abandoned. "Mr. Frieze, I thought maybe you didn't recognize me. We've met before several times."

"A lot more than 'several' times, I think, Mr. Duggan," Frieze said sarcastically.

Tommy nodded. "That's absolutely true. Did you happen to go jogging this morning, Mr. Frieze?"

Did I? Bob Frieze asked himself. I had my sweats on. When did I change into them? Yesterday afternoon? Last night? This morning? Did I follow Natalie home when she left the restaurant? Did we have another fight?

He stood up. "Mr. Duggan, I am sick and tired of your accusatory manner. I have been sick and tired of it for a very long time, four and a half years to be exact. I will no longer submit to questioning by you or anyone else. I intend to start phoning friends in Palm Beach to see if any of them have seen my wife or has my wife staying as a guest in their home."

He paused. "However, Mr. Duggan, my first call will be to my lawyer. Any further questions you have for me should be addressed to him."

seventy-five

Joan Hodges was going through the computer files and making lists of all Dr. Madden's patients for the past five years.

A police technician had been assigned to help her. Two psychologists, both friends of Dr. Madden, had volunteered to come over to assist in trying to reassemble the confidential files of the patients that had been scattered about the office.

The accelerated pace of the activity had been requested by Tommy Duggan. If the file of Dr. Clayton Wilcox remained missing, he reasoned, it would point to the strong possibility that he had been the killer.

Joan had already been able to ascertain that no one else on the list Duggan gave her to check had been one of Dr. Madden's patients.

"But that doesn't mean someone didn't use a phony name," Tommy had cautioned her. "We need to know if the file of anyone else listed in the computer is missing, because if so, we'll check that person out."

They had laid the file folders in alphabetical order on long metal tables that had been set up in Dr. Madden's living room. In some cases the adhesive name tags on the folders had been torn or pulled off, so they knew that the results would be inconclusive at best.

"Police work is tedious," the police technician told Joan with a smile.

"I can see that."

More than anything else, Joan wanted now to finish up here and find a new job. She had called the employment agency already. Several of the psychologists who knew Dr. Madden had hinted they'd like to talk to her about working with them, but she knew she needed a complete change. Continuing in an office with the same atmosphere would only bring back to her the grisly sight of Dr. Madden sitting in her chair, the cord pulled tightly around her neck.

She came across a name with a Spring Lake address and frowned. She read the name and couldn't place him, although she realized that she didn't know them all. He could have been one of the evening patients; she never did meet most of them.

But wait a minute, she thought.

Is he the one who only came once, about four years ago?

I got a glimpse of him getting in his car when I came back that evening to pick up my glasses, which I left here. I remember him, she thought, because he seemed to be upset. The doctor said he left abruptly. She handed me a one-hundred-dollar bill that she said he'd thrown on her desk, Joan thought. I asked her if she wanted me to bill him for the rest of her fee, but she said to forget it.

I'd better pass his name along to Detective Duggan immediately, she decided as she picked up the phone.

Douglas Carter of 101 Hayes Avenue, Spring Lake.

seventy-six

TOMMY DUGGAN AND PETE WALSH were in the prosecutor's office, where they had just given him a rundown of their findings in the Bernice Joyce murder and on the disappearance of Natalie Frieze. "So the husband told us she's probably in Palm Beach, and now he won't talk to us except through his lawyer," Tommy concluded.

"What's the likelihood that she'll turn up in Palm Beach?" Osborne asked.

"We're checking the airlines to see if she flew out on

any of them. I think it's a thousand to one against it," Tommy replied.

"The husband invited you to look around the house?"

"The Spring Lake cops went through it. No sign of any struggle or violence. It looks as if she might have been in the middle of packing, then left."

"Cometics? Pocketbook?"

"The husband said that when he saw her at his restaurant yesterday, she was wearing a gold leather jacket, a brown-and-gold striped silk shirt, and brown wool slacks, and she was carrying a brown shoulder bag. There was no sign in the house of either the shoulder bag or the gold leather jacket. He admits they quarreled and that she slept in the guest bedroom the night before. That would be Wednesday night. There were enough cosmetics and perfumes and lotions and sprays in the master and guest bathrooms to open a Macy's outlet."

"More likely an Elizabeth Arden outlet," Osborne observed. "We'll have to wait and see if she shows up. As an adult, she has the right to pick up and go whenever she wants. You say her car was in the garage? Somebody must have picked her up. Is there a boyfriend in the picture?"

"None that we're aware of. I spoke to the housekeeper," Walsh said. "She comes in three afternoons a week. Thursday wasn't one of them."

The prosecutor raised his eyebrows. "She comes in afternoons? Most housekeepers come in during the morning."

"She was arriving when we left today. She explained that Mrs. Frieze often sleeps late, so she didn't want to be bothered by someone puttering around or vacuuming. I didn't get the idea the housekeeper was too fond of Natalie Frieze."

"Then for the moment we have to just wait and see," Osborne said. "What's the matter, Duggan? You don't look happy."

"I don't have a good feeling about Natalie Frieze," Tommy said flatly. "I'm wondering if somebody has anticipated the 31st by a couple of days."

For a long moment there was silence. Then Osborne asked, "Why do you think that?"

"Because she fits the pattern. She's thirty-four, not twenty or twenty-one, but like Martha Lawrence and Carla Harper, she's a beautiful woman." Duggan shrugged. "Anyway, I've got a very, very bad feeling about Natalie Frieze, plus I don't like the husband. Frieze has a weak, unsubstantiated alibi for where he was when Martha Lawrence disappeared. Claims he was in his backyard working on his flower beds."

Welsh nodded. "He lived the first twenty years of his life in the house where the remains of Carla Harper and possibly Letitia Gregg were found," he said. "And now his wife is missing."

"Sir, we'd better get to Dr. Wilcox," Tommy Duggan suggested. "He's coming in at three o'clock."

"What have you got?" Osborne asked.

Tommy leaned forward in his chair with his hands joined, a position which meant he was weighing and measuring his options carefully.

"He was willing to come. He knows he doesn't have to. When he gets here, I'll emphasize again that he's free to leave at any time. As long as he's fully aware of that, we don't have to give him Miranda warnings, and frankly I'd rather not have to give it. He may button up if we do."

"What's your take on him?" Osborne asked.

"He's hiding a lot, and we *know* he's a liar. Those are two big handicaps in my book."

CLAYTON WILCOX ARRIVED promptly at three o'clock. Duggan and Walsh escorted him to a small interrogation room, where the only furniture was a table and several chairs, and invited him to sit down.

He interrupted them when they once again assured him that he was not in any way being detained, and that he was free to leave.

A glint of amusement in his eyes, he said, "You have probably debated about whether or not to give me the Miranda warnings and come to the conclusion that emphasizing my freedom to leave has covered you sufficiently as far as the law is concerned."

He smiled at the expression on Pete Walsh's face. "Gentlemen, you seem to forget that I spent the better part of my life in academia. You have no idea how many debates on civil liberties and the court system I heard, or how many mock trials I attended. I *was* the president of a college, you know."

It was the opening Tommy Duggan wanted, and he jumped in. "Dr. Wilcox, in looking at your background, I'm surprised to see that you retired from Enoch College at age fifty-five. Yet you had just signed a new five-year contract."

"My health would not permit me to carry on my duties. Believe me, the role of president of a small but prestigious institution requires a great deal of energy, as well as time."

"What is the nature of your ill-health, Doctor Wilcox?"

"A serious heart condition."

"Have you discussed this with your physician?"

"Certainly."

"Do you have regular checkups for your heart condition?"

"My health has been stable of late. Retirement has removed a great deal of stress from my life."

"Doctor, that doesn't answer my question. Do you have regular checkups?"

"I have been careless about having them. However, I feel very well."

"When was the last time you went to a doctor?"

"I'm not sure."

"You weren't sure about whether or not you ever had an appointment with Dr. Madden. Do you still claim that, or have you changed your mind?"

"I may have had an appointment or two."

"Or nine or ten, Doctor. We *have* the records."

Tommy proceeded carefully in conducting the interrogation. He could tell that Wilcox was becoming rattled, but he didn't want him to get up and leave. "Doctor, does the name Gina Fielding mean anything to you?"

Wilcox paled as he leaned back in the chair and, obviously playing for time, looked up at the ceiling with a thoughtful frown. "I'm not sure."

"You gave a one-hundred-thousand-dollar check to her twelve years ago, just at the time you retired, Doctor. You marked the check 'Antique desk and bureau.' Does that refresh your memory?"

"I collect antiques from many sources."

"Miss Fielding must be pretty smart, Doctor. She was only twenty years old at the time, and a junior at Enoch College. Isn't that right?"

There was a long pause. Clayton Wilcox looked directly at Tommy Duggan, then moved his gaze to Pete Walsh.

"You are quite right. Twelve years ago Gina Fielding was a twenty-year-old junior at Enoch College. A very worldly twenty-year-old, I might add. She worked in my office and was very flattering in her attention to me. I began to visit her occasionally at her apartment. A consensual relationship developed for a brief time, which of course was entirely inappropriate and potentially scandalous. She was a scholarship student from a low-income family. I began giving her spending money."

Wilcox looked down at the table for a long minute as if he was finding the scratched surface totally facinating. Then he looked up again and reached for the glass of water they had put on the table for him.

"Eventually I came to my senses and told her that the relationship would have to end. I said I would have her placed in a different office job, but she threatened a lawsuit against me and the college for sexual harrassment. She was prepared to swear that I had threatened to have her scholarship taken away if she did not have a relationship with me. The price of her silence was one hundred thousand dollars." He paused for a moment, taking a deep breath.

"I paid. I also resigned my presidency because I did not trust her, and if she broke her word and sued the college, I knew there would be much less media interest were I no longer the president."

"Where is Gina Fielding now, Doctor?"

"I have no idea where she lives. I do know that she is going to be in town tomorrow, looking for another hundred thousand dollars. She obviously has been following the tabloids, and she has threatened to sell her story to the highest bidder."

"That's extortion, Doctor. Are you aware of that?"

"I'm familiar with the word."

"Were you planning to pay her off?"

"No, I was not. I cannot live the rest of my life like this. I am going to tell her that I will not give her one more penny, knowing, of course, the consequences of that decision."

"Extortion is a very serious crime, Doctor. I would suggest that you allow us to equip you with a taping device. If you can get Miss Fielding on record demanding the money to buy her silence, we can press charges against her."

"Let me think about it."

I believe him, Tommy Duggan thought. *But that still doesn't let him off the hook, as far as I'm concerned. If anything, it's proof that he's attracted to young women; besides, it's still his wife's scarf that is the murder weapon. And he still doesn't have an alibi for the morning of Martha Lawrence's disappearance.*

"Doctor, where were you between seven and eight this morning?"

"I was out walking."

"Were you on the boardwalk?"

"At some point I was, yes. As a matter of fact, I started on the boardwalk, then walked around the lake."

"Did you happen to see Mrs. Joyce on the boardwalk?"

"No, I did not. I was very sorry to learn of her passing. A brutal crime."

"Did you see anybody you know, Doctor?"

"Frankly, I didn't pay attention. As you can now understand, I have had a great deal on my mind."

He stood up. "I am free to go?"

Tommy and Pete nodded. As Tommy got up, he said, "Let us know about taping your talk with Miss Fielding. And something I must tell you, Doctor—we are vigorously pursuing the investigation into the deaths of Miss Lawrence, Miss Harper, Dr. Madden, and Mrs. Joyce. Your responses to our questions have been evasive, to put it in the most generous terms. We will be talking to you again."

Clayton Wilcox left the room without responding.

Walsh looked at Tommy Duggan. "What do you think?"

"I think he decided to come clean about the Fielding woman because he has no choice. She's the kind of woman who'll buy his silence and go to the tabloids anyhow. For the rest of it, he does seem to have a habit of going on those long walks of his and never meeting anyone who might verify where he was at a particular time."

"And he also seems to have a thing for young women," Walsh added. "I wonder if there's more to the Fielding story than he fed to us?"

They went back to Tommy's office where the message from Joan Hodges was waiting for them. "Douglas Carter," Tommy exclaimed. "The guy's been dead for over one hundred years!"

seventy-seven

Eric Bailey had planned to drive down to Spring Lake on Friday evening, but changed his mind after making a phone call to Emily. She told him she was having dinner with the owner of the inn in which she had stayed during visits while she was in the process of buying the house.

There was no point, Eric decided, in spending time in Spring Lake if he didn't know where Emily was. Just to get a glimpse of her coming home at the end of the evening wasn't worth it.

He would drive down tomorrow, and get there by midafternoon. He'd park the van in an inconspicuous spot. There were plenty of parking spaces on Ocean Avenue, and no one would pay attention to a late model navy-blue RV. It would blend in with all the other moderate to expensively priced vehicles entering and leaving the parking spaces near the boardwalk.

Faced with an empty evening ahead of him, Eric felt himself growing increasingly impatient. He had so much on his mind, so much to deal with in the days ahead of him. The sky was crashing down. Next week the company's stock would be downgraded to junk. Everything he had would have to be sold. Shirtsleeves to shirtsleeves in five years, he thought angrily.

He was engulfed in this nightmare because of Emily Graham. She had started the selling trend on his company's stock. She had not put a penny of her own into the company but had made ten million dollars because of his genius. She had then rejected his offer of love with a dismissive smile. And she was set for life.

He understood that soon it would not be enough to make her fearful.

There was another step he would be forced to take.

Saturday, March 31

seventy-eight _____

A SENSE OF FOREBODING had settled over a town reeling with the series of events of the past ten days.

"How is it possible that this is happening here?" the early risers asked each other as they met at the bakery. "It's March 31st. Do you think that something will happen today?"

The weather contributed to the sense of unease. The last day of March was proving to be as capricious as the rest of the month had been. Yesterday's warm breeze and sunny skies had disappeared. The clouds were now heavy and gray. The wind from the ocean was sharp and biting. It seemed impossible that in a few weeks the trees would once again be laden with leaves, the grass would turn velvety green, and flowering shrubbery would again surround the foundations of century-old homes.

After a pleasant evening with Carrie Roberts, Emily spent a restless night filled with vague dreams, not as terrifying as they were mournful. She awoke from one of them with tears in her eyes and no memory of what had brought them on.

Ask not for whom the bell tolls; it tolls for thee.

What brought *that* on? she wondered as she settled

back on the pillow, unwilling as yet to start the day. It was only seven o'clock, and she hoped she could sleep for a little while longer.

It was difficult, though; she had so much on her mind. She had the tantalizing feeling that she was very close to finding the link between the past and the present, and being able to make the connection between the two sets of murders. She was also hopeful that she might find the clue she needed in one of Julia Gordon Lawrence's diaries.

The handwriting was exquisite, but small and spidery and therefore difficult to read. In many places the ink had faded, and she had had to focus intensely on whole sections of the diaries.

Detective Duggan had called while she was at dinner and left a message that the photo lab would have the enlargement of the group picture for her by late today. She was looking forward to seeing it.

Getting that photo would be like finally meeting people that she'd heard a lot about, she thought. I want to see their faces clearly.

The overcast morning meant that the room was in semidarkness. Emily closed her eyes.

It was 8:30 when she woke again, this time without the lingering sense of fatigue and feeling all around more cheerful.

It was a state of mind that lasted only an hour. When the mail was delivered, in it was a plain envelope with her name printed in childish letters.

Her throat closed. She had seen that printing on the postcard with the tombstone drawings that had come in the mail only a few days ago.

With trembling fingers she ripped open the envelope and pulled out the postcard inside it.

Even though it had come in an envelope, the postcard was addressed to her. She turned it over and saw a drawing of two tombstones. The names on them were Natalie Frieze and Ellen Swain. They were placed in the center of a wooded area adjacent to a house. The address printed across the bottom of the card was 320 Seaford Avenue.

Shaking so violently that she misdialed twice, Emily phoned Tommy Duggan.

seventy-nine _____

MARTY BROWSKI WENT INTO THE OFFICE on Saturday afternoon to try to clear his desk, looking forward to a few hours without interruption. But after only a few minutes there he decided he might as well have stayed home. He simply could not concentrate. All of his attention was focused on only one person. Eric Bailey.

The financial page of the morning newspapers plainly stated that Bailey dot-com would be forced into bankruptcy and that the misleading statements of its founder about new product developments were a matter of great concern to the director of the New York Stock Exchange. The article speculated he might even be facing criminal charges.

He fits the profile of a stalker so well he could have posed for it, Browski thought. He had the EZPass records checked again, only to find that neither one of Eric Bailey's vehicles had been recorded as driving south of Albany.

There was absolutely no additional car registered to him, and it was unlikely that he would rent a car and risk leaving a paper trail.

But what about a *company* car?

The thought hit Browski as he was about to give up the attempt to work and go home. I'll get the guys to run through that one, he decided. They can call me at home if they find anything.

There was just one more possibility: Bailey's secretary. What was her name? Marty Browski looked up to the ceiling as though expecting a voice from the heavens to answer him.

Louise Cauldwell—the name came to him suddenly.

She was in the phone book. Her message machine was on. "Sorry, I'm not answering the phone right now. Leave a message, please. Your call will be returned."

Meaning maybe she's out and maybe she's not, Marty thought irritably as he identified himself and left his home number for her. If anyone knew whether or not Bailey had other means of getting around than the two vehicles registered in his name, Ms. Cauldwell just might be the one.

eighty

FOR THE THIRD TIME IN TWO DAYS, tapes marked CRIME SCENE went up on the property of a Spring Lake home owner.

This residence, one of the oldest in town, had originally been a farmhouse and still retained the simple lines of its early nineteenth-century design.

The spacious property was composed of two building lots. The house and garden were on the left, while the area to the right was unchanged from its natural wooded state.

It was there, in the shadow of a cluster of sycamore trees, that the body of Natalie Frieze, encased in heavy plastic, was found.

For area residents, the events that followed had the feeling of déjà vu. The media flocked to the scene in large vans with antennas. Helicopters hovered overhead. In contrast, the neighbors gathered in quiet dignity on the sidewalk and on the closed-off road.

After receiving Emily's shocked phone call, Tommy Duggan and Pete Walsh immediately alerted the Spring Lake police, passing on to them the message on the postcard. Before they had reached Emily's home, they received confirmation that the postcard was not a hoax. The difference was that this time the remains had not been interred.

"Wonder why he didn't bury her?" Pete Walsh asked soberly, as once more they watched the forensic team perform the grim task of examining and photographing the victim and the surroundings.

Before Tommy could reply, a squad car pulled up to the site. A pale and shaken Bob Frieze emerged from the back-seat, spotted Duggan and rushed to him. "Is it Natalie?" he demanded. "Is it my wife?"

Duggan nodded, but didn't speak. He had no intention of offering even perfunctory sympathy to the man who might well be the murderer.

A few feet away, Reba Ashby, her identity camouflaged by dark glasses and a scarf that covered her head and shadowed her face, was scribbling in her notebook: "Reincarnated serial killer claims his third victim."

Nearby, Lucy Yang, a reporter from New York's Channel 7, was facing the camera, holding the microphone and quietly saying, "The eerie repetition of the crimes of the late nineteenth century has claimed its third, and possibly last, victim. The body of thirty-four-year-old Natalie Frieze, wife of restaurateur and former Wall Street executive Robert Frieze was found today . . ."

Duggan and Walsh followed the hearse conveying Natalie's body to the medical examiner's office.

"She's been dead between thirty-six and forty hours," Dr. O'Brien told them. "I can narrow it down more when I do the autopsy. Cause of death appears to be the same as the others—strangulation."

He looked at Duggan. "Are you going to dig for the remains of the March 31st, 1896, victim now?"

Tommy nodded. "We have to. We'll probably find her there. This killer is running true to form, copycatting the 1890s crimes."

"Why do you think he didn't wait until the 31st to kill

her?" the medical examiner asked. "That would have followed his pattern of matching the dates on which the earlier victims died."

"I think he wanted to be sure he got her when he had the opportunity, and with so much added security in town, he didn't figure he could take the chance of digging a grave. His need probably was to have her *discovered* today, the 31st," Tommy told him.

"There's one more factor you'd better consider," the ME told him. "Natalie Frieze was strangled by the same kind of cord the killer used on Bernice Joyce. The third piece of the scarf that was used on the Lawrence and Harper women is still out there somewhere."

"If that's the case," Tommy said, "it may not be over yet."

eighty-one

WHEN EMILY PICKED UP THE PHONE she was not sorry to hear Nick Todd's voice.

"I've been listening to the radio," he said.

"It's so awful," Emily told him. "Just a few days ago I sat with her at the luncheon the Lawrences gave after the memorial Mass."

"What was she like?"

"Strident good looks. The kind that make other women feel they need a makeover."

"What kind of *person* was she?" he asked.

"I'll be honest. I wouldn't have chosen her as a friend. She had a hard edge that was inescapable. It's just impossible to think that I was sitting across the table from her a week ago, and now she is dead—murdered!"

Nick caught the distress in Emily's voice. He was in his

SoHo apartment and had been planning to catch a movie, followed by dinner at the hole-in-the-wall pasta restaurant in the Village that was his favorite.

"What are you up to tonight?" he asked, trying to make his voice sound casual.

"Absolutely nothing. I want to finish reading the old diaries I've been loaned and then rejoin the twenty-first century. Something inside me is telling me it's time."

Afterward Nick asked himself why he hadn't suggested he drive down for dinner that evening. Instead, he confirmed that he would pick her up at 12:30 on Sunday for brunch.

But when he hung up, he found he was too restless to even consider going to a movie. Instead, he had an early dinner, phoned and made a reservation at The Breakers, and at seven o'clock got in his car and started driving to Spring Lake.

eighty-two _____

MARTY WAS FINISHING DINNER when the phone rang. Louise Cauldwell, Eric Bailey's secretary, had just returned home and picked up her messages. Marty got straight to the point. "Ms. Cauldwell, I must ask you something. To your knowledge, does Eric Bailey drive any vehicle other than the two registered in his name?"

"Oh, I don't think so. I've been with him since the company started, and I've never seen him in anything other than the convertible or the van. He trades them in every year, but it's always for the newer model."

"I see. Do you know if Mr. Bailey plans to be away this weekend?"

"Yes, he's going to Vermont to ski. He does that frequently."

"Thanks, Ms. Cauldwell."

"Is there anything wrong, Mr. Browski?"

"I thought there might be, but I guess not."

Marty settled in the den for an evening of television, but after watching the tube for almost an hour, he realized he had no idea what he was seeing. At nine o'clock he bolted up and announced to Janey, "I've just thought of something," and hurried to the phone.

EZPass confirmed his hunch. Neither one of Eric Bailey's vehicles showed any activity for the day.

"He has a third car that he's driving," Marty muttered. "He *has* to have a third car."

She's probably out, he thought as he tried Louise Cauldwell's number again. It's Saturday night, and she's an attractive woman, he reminded himself.

But Louise Cauldwell picked up on the first ring.

"Ms. Cauldwell, is there a company car that Eric Bailey might be using?"

She hesitated. "We *do* have company cars leased in the names of some of our executives. A number of them have left recently."

"Where are the cars they used?"

"A couple are still in the parking lot. You can't break those leases, you know. I guess it's possible Mr. Bailey might be using one of them, although I can't imagine why."

"Do you know the names they'd be registered under? This is very important."

"Is Mr. Bailey in some kind of trouble? I mean he's been under so much pressure lately. I've been worried about him."

"Is there something in his behavior that troubles you, Ms. Cauldwell?" Marty asked quietly. "Please don't think about confidentiality now. You won't be doing Eric Bailey a favor if you don't cooperate."

There was a moment of hesitation. "The company is going under and he's cracking up," she said finally, emotion in her voice. "The other day I went into his office and he was crying."

"He seemed fine when I saw him the other day."

"He puts on a good front."

"Did you ever hear him mention Emily Graham?"

"Yes, just yesterday in fact. He seemed upset after you left. He told me that he blames Ms. Graham for ruining the company. He said that when she sold her stock, other people got nervous and followed her example."

"That's not true. The stock went up another fifty points after she sold."

"I'm afraid he forgets that."

"Ms. Cauldwell, I can't wait until Monday to get the number of a car he may be driving. You've got to help me."

Thirty minutes later, Marty Browski met Louise Cauldwell in the darkened offices of Bailey dot-com. She turned off the alarm, and they went upstairs to the accounting office. In a few minutes she had the license plate numbers of the leased cars and the names of the men for whom they were registered. Two of the cars were in the parking lot. The third one Marty checked out with EZPass. It had been on the Garden State Parkway and at 5:00 P.M. it had gotten off the parkway at Exit 98.

"He's in Spring Lake," Marty said flatly, as he picked up the phone to dial the police there.

"We'll keep an eye on her house," the desk sergeant promised. "The town is crowded with media, and the curiosity seekers doing a drive-through, but I promise you—if that car is here, we'll find it."

eighty-three

EMILY'S PLEASURE ON HEARING Marty Browski's voice changed to shock when she realized why he was calling.

"That is absolutely impossible," she said.

"No it isn't, Emily," Marty said firmly. "Now listen,

the local police are going to keep the house under surveillance."

"How are they going to do *that?*"

"They'll drive by your house every fifteen minutes. If Eric calls and wants to see you, put him off. Tell him you have a headache and are going to bed early. *But don't open the door for him.* And I want you to keep your alarm on the 'instant' setting. The Spring Lake cops are looking for Bailey. They know what vehicle he's driving. Now, check those locks!"

"I will." When she hung up, Emily went from room to room, testing the doors that opened to the porch, then the front and back doors. She pushed INSTANT and ON, and watched the signal on the alarm box switch from green to a flashing red.

Eric, she thought. Friend, buddy, little brother. He was here Monday, installing the cameras, acting so worried about me, and all the while . . .

Betrayal. Hypocrisy. Putting in security cameras and laughing at me while he was doing it. Emily thought of all the nights in the past year during which she had awakened, startled, sure she'd heard someone in the house. She thought of all the times it had been so hard to concentrate on preparing a defense for a client, because a picture Eric had taken of her had been slipped under her door, or stuck to her windshield.

"I hope when they find that wacko, they throw the book at him," she said aloud, not knowing that at that very moment she was looking directly into a camera, and that Eric Bailey was parked in his van six blocks away, watching her on his television screen.

eighty-four

"ONLY YOU WON'T BE AROUND when they do throw the book at me," Eric responded aloud.

The shock of realizing that he had been found out, and of having Marty Browski phone Emily Graham and tell her he was the stalker stunned Eric. I've been so careful, he thought, looking at the carton that contained the woman's coat and dress and wig he had worn into St. Catherine's Church on Saturday, and thinking of all the disguises he had used to get close to Emily in the past without being detected.

And now the police were looking for him and no doubt soon would arrest him. He would be sent to prison. His company would collapse in bankruptcy. The people who had praised him so lavishly would turn on him like dogs.

Then he focused on the screen again and leaned forward, his eyes suddenly wide, excitement rushing through him.

Emily had gone back to the dining room and was on her knees going through the box of books, obviously looking for something in particular.

But on the split screen, he could see that the handle of the door leading from the porch to the study was turning. I know she has the alarm on, he thought. *Someone must have tampered with it!*

A figure wearing a ski mask and a dark sweatsuit stepped into the study. In a quick, furtive move, the intruder got behind the club chair in which Emily always sat and dropped to his knees. As Eric watched, the masked man took a piece of material from his pocket, held it in both hands and pulled it taut, as if testing it.

Emily came back into the study carrying a book, settled down in the club chair, and began to read.

The intruder did not move.

"He's *enjoying* this," Eric whispered to himself. "He doesn't want it to be over too soon. I understand. I understand."

eighty-five

TOMMY DUGGAN AND PETE WALSH WERE still in the office at 8:30 on Saturday evening. Bob Frieze had steadfastly refused to answer any questions about his whereabouts on Thursday afternoon and evening, and now, claiming chest pains, he had been admitted to the Monmouth Hospital for observation.

"He's stalling until he can get a story together that will hold up in court," Tommy told Pete. "There are a couple of ways this could play out. One is Frieze is the serial killer and is responsible for the deaths of Martha Lawrence, Carla Harper, Dr. Madden, Mrs. Joyce, and his wife, Natalie. Two is he may have killed his wife but *not* the others. And, of course, there is a third possibility—that he is innocent of all these deaths."

"You're worried that the third piece of scarf is still missing," Pete said.

"You bet I am. Why do I have a feeling that Natalie Frieze's murder was a ploy to trick us into thinking that the killer had completed the cycle?"

"Unless, of course, Natalie's murder was the result of a quarrel between husband and wife, disguised to look like one of the serial murders. That would point toward Bob Frieze as a suspect but would take it out of the serial killer loop."

"Which also means that another young woman may

die in Spring Lake tonight. But who? I checked a short while ago—no one has been reported missing. Let's call it a day. It's getting late, and we can't accomplish anything more here," Tommy said.

"Well, *something* was accomplished. While we were at the crime scene, Wilcox called and allowed our guys to wire him. We've got Gina Fielding on tape, trying to extort money from him."

"And now his guilty secret will be featured in *The National Daily* the day after tomorrow. I still say he was trying to get one jump ahead of us by agreeing to implicate her. In a way, it makes him sympathetic. But I still don't trust him. And so far as I'm concerned, he's still very much in the running as a suspect."

They started to leave when Pete said, "Wait a minute," and pointed to an envelope on Tommy's desk. "We never did drop this enlarged photo at Emily Graham's like we promised."

"Take it with you and run it over tomorrow morning."

As Pete picked up the envelope, the telephone rang. It was the Spring Lake police, relaying the message that Emily Graham's stalker had been identified and was believed to be somewhere in town.

On hearing the news, Tommy said, "On second thought, maybe we'll drop that photo off tonight."

eighty-six _____

EMILY HAD HER CELL PHONE in her pocket, a habit she had developed since the picture of her in church was slipped under the door last Sunday. She reached for it now, hoping that her grandmother hadn't turned in early and shut off the phone. She had been reading the final diary of Julia Gordon Lawrence that had been included in the material the Lawrences had loaned her, and she had a question about it she hoped her grandmother could help answer.

She had read earlier that Richard Carter's second wife gave birth to a baby girl in 1900. In relation to that, an entry in 1911 puzzled her. In it Julia had written: "I have heard from Lavinia. She writes that she is very happy to be home in Denver. After a year, her little daughter has quite recovered from the loss of her father and is flourishing. Lavinia herself confesses to being tremendously relieved. In fact she was rather astonishingly frank when she took pen to paper. She writes that Douglas had a deep well of coldness within him, and at times she was quite frightened of him. She feels that it was a blessing that his death released her from that marriage and has given her child a chance to grow up in a more congenial and warm atmosphere."

Emily put down the diary and snapped open the cell phone. Her grandmother answered with a quick hello, a sure sign that she was watching television and wasn't thrilled to get a call.

"Gran," Emily said. "I have something I have to read to you because it simply doesn't make sense."

"All right, dear."

Emily explained the entry and read it to her. "Why would she refer to him as Douglas when his name was Richard?"

"Oh, I can tell you that. His name was Douglas Richard, but in those days it was common to call a man by his middle name if he had the same name as his father. Madeline's fiancé was actually Douglas Richard III. I understand the father was a very handsome man."

"He was a handsome man, with an invalid wife, and she was the one who had the money. Gran, you've been a great help. I know you were watching television, so go back to it. I'll call you tomorrow."

Emily clicked off the phone. "It *wasn't* young Douglas who was the killer," she said aloud. "It wasn't his cousin Alan Carter either. It was his *father*. And when he died, his wife and daughter moved to Denver."

Denver! Suddenly she saw the connection.

"Will Stafford was *raised* in Denver! His mother *lived* in Denver!" she said aloud.

Emily suddenly felt a shadowy presence hovering over her and froze in stunned terror as she heard a voice whisper in her ear.

"That's right, Emily," Will Stafford said. "I *was* raised in Denver."

Before she could make a move, Emily felt her arms being pinned to her sides. She tried to struggle to her feet, but a rope was quickly looped around her chest, holding her to the back of the chair.

Moving with lightning-swift efficiency, Stafford was on his knees before her, tying her feet and legs.

She forced herself not to scream. It would be useless, she realized, and he might decide to put tape over her mouth. Make him *talk* to you, an inner voice whispered, keep him talking! The police *do* have the house under surveillance. Maybe they'll ring the bell, she thought, and when they don't get an answer, they'll force their way in.

He stood up. Pulled the ski mask off his face. Unzipped his jacket. Stepped out of the baggy ski pants.

Underneath his outer layer of clothing, Will Stafford was wearing a very old-fashioned high-collared shirt and string tie. The wide lapels of his turn-of-the-century dark blue suit accentuated his stiffly starched white shirt. His hair was combed in an uncharacteristic side part and brushed tightly across the top of his head. It was also somewhat darker than his natural color, as were his eyebrows.

Then Emily noted with a start that he had painted a narrow mustache above his upper lip.

"May I introduce myself, Miss Graham?" he asked with a short, formal bow. "I am Douglas Richard Carter."

Don't panic, Emily warned herself. It's all over if you panic. The longer you can stay alive, the better chance you have that the police will check on you.

"I am very pleased to meet you," she said, struggling to mask her terror, managing to speak through lips almost too dry to form the words.

"You do know, of course, that you must die? Ellen Swain has been waiting for you to join her in her grave."

His voice is different too, Emily thought. The words are more precise, clipped almost. It sounds as if he has a slight British accent. *Reason with him,* she ordered herself fiercely.

"But Natalie Frieze is with Ellen," she managed to say. "The cycle is complete."

"Natalie was never meant to be with Ellen." His tone was impatient. "It was always you. Ellen is interred near the lake. The drawing I sent showing Natalie's tombstone next to Ellen's was meant to mislead. They are not together. But you will sleep with Ellen soon."

He bent down and caressed Emily's cheeks. "You remind me of Madeline," he whispered. "You, with your beauty and youth and vitality. Can you understand what it was like for me to look across the street and see my son with you and to know that I was condemned to live my life with an ailing woman whose beauty was gone, whose sole attraction was her wealth?"

"But surely you loved your son and wanted him to be happy?"

"Surely I would not allow someone as exquisite as Madeline to be in his arms while I sat at the bedside of a besotted invalid."

There was a flash of light from a passing police cruiser. "Our police in Spring Lake do their best to secure our safety," Will Stafford said as he reached in his pocket and brought out a piece of silvery material edged with metal beading. "Since they have just checked this house, we will have at least a few minutes more. Is there anything more you would like me to explain to you?"

eighty-seven _____

THE SPRING LAKE POLICE SQUAD CAR was cruising along Ocean Avenue. "There it is!" Officer Reap said, pointing to a dark blue van parked in one of the spots that faced the boardwalk.

They pulled into the space beside it and rapped on the front window. "There's light coming from the back," Phil said. He rapped again, harder.

"Police, open up!" he called.

Inside, Eric was watching the screen in rapt fascination, and he had no intention of being interrupted. The key to the van was in his pocket. He pulled it out and pressed the remote button that unlocked the doors.

"Come in," he said. "I'm right here. I've been expecting you. But please let me finish watching my show."

Reap and his partner slid open the door and immediately saw the television screen. What does he think he's doing? This guy must be a nut, Reap thought, as he glanced at the screen. For an instant he thought he was watching a horror movie.

"He's going to kill her," Eric said. "Be quiet, he's talking to her. Listen to what he has to say."

The two officers stood immobile for a moment, transfixed by the shocking realization of what was unfolding in front of them and by the calmness of the voice that came through the speaker.

"In my current incarnation I had only expected to repeat the pattern of the past," Will Stafford was saying, "but it was not to be. I thought Bernice Joyce was a threat that had to be eliminated. Her last words to me as she died were that she was mistaken. She thought she had seen someone else pick up the scarf. A pity. She did not have to die after all."

"Why Natalie?" Emily asked, fighting for time.

"I am sorry about Natalie. The night of the Lawrence party, she had stepped onto the porch to have a final cigarette before she gave them up for good. From that vantage point, she may have seen me carrying the scarf to the car. When she started smoking again at our luncheon last Wednesday, I could sense that she was starting to remember. She had become a danger. I could not allow her to live. But don't worry. Her death was mercifully swift. It always has been that way. It will be for you too, Emily, I promise."

Astounded, Officer Reap realized suddenly that he was about to see a murder committed.

". . . when I was fourteen, my mother and I first came to Spring Lake. A sentimental journey for her. She never stopped loving my father. We walked past the house where her mother, my grandmother, had been born."

"God Almighty, that's Will Stafford and Emily Graham!" Reap snapped. "I was by her house last Sunday after that picture of her at the memorial Mass was pushed under her door. Stay here with him!" he shouted to the other officer, as he leapt out of the van and broke into a run.

". . . The woman who lived in my great-grandfather's house invited us in. I became bored and started rummaging around on the second floor of the carriage house. I found his old diary. I was *meant* to find it, you see, because I am Douglas Richard Carter. I have returned to Spring Lake."

Don't let me be too late, Phil Reap prayed as he got back in the squad car. As he raced to 100 Hayes Avenue, he radioed headquarters for backup.

eighty-eight _____

NICK TODD DECIDED that for his own peace of mind, he would drive past Emily's house just to reassure himself that all was well inside. He was just approaching it when a police car came racing down the street from the other direction and pulled into the driveway.

With a sense of dread, Nick pulled in behind the police car and quickly jumped out. "Has anything happened to Emily?" he demanded. Please, God, please, don't let anything happen to her, he begged silently.

"We hope not," Officer Reap said tersely. "Stay out of my way."

THE POLICE WILL DRIVE BY AGAIN, Emily promised herself. But then if they didn't see him come in, what good is that? she reasoned. He's managed to get away with the murders of Martha, Carla, Natalie, Mrs. Joyce, and probably others. I'm next. Oh, dear God, *I want to live!*

"Tell me about the diaries," she said. "You have kept a record of everything, haven't you? You must have written down every detail of the way everything happened, of your emotions at the time, of the reactions of the families of the girls?"

"Exactly." He seemed pleased that she understood. "Emily, for a woman you are very intelligent, but your intelligence is limited by a woman's natural enemy—her generosity of spirit. With compassion visible in your eyes, you drank in my story about taking the blame for a friend who had been the real driver in an accident. I told you that because my receptionist admitted she had revealed too much to that gossip columnist, and I was afraid if something was printed, it would put you on your guard."

"Whatever you did, the juvenile record would have remained sealed."

"What I did was to follow my great-grandfather's example. I overpowered a young woman, but before I could complete my mission, her screams were heard. I spent three years in juvenile detention, not one as I told you."

"It is time, Emily—time for you to join lovely Madeline, time for you to rest with Ellen."

Emily stared at the tattered shreds of cloth in his hands. *He's enjoying himself,* she thought. Make him keep answering questions. He wants to brag.

"When I am with Ellen, will it be over?" she asked.

He was behind her now, gently wrapping the remnant of scarf around her neck.

"I wish that could be true, but alas there is at least one more. Dr. Madden's secretary unfortunately caught a glimpse of me the night I visited Dr. Madden. In time, she might remember me. Like Bernice Joyce and Natalie Frieze, she poses an unacceptable risk."

He leaned forward and brushed her cheek with his lips. "I kissed Madeline as I tightened her sash," he whispered.

TOMMY DUGGAN AND PETE WALSH arrived at Emily's house just in time to see Officer Reap running up the steps to the porch, followed by another man.

Reap quickly reported what he had seen on the monitor in Bailey's van.

"Forget the front door. Take one of the porch doors on the right," Duggan shouted. He and Walsh, followed by Nick, ran to the left. Reaching the door to the study, the three men looked in the window and saw the scarf being tightened around Emily's neck.

Tommy knew that in another few seconds it would be too late. He drew his pistol, took aim, and fired through the glass.

The impact of the bullet caused Will Stafford to jerk back, then crumple to the floor, the remains of the scarf that had snuffed out the lives of Martha Lawrence and Carla Harper still clutched in his hand.

Sunday, April 1 ═══════════════

eighty-nine _____

ON SUNDAY MORNING, Tommy Duggan and Pete Walsh joined Emily and Nick at a quiet corner table in The Breakers breakfast room.

"You were right, Emily," Tommy said. "There was a complete written record of what his great-grandfather did. In addition, Stafford kept his own journal and wrote the details down in the same clinical fashion his great-grandfather did."

"We got a search warrant for Stafford's house and we found the original Douglas Carter's diary as well as the one Stafford kept," Tommy Duggan said. "I stayed up all night reading it. It was exactly the way you had figured it out. Douglas Carter's wife was out of it with the amount of laudanum she was taking. And maybe he was feeding her more. He writes in his journal that he had beckoned Madeline over to his house, saying that his wife was having a seizure. When he put his arms around her and tried to kiss her, she began to struggle, and he knew he'd be ruined if she talked."

"I find it hard to think that it was Will Stafford's great-grandfather who did this," Emily said. It was like being touched by fingers from the grave. I still feel so frightened, she thought. Will I ever feel safe again?

"Douglas Carter was nearly fifty years old when his

second wife, Lavinia, gave birth in 1900 to a baby girl, Duggan said. "They named her Margaret. After Douglas died, in 1910, Lavinia and Margaret moved back to Denver. Margaret married in 1935. Her daughter, Margo, was Will Stafford's mother."

"He told me that he found that diary by chance when he and his mother were visiting Spring Lake and stopped at the house where his great-grandparents lived," Emily said.

"Yes, and he rummaged in that loft over the carriage house and found his great-grandfather's journal," Duggan confirmed.

"It seems to me," Nick said, "that the seeds of corruption were in him then. A normal kid would have been horrified and would have shown the journal to an adult."

Listening to the discussion, Emily felt as though she was still in a kind of dream world. Will had obviously arrived early the night he had taken her to dinner so that he could remove the sensor from the alarm system for the door that led into the study. He must have taken the key for that door from the ring the Keirnans gave him to enter the house before the closing.

Last night, after Stafford's body had been removed and the forensics team was finishing the painstaking sifting for evidence, Nick told her to pack an overnight bag and took her to The Breakers Hotel where he was registered.

"Once again my home is a crime scene," she told him.

"It won't be after this," he assured her. "It's all over now."

But even in the safety of The Breakers, Emily woke at 3:00 A.M., startled, frightened, remembering, sure she had heard footsteps in the hallway. Then the certainty of Nick's presence in the next room had been enough to make the trembling stop, to allow sleep to claim her.

"Did Douglas Richard Carter kill his son?" Emily asked.

"His diary isn't really clear on that point," Duggan answered. "He says that Douglas had a gun and he struggled with him. After it went off, he managed to make it look like a suicide. I wouldn't be surprised if Douglas had figured out what his father had done and confronted him. Maybe even that guy couldn't face the fact that he'd murdered his only son. Who knows?"

"What about Letitia and Ellen?" Emily knew she had to know their fates as well if she were ever to be able to put all this behind her.

"Letitia was on her way to the beach," Pete Walsh said. "She had brought a bouquet of flowers from her garden for Mrs. Carter, and Carter happened to be home. Again his advances were rebuffed and again he killed a young woman.

Tommy Duggan shook his head. "The diary makes for pretty nasty reading. Ellen Swain was visiting Mrs. Carter and began to ask questions, apparently having come to suspect that Carter was the cause of her two friends' disappearances. She never got out of the house that day, although given his wife's befuddled state, it was easy enough for Carter to convince the poor woman that she actually had seen Ellen leave."

Duggan frowned. "He's very specific about where he buried Ellen. We're going to try to find her remains and put them in her family's plot. She died trying to find out what happened to her friend Letitia. So in a way it's especially fitting that the two family plots are side by side in the cemetery."

"*I* was supposed to be buried with Ellen," Emily said. "That was his plan for me."

She felt Nick Todd's arm around her shoulders. This morning he had knocked on her bedroom door with a cup of coffee for her in his hand. "I'm an early bird," he explained. "This is one of the things you'll miss at the office, because if I get the job I think I'm going to get, I'll be downtown. I invited my dad to have lunch with me at the cafeteria at the U.S. Attorney's office. You can come too. Better yet, you can come down *without* him."

I'll be there, she thought. You bet I will.

Pete Walsh had just finished a double order of scrambled eggs, sausage, and bacon. "Your study is being cleaned right now, Emily. I think from now on you'll find peace in your home."

Tommy Duggan's breakfast had been orange juice, black coffee, and a banana. "I have to be on my way," he said. "My wife, Suzie, has great plans for me. She's been threatening that on the first warm weekend day I'd get to clean the garage. This is it."

"Before you go," Emily said quickly, "what about Dr. Wilcox and Bob Frieze?"

"I think Dr. Wilcox is one relieved guy. It's out in the open that he got too cozy with a student years ago. Her picture is in all the papers today. Although he was way out of line getting involved with a college student when he was president of the university, no one looking at her picture today would think he took advantage of an innocent young maiden."

"What about his wife's reaction?"

"My guess is that the public humiliation will finish that marriage. She *did* know why he resigned the college presidency so abruptly. There was no way he could have hidden it from her, and I guess she's been throwing it up to him on a regular basis. Actually, I think he's relieved about everything. He *did* tell me that he thinks his novel is damn good. Who knows? The guy may end up with a whole new career."

Tommy was pushing back his chair. "As for Frieze, he can thank Natalie that he's in the clear. She gave him a piece of paper she'd found in his pocket, with a phone number and the name Peggy, asking him to call her. Our guys checked her out. Frieze was in the habit of dropping into some bar in Morristown. Claims he didn't remember any of it, but obviously he didn't waste time during his blackouts. Peggy's pretty cute. Between Peggy's testimony and Will Stafford's diaries, Frieze is in the clear."

Tommy Duggan stood up. "A final piece of information. Stafford accosted Martha after she left the boardwalk. Drove up to where she was walking and told her he was having chest pains. Asked her to drive him home. She knew him and fell for it, of course. He forced Carla to ride with him when she was on the way to get her car after leaving the Warren. Then he went back and got her car later. Nice guy, huh?"

He turned to go. "Enjoy the rest of your breakfast, folks. We're off."

After they left, Emily was silent for a long moment. "Nick, the reason Tom Duggan came to my house last night was to deliver an enlarged photograph. I looked at it this morning."

"What did you find?"

"The police lab did a magnficent job of enlarging and enhancing the photograph. The faces are very clear now, and I can match them with all the names that are on the back of the original. Madeline and Letitia and Ellen and Phyllis and Julia. And the men. George and Edgar and young Douglas and Henry and even Douglas Carter, Senior, or Will Stafford as we knew him in the present."

"Emily," Nick protested, "you *can't* mean that you believe he really was reincarnated."

She looked directly at him, her eyes pleading for understanding. "Nick, Will Stafford was the image of his great-grandfather as he appeared in that picture, but . . ."

"What is it, Emily?"

"I found that picture in the Lawrence family memorabilia. It's a million to one Will never saw it."

His hand, reassuring and firm, was over hers.

"Nick," Emily whispered, "in that picture, Douglas Carter was holding what appeared to be a woman's scarf with metal beading."